Side Tracked

A Novel

By Yonder Blair

Side Tracked

A Novel

By Yonder Blair

POLYVERSE
PUBLISHING

polyversepublishing.com

Library of Congress Cataloging-in-Publication Data
Names: Blair, Yonder, author.
Title: Side Tracked, A Novel / Yonder Blair
Description: Santa Barbara : Polyverse Publications, 2024.

Identifiers: LCCN pending (print) | LCCN pending (ebook)
ISBN 978-1-959111-15-3 (paperback) | ISBN 978-1-959111-16-0 (ebook)

Subjects: General Fiction. | Mystery.

Book design by Louis Force Torres
Published by Polyverse Publishing

Printed in the United States of America
DOC 10 9 8 7 6 5 4 3 2 1

Tenure: the right or guarantee to hold something, such as a position or an office.

Tenure track: the path towards such a right or guarantee

Don't wake up at 32, 35, or 40, tenured to a life that happened to you when you weren't paying strict attention.
—Richard Russo

Only God's tenure is eternal.
—Oche Otorkpa

PROLOGUE

The following article appeared in the
Syracuse Post-Standard.

Dateline March 13.

Officials at Macallan University announced that they have filed a missing person's report with the Oban police department regarding one of their senior faculty members. Aaron Randolph, dean of the humanities division, has not been seen on campus for several days. His estranged wife says she knows nothing about his whereabouts. Faculty colleagues and administrators have been interviewed to determine if Prof. Randolph had plans to be out of town. No one knows of any conferences he was scheduled to attend or any other reason for him to be away from campus.

Oban police secured a warrant today to search the professor's house and ascertained it had not been lived in for several days. They would not elaborate except to say it seemed the professor had left things in an unfinished state. They are actively seeking information about when and where he was last seen.

The Post-Standard has learned that Prof. Randolph is a controversial figure on campus and could have a number of enemies. The FBI is scheduled to join the investigation tomorrow.

CHAPTER 1

The town of Oban, New York, was established in the mid-nineteenth century and formally chartered in 1843. It was founded by an immigrant Scotsman named Macalister, for whom the Finger Lakes region of upstate New York reminded him of the Lochs in the Scottish Highlands where he grew up. So enamored was he of the site, he named it Oban after the city of his birth, on the Scottish coast not far from Glasgow.

The Oban of Macalister's upbringing is a small but important port on the west coast of Scotland. It serves today, as it did during his childhood, as the gateway to the islands known as the Hebrides. It is also famous for its eponymous distillery, producing one of the country's finest Scotch whiskeys. Though Macalister's American Oban didn't have a seacoast, and he would have to substitute the cold and snow of an upstate New York winter for the relatively more moderate climate on the west coast of Scotland, he figured he couldn't have everything. He could still import his Oban Scotch whenever he wanted to keep warm.

It didn't take long for the little town Macalister had founded to outpace his hometown in both size and importance. Thanks in no small measure to his personal leadership, it soon became a respectable commercial and cultural center in upstate New York just west of Syracuse. Not a major city by any means, but one large enough to support his pet project, the establishment of a liberal arts college. His inspiration in this regard came from his days as a student at the University of Glasgow, the institution which provided him a future well beyond his wildest dreams as a kid growing up in Oban by the sea.

Initially, Macalister wanted to name the college after himself and his family, but he discovered that some folks in Minnesota had beat him to it by just a few years, establishing their own Macalister College in 1874. Under the circumstances, he could have used the Oban name for his college as well as his town, but being a true Scot, and therefore a man who knew his whiskey, he decided to expand upon the spirit of things, so to speak, and named it after his other favorite Scotch, Macallan. Now he had both a town and a college evoking his love for two of the world's finest of libations.

When Macalister first came to America, he had difficulty adjusting to the version of his language he was being subjected to in the colonies, as he still called the States. He could be heard muttering under his breath things like "these people haven't spoken English in years". Which was of course true, the King's English being as remote from upstate New York as England itself. Old man Macalister had special difficulty grasping the sense of the many local colloquialisms. He tended to take them literally, often to his own embarrassment and the amusement of others.

After recounting something that happened to him one day, for example, his companion responded in a completely natural way by saying, "Well, what do ya know about that!" Macalister looked at him incredulously and answered, "I just told you what I know."

It particularly irked him when people would say "you're welcome" after he said "thank you". He claimed it was like "throwing the thank you back in your face."

Needless to say, most of his newfound American friends likewise found his English to be even stranger. His Scottish brogue was so thick they often couldn't make out what he was saying in the first place. Fortunately in the long run, as the success of his endeavors demonstrated, the medium did not mangle the message.

Macalister was also astonished to see so many buildings in his adopted country made of wood instead of stone, as in his European homeland. He would wonder out loud why the Americans were building such temporary structures.

"When," he would say, "are they going to build permanent ones? Do they not think their country is going to last that long?"

But Macalister had great faith in the ultimate longevity of his adopted country and insisted his new college campus be built with the finest stone available in the region. Not only that, he insisted his buildings be modeled after the gothic revival architecture of his beloved University of Glasgow.

Eventually the town of Oban, New York, would become a thriving commercial and intellectual community; and its once modest liberal arts college became Macallan University. It encompassed substantial humanities, social and natural science divisions augmented by impressive, state-of-the-art computer science and engineering facilities. Over time tastefully designed modern structures were added to the original gothic center of the campus, complementing the original buildings nicely. While their architecture was necessarily different, they did not look out of place, being constructed with the same stone as the original ones. All of which would have made the founder proud.

Among its faculty, Prof. Aaron Randolph was one of the best known, if not the most respected professors. Despite a relatively modest publication record, or maybe because of it, he seemed bent on making his way into the administrative side of the university. He succeeded in becoming chairman of the Romance Studies department, a position his own colleagues found less than palatable. His abrupt personal style and idiosyncratic decision making made him more enemies than friends among the faculty.

He was a burly fellow, with all the mannerisms that complemented his physique. One would often hear his colleagues utter things like, "Aaron likes to throw his weight around." One of their favorites was, "Aaron has now added some official height to his physical girth."

His students were not terribly fond of him either. He taught French history with a perspective that suggested some kind of personal bias. He dwelt heavily on the marvels of the monarchy while treating the French revolution almost as a destruction of what was once great about the country.

Randolph's personal life had also been as contentious as his professional one. His third wife left him some time ago, under circumstances that were never made clear. The faculty rumor mill was for years rife with stories ranging from obnoxiousness to infidelity and even to wife beating. Only the first, of course, had any evidence to support it, and there was plenty of that. But to be honest, Randolph wasn't by any means the only obnoxious member of the faculty, depending on how one defines obnoxiousness. A person can be inherently obnoxious, as Randolph surely was, but in the rarefied atmosphere of academia, even the nicer ones are obnoxious to one another depending on the stakes involved. The pettier the issue, the more intense the politics. It's not as if it's built into their DNA. It seems to be an acquired characteristic, something assumed once the privilege of tenure has been bestowed.

CHAPTER 2

It was into this community that I, Isaac Bell, entered as an assistant professor, fresh out of graduate school at the age of twenty-six.

I must admit I was highly motivated and determined to achieve what I thought was the silver chalice of academia, the coveted goal of tenure. I had set specific goals for myself even while still in college. That was during my junior year, which I spent on a study abroad program in France. I was majoring in foreign languages, and was sure a year at the Sorbonne in Paris would solidify my knowledge and use of the language.

Things did not go quite as I planned, however, because the program I was on had its own rather antiquated ideas of the language learning process. As I saw it, I had already achieved all I could learn inside a college classroom in the States. This was supposed to be my opportunity to benefit from being immersed in the culture itself, learning by experience on the streets of Paris. Or so I thought.

Unfortunately, my program director had other ideas. He insisted on attendance in language classes, with an additional hour each day in something called a language lab, where we all were told to put on headphones and interact with an anonymous, pre-programmed speaker on the other end of the line. This, for me, was the last straw.

"Why," I asked, "should I be talking with a mannequin I can't even see, when I could be out in the streets interacting with real people?"

It wasn't long therefore before I started skipping class. Instead, I spent my time devising projects to pursue in the city. As a result, I ended up effectively inventing an intensive language learning program of my own, of which I was rather proud.

As great a solution as that turned out to be, however, it got me in a lot of trouble with my director, something that would come back to haunt me later in life. Midway through my year abroad, I had a rather contentious meeting with my director when he called me into his office.

"I understand you've been missing a lot of classes lately, Ike. Is my information correct?"

"Up to a point, yes sir."

"What do you mean by 'up to a point'? Which point is that?"

"The point where the language classes become pointless, I guess."

"Don't get smart with me, young man, or you'll get yourself an early exit back to the States."

"What I meant to say was that I don't miss all my classes. I find the history and culture classes very valuable. It's just the language ones, especially that ridiculous language lab, that I find useless."

"Useless, in what way?"

"I came all the way over here to learn from real-life situations, not from contrived ones pretending to mimic what I can experience out in the streets."

"We did not send you here to spend time playing tourist or whatever it is you are doing out in the streets, as you say."

"Well, I am not like the other students who sit through classes and then spend the rest of their time partying and getting drunk, speaking English most of the time. I have devised a series of projects for myself where I have to use French. I'm learning a lot more about how the language works that way."

"Well, you may think that is so, but here we have rules. And from now on you will attend all the classes or be excused from the program."

I did do what he told me for the rest of the summer, but that only made me more determined than ever to devote my life to improving the language teaching profession.

While my experience in Paris that year left much to be desired, the projects I had devised for myself created a love of the city like none I had ever felt in any other place. From that moment on, Paris would always be "my beloved Paris", the place I would have to return to someday to make my life complete.

Once back in the States, I spent my senior year looking for graduate schools to pursue my newfound passion. Ultimately I settled on the Graduate School of Education at a prestigious university. I was going to get a doctoral degree that would assure me a teaching position in the future. By the time I finished my Ph.D. dissertation I had already secured a name for myself as someone they said had great promise in the field of intensive language training.

Much to my consternation, however, I discovered that a doctoral degree from a School of Education, even one at a prestigious university like mine, would not guarantee me a faculty position at an equally prestigious university. I guess if I had been more attentive, I would have realized how much a doctoral degree from a School of Education does not pass muster as a genuine degree among the elites of the university establishment. The tip-off should have come when the professors from my school insisted on being called Doctor, while those from other parts of the university never thought to use the title. In fact, the ones from the Arts and Sciences faculty insisted on being called Mister. For them, using the title of Doctor was considered a sign of an inferiority complex.

Having ignored all this, I remained self-assured, not letting the prejudices of the academic system faze me. So when I finally secured a position as Assistant Professor at the relatively unknown Macallan University, I didn't perceive it as a slight at all. Rather, it was an opportunity to show what I was worth. Maybe not a big fish in a small pond, just a future big fish.

CHAPTER 3

In my first year as a junior professor at Macallan, I tried my best to be perceived as a cool and assured guy. My students even took to calling me Likable Ike. I could, of course, get worked up at times, as I certainly had with my study abroad director, but my normal demeanor, if I say so myself, was rather laid back. I definitely didn't want anyone calling me Doctor. I liked being called Likeable Ike.

As I would understand later, however, that gave me a somewhat overinflated sense of security, something I should have been wary of as an untenured junior professor. Obviously, I still had a lot to learn about how the system works, and my initial naivete in that regard would eventually test my ability to remain true to myself.

It may sound egotistical, but you'll understand if I say what I also had going for me was my basic good looks. Being relatively tall, just under six feet, with an olive complexion and curly dark hair, I had no trouble becoming a hit with the female students. The way I dressed helped as well, casual but just tasteful enough not to offend the older members of the faculty, who I noticed always dressed more formally. Though I had never been very athletic, I did try to stay in shape. That was important because I had been diagnosed with an irregular heartbeat as a child, which kept me from engaging very much in sports. So the relatively sedentary life of a professor, I figured, should suit me pretty well.

Unfortunately, as it turned out, I joined the Romance Studies department at Macallan just at the time Aaron Randolph was installed as chairman. Thus I was forced to spend my untenured, shall we say neophyte, years under the watchful eye and judgmental thumb of the overbearing

Professor Randolph. I would come to realize just what that meant for my future more and more each year as I tried to build a case for ultimately obtaining tenure. I knew I had exactly six years, according to the academic rulebook, to make my case or start looking for another career.

Honestly, I had every reason to believe I had been hired at Macallan because of my specialty. My dissertation and the articles I managed to get published while in graduate school had already earned me and my ideas about language training a certain degree of national attention. It came as a surprise, therefore, that the reception I got from the faculty in my own department turned out to be mixed, even hostile at times.

The objections they threw at me came on three fronts. In the first place, the die hard academicians insisted that real learning could only take place inside their classrooms. That was the very attitude I had found untenable during my year abroad, that had prompted me to launch my career in the first place.

The second criticism came from the classical grammarians, one of whom actually insisted that "only being able to write sentences with perfect grammar is the proper subject of a university education. Being able to speak a language fluently," this person went on, "may be a laudable thing, but the substandard phrases and colloquialisms involved have no place in a university setting."

I would wince every time I heard one of my esteemed older colleagues speaking in grammatically correct but obviously archaic French with an atrocious American accent.

Both of these objections, however, paled by comparison with the third, the coup-de-grace, if you will. This unfortunately was championed by none other than chairman Randolph himself.

"Language teaching," he would say, "did not belong in a university in the first place. That was something one might do in high school or on one's own. University training should be devoted to the scholarly study of the literature and culture of a foreign country."

Faced with this sort of parochial thinking, I could have countered with the obvious notion that a culture cannot be understood without knowledge of its language, nor a language without appreciation of the culture in which it is embedded. But I could not afford to offend the domineering Aaron Randolph.

Not surprisingly, this three-pronged attack came from the older, established professors in my department. Aside from Randolph, there were four of them: Fielding, Higgins, Truesdale and Doyle. While their idea of academe was uniformly antiquated, you could still tell them apart by their mannerisms and their dress, which were so cliché the students took to mocking them mercilessly.

Professor Fielding, for example, came to class every day dressed in the same dark suit so powdered with dandruff it seemed he must have just come in from a snow storm. The students would sometimes make a show of looking out the window to check the weather as he walked in. That would invariably produce a puzzled look on the professor's face, amid a chorus of muffled giggles from the gallery. His lectures bored the students to death and his articles on French literature, published in obscure journals, were little more than a litany of footnotes to other people's work. Thus he quickly became tagged as Footnote Fielding.

Professor Higgins was a short and balding man whose clothes often looked like he had slept in them. It seemed to have been more than twenty years since he had read the Spanish novels he taught, and the students often had to correct him when he got the plots wrong. These constant corrections earned him the nickname Hopeless Higgins.

Then there was Professor Truesdale, the oldest member of the faculty, who had sported the same bow tie for some thirty-odd years. He read the same lectures on Italian history and culture every year from the same, worn and stained yellow legal pads. Due to the age and ancient nature of Truesdale, the students began to call him T-Rex Truesdale.

Finally, the only woman in the department was so protective of her status as such, she did everything she could to ensure no female candidate ever got past the preliminary screening stage. Though they had their fun, the students, not wanting to be seen as sexist, stopped short of calling her anything but Professor Doyle.

As for Randolph himself, the students had a field day. Because he had never had children despite being married three times, he became Barren Aaron. Because he pursued women with evidently little success, he earned the title Randy Randolph. There were several other racier monikers, but the students were especially careful not to be overheard uttering them.

What saved my sanity during these untenured years were my younger colleagues. They were quite a colorful mix, in more ways than one. Jim Taylor was the token black person in the department, a cool guy everyone wanted to be around. He had a razor-sharp intellect and little patience for the stale traditions of academe. He joined the department the year after me. Everyone thought he would be a shoe-in to get tenure and was destined to become a star in his field, the literature of the French African diaspora. Despite the exotic nature of his subject, or more likely because of it, his classes were invariably filled to capacity.

Tom Bradford was unmistakably but not flamboyantly gay, and a veritable hoot to be around. He taught both French and Spanish language classes, and had managed to make peace with old man Randolph enough to get tenure despite the chair's disdain for language teaching. It was rumored that Randolph had been afraid to deny him tenure, lest he be charged as homophobic. Tom soon became a good friend and counsel for me as I struggled to comprehend what I had got myself into.

Bill Bransing was the Romance linguist in the department, known nationally for his work on the history and structure of languages. He had escaped the wrath of Randolph because his work was theoretical rather than practical, and because he had already gotten tenure when Randolph assumed the chairmanship.

This was the world I inherited when I accepted the position as Assistant Professor at Macallan University.

CHAPTER 4

During my first year at Macallan, I enjoyed teaching both French and Italian language courses. I also managed to complete two articles for publication that year, which put me in good graces with the chairman. The attitudes of my senior colleagues didn't faze me then, since I could pursue my teaching and publishing without their interference. I could also afford to ignore their antiquated views in faculty meetings, since so far at least, the issues being discussed there did not affect my work.

What bothered me, though, was not being able to put in action the central ideas I had been promoting in my publications. My teaching had necessarily been confined to classwork with the students, there not being any other venues available for learning outside the classroom. I needed the proper conditions for the kind of language training I was championing, either my own program abroad for Macallan students or at least an intensive summer course on the Macallan campus, where I could create a simulated foreign atmosphere when there were no other students on campus at the time.

I broached the subject informally a couple of times with Randolph, but each time he simply told me to be patient. "It will take time to build the kind of support you will need to convince your colleagues," the chairman told me. "I would have to set aside some of the department's precious resources to make that happen."

Slowly I began to realize that the views of the old guard would indeed impact my work, indirectly if not directly, and eventually affect my chances for proving myself worthy of getting tenure. I could not simply continue publishing ideas I had never had the opportunity to put into action myself.

As my second year at Macallan began, I became more and more impatient. I considered either confronting Randolph more aggressively or waiting another year to try and ingratiate myself somehow with my senior colleagues. After all, my research and teaching were going well, and I had several, very supportive younger colleagues to take refuge with. I figured I could afford to spend one more year enjoying their friendship and taking advantage of their counsel as to how to proceed.

Relations with my younger colleagues, especially Tom Bradford and Jim Taylor were not only gratifying, they also provided a welcome relief from the pressures of academe. Tom and Jim, the two token minorities, were serious scholars, but they also knew how to relax and unwind. There were great get-togethers, usually at Tom's place, almost every weekend, with plenty of booze, nothing stronger than pot, and lots of young friends and colleagues from other departments. I never laughed so hard as when Tom got on a tear at one of these parties with his famous stories, often told at the expense of the older faculty.

There was one about Higgins, who used to smoke cigars in class, back before they banned smoking inside the university buildings. As Tom would tell it, mimicking Higgin's movements, the old geezer was always writing things on the blackboard and puffing his cigar at the same time.

"Since he was right-handed," Tom related, "he would hold the cigar in his right hand and puff on it once in a while as he lectured. When he thought of something he wanted to write on the board, he would whip around and start to write, forgetting that what he had in his hand was the cigar. It would take him several seconds to realize what he'd done, during which time half the cigar would have crumbled apart, with pieces falling all over the floor. Oblivious to the audible amusement from the students, he would resume writing, with the chalk this time, as if nothing had happened, trampling underfoot the pile of ashes and tobacco remnants for the remainder of the class."

Once Tom said he asked Higgins himself if the story was true.

"His answer," Tom relayed, "was as priceless as the story itself. 'Don't you know,' he told me, 'I do that on purpose, to see if they're paying attention in class. Wakes them up a bit, don't you know.' To which I answered, 'you don't say'!"

Tom also had several jokes about his dad, whom everyone knew he adored, so they were never hurtful. His father had a mild case of dementia and occasionally did some weird things that Tom would turn into great tales. There was one about his dad insisting you could hard-boil an egg in the microwave.

"My claiming otherwise only made him more determined to prove me wrong. Before I could stop him, he popped an egg in there and pushed the button for one minute on high. Not knowing how big the explosion might be, I yelled at him not to stand so close to watch. Good thing, too, because a couple seconds later there was a loud bang and the door to the microwave came whizzing by dad's ear. Not so with the egg, though. It showered him with so many pieces of half-cooked egg, it took him the better part of an hour to get them off."

Then there was the story about his dad and the phone. "He heard it ring," Tom began, "picked it up and immediately started yelling into it. When I asked him what was wrong, he insisted it was a crank call because there was no one on the other end. That's when I took the TV remote away from him and handed him the phone."

It was also at these parties that I met many bright, good-looking women. And I have to admit I rarely went home alone. But I learned early on that the women I met at these parties, often graduate students who were not much younger than myself, were primarily interested in furthering their academic careers, not in anything like a serious relationship. So my after-party dalliances invariably ended up as one-night stands.

Eventually Tom and I began to establish a special relationship of our own. In fact, he became not only a friend but a mentor as well. His insights and advice about how to succeed as a faculty member were invaluable. As he put it, "dealing as a gay person navigating the straight world outside has actually improved somewhat over time, with the push for LGBTQ rights and all. But dealing with colleagues in the academic world never gets any better."

As he explained it, the way academics are trained virtually guarantees the system won't change.

"It has a lot to do with the very institution of tenure," he claimed. "To have a career practicing law, for example, you have to pass the bar exam. It's the same test everyone takes, so you're on a level playing field there. But getting tenure in academe is a highly subjective process. It takes only one prejudicial judgment by a faculty member to put the kibosh on someone's career."

Much like the US congress, I thought to myself, where one senator's personal agenda can destroy an entire country's hopes to get a much-needed bill passed.

"Young scholars," Tom went on, "are trained from the git-go to view tenure as the pinnacle of success, and to ignore everything but their own survival in order to get there. Once they do, if they do, they feel they have gained the right to forever guard their own prerogatives. There could be no more self-centered process than that."

Over the course of those first two years, I also became friends with Phil. Phillip Cranston was a young, untenured professor like myself, working as a linguist in the anthropology department. We had many conversations together, comparing notes on what it was like to be in our situation. Phil's issues were oddly the converse of mine, however. I had relatively good success getting my work published, but more difficulty getting members of my own department to appreciate me. Phil on the other hand was respected by just about every colleague in the anthropology department but had little luck getting his work published.

Phil's problems stemmed from the very nature of academic publishing. "Every time I submit an article to a journal," he would lament, "I am told my approach is not compatible with the ideology of that particular publication. It seems each journal is controlled by cliques of scholars promoting their preferred points of view. Under these circumstances," Phil wondered out loud, "how can anyone with truly original ideas possibly get a foot in the door."

After more than two years trying, Phil had become despondent about ever being able to publish enough to gain tenure in the publish-or-perish world we both had chosen as a career. Several colleagues in his department had suggested he write a book instead of articles, but that, he rightly concluded, "would amount to putting all my eggs in one basket, and in the end I'd still be at the mercy of the publishing industry, just at a different level."

Listening to Phil made me feel I was the luckier one, and I did my best to try to cheer Phil up whenever we got together. Phil was not much of a partier, so we would get together at each other's homes instead, where I would try to steer the conversation away from anything to do with the university as much as possible. We really enjoyed each other's company, talking about language, looking for ways his theoretical approach could be of value in my practical world of language training, and vice versa. We even toyed with the idea of publishing a book together, but unfortunately, I couldn't spare the time just then. I had already secured a commitment from a publishing company to produce a textbook and was already hard at work on it.

CHAPTER 5

With the help of conversations like this, I began to understand more about the academic system by the end of my second year at Macallan. But I was growing weary of waiting for the department to adopt one of my projects. So I vowed to confront the chair about it first thing in my third year.

Two months into the new term I managed to screw up enough courage to request a formal meeting with Randolph. I had never been in his office before. The departmental secretary asked me why I wanted the meeting and a time was finally set. When I entered, I noticed right away how relatively few books there were on the shelves. It felt more like a doctor's than a professor's office, with framed certificates on the walls attesting to Randolph's degrees and such. Nothing like the walls of books I was used to seeing. I was also surprised not to find a single photograph of a personal nature anywhere in the room either, no family pictures, not even ones of professional gatherings that might otherwise give a sense of collegiality. This was evidently a personal power center and little else.

Randolph asked me to close the door and take one of the two chairs in front of his imposing desk. Then in a gesture that struck me right away, he came out from behind the desk himself and sat in the chair next to me. I understood this was meant to imply we were now on a level playing field. But I knew better.

"I'm sorry we haven't been able to see more of each other," he began with a practiced smile, "but these past two years have kept me pretty tied up just trying to retain the money needed to keep the department running."

That smile, I had been warned, was known in the department as the smiling shaft. So I understood right away that what I had just heard was intended to serve as a shot across the bow, a warning that if I were to ask for the funds I needed to launch one of my projects, it would not come easily, if at all.

Being out of my element, I wasn't sure how to proceed, since the stage was already set. Randolph seemed to sense my discomfort and filled the silence himself.

"I understand," he offered, "you're here to talk about your projects, no?"

"Yes, that's right."

"Which one, if I may ask? I know you've been thinking of two different ones, the summer course and the program abroad."

"Well, I'm not greedy," I responded with a smile of my own, trying to sound confident, "but I presume the summer session idea would be the simplest to implement and require the least funding."

"How so?" Randolph asked, knowing full well, I presumed, what each of my proposals would cost him.

"Well, the department is already offering summer session courses, and we could start off modestly the first year by adding just one new course."

"I see," Randolph said, assuming a pensive expression by bringing his hand to his face and stroking his cheek. "You realize, of course, that you'd put me in a bit of a bind that way. Either I find the extra money or I have to tell one of the other faculty members his or her course is not going to be offered this time around."

"I appreciate what you're saying," I responded. Then, determined not to let him get the best of me, I added, "but with all due respect, I will have been here now for three years and maybe it's my turn to get some of the summer funding. I am willing to do all of the added administrative work the course would require myself without compensation if that would help. Actually, I would need to do that anyway, since my system would require establishing a series of extra-curricular activities only I could organize to complement the class."

"Well, I see you've thought this through," he said, shifting in his chair, "so let me make you a proposition. If you will agree to put this to a vote at our next faculty meeting, I'll go along with what the faculty say. How about that?"

I sensed immediately this could be a trap, but it was either this or nothing.

"OK, fine, let's do that then. I guess it's only fair," I said. "Thank you."

On my way back to my office, an array of thoughts went through my head. What have I just gotten myself into, was the first. I'll be up against the old farts and at the mercy of the system yet again with that vote, was the second. But if I win, I will have gained stature in the department, was the third. Then the fourth and most likely one: Randolph will surely take it out on me, one way or another, if he loses that vote.

Once I got back to my office, all I could think of was: I need a drink.

CHAPTER 6

I did get the vote on my summer session proposal at the next faculty meeting, as Randolph promised. Not surprisingly, the three older men voted against, and the three younger ones for. That left Doyle to break the tie, since Randolph chose not to insert himself into the process. By abstaining, he left the decision up to Doyle, knowing full well he would still have the option to implement the decision or not, depending on how things went later on. So he let Doyle do what he knew she would, stick it to him when the chips were down.

As we left the meeting room, Tom took me aside and asked if I wanted to go for a drink to celebrate. He used air quotes around the word "celebrate", which I took to mean there was still a lot I needed to learn about what just happened.

What Tom told me while we were seated at a corner table away from prying ears in his favorite bar did come to pass exactly the way he predicted it would. A week after the positive vote, Randolph announced he had found the funding and would approve one course for me in the next summer session. Then, about two-thirds of the way through that third year, I got a message, from Randolph's secretary, not Randolph himself, saying he was terribly sorry, but the university had cut the summer budget at the last moment and he had no choice but to drop my course after all.

In the meantime, I had worked feverishly to prepare the syllabus and the extra-curricular projects for the course. To manage this, I had to delay working on my textbook, but I figured the success of that summer course would be worth it on my resume. Utterly dejected by this last-minute turn of events, I left my office early that day and headed home.

The moment I walked through the door I heard the phone ring. It was Tom, asking if I needed another drink.

"Probably two," I responded, and headed over to Tom's favorite bar.

Once again we sat at the corner table. I was about to order a double Scotch on the rocks when Tom, trying to lighten the mood a bit, asked if I knew about the tradition at this bar.

"No," I answered, "I can only imagine."

"Well," Tom said, "this town and the university were both named by a Scot who knew his whiskey. And this bar honors the tradition by giving discounts on both Oban and Macallan Scotch. So take your pick, dear colleague, and the treats on me."

"In that case, let's order one for you and the other for me."

"Sounds like a plan."

The drinks came almost instantly, with a wink from the waitress, as if she had poured them in advance. Tom raised his glass and offered a sarcastic toast.

"Here's to the spirits which keep this town and its beloved university going."

"In its own inimitable way," I responded, still dejected.

Then, getting serious, Tom said, "Tell me you didn't see this coming. I tried to warn you to look out for him doing something just like this."

"I suppose I did, but I still can't believe this is the system I have dedicated my life to."

"Well, it is what it is, but you have to persevere. You've still got three years before your tenure decision, and with your publication record, you should be able to write your own ticket. Personally, I think you have a bright future, and I'm putting my money on you."

After a second round of Scotch and with this encouragement still ringing in my ears, I went back to my apartment determined to finish working on my textbook. I loved writing and I loved teaching my classes. So I buried myself in my work for what was left of the spring semester.

Then, just as the semester was about to end and I was finishing grading final exams, Randolph asked to see me again. This time, when I entered his office, he stayed seated behind the big desk. He told me he wanted to make it up to me for what happened and had a proposition.

The way Randolph phrased his "proposition" put me even more on guard than usual. What he offered was nothing less than a position as assistant chair of the department, starting in the next academic year.

Right away I sensed the smiling shaft at work, but remained speechless. Randolph filled the silence with an explanation.

"The thing is," he said, "I need someone to help me take the edge off my relations with the faculty. Despite the budgetary issues we all face now, there are still some things we can accomplish. But with a faculty as divided as ours, the job is even more difficult. I need someone whom the faculty likes who can help me get things done. There is a reason you are called Likable Ike—yes, I know all about that—and you can help me make things happen."

Not knowing what else to say, I responded, "What sort of things, sir, if I may ask?"

"Well, I have thought some more about the summer session course you proposed and think it could provide us a national reputation for specialized language training in the summer. We could become a center of sorts for that kind of thing outside the normal academic year. But I can't sell it to the administration because it's not in my area of expertise. Obviously, I failed this time around, and you have had to pay the price. So I am trying to make it up to you."

"I certainly appreciate that, sir, but what other types of things are you contemplating?" I asked.

"Well, those are still in the incubational stage, and I can't elaborate unless you are willing to accept this responsibility. Then we can pursue them in earnest together."

Hmm, I thought. Other things he can't divulge. What does that mean? If I had an ounce of brains, I should walk right out of the room. But then I would also all but certainly ruin my chances for tenure. I needed some time to think about this, and told Randolph so. Randolph said he understood and would wait for my response.

Clearly it was time for a third drink with Tom, but not in the bar this time. We decided to meet at Tom's place and he invited Bill Bransing to join us. Bill would be able to give us additional perspective on the situation, since he was the most experienced of Tom's friends.

I had of course been to Tom's place before, but it was always at one of his parties with lots of people milling around. So this was my first opportunity to appreciate what a really nice place it was. The house was located among the tree-lined hills just above the town. It seemed a bit large for a single person, but it was tastefully decorated to create a warm and inviting atmosphere just the same. There was an open floorplan in the part of the house where the kitchen, dining area and living room were. But then there were several smaller, more intimate nooks whose walls were lined with built-in bookshelves. The one with the fireplace was the coziest, where Tom suggested we sit and talk, in his comfy leather chairs.

Tom offered to bring out the Scotch, but I declined, saying this was too serious a discussion and I needed to keep my wits about me. Bill agreed and we all settled on a glass of wine instead. Tom began by asking me to describe in as much detail as possible the conversation in Randolph's office.

As they listened, both Tom and Bill's facial expressions gave away what they were thinking. But they stayed quiet until I finished.

"Wow," was the first expression out of Bill's mouth.

"What a son-of-a-bitch," was Tom's. "You do know what he's up to, right Ike?" Tom asked me.

"I think so, but I have no idea how to deal with it."

"That's what we're here for," Bill assured him. "I suggest we start with risk assessments for each of the choices he gave you, yes or no, accept or don't accept, with pros and cons for each."

"That's what I was trying to do in my own mind last night," I said, "but I'm sure there's a lot I didn't think of."

Then Tom said, "OK, where do we start, with yes or with no?"

"Maybe with the one most likely to get me tenure?" I suggested, trying to laugh.

"Ah, my friend," Tom said, "unfortunately there's the rub. Either may lose you tenure and neither will guarantee you anything."

"Oh gee, thanks," I said, taking another sip of wine. "Now I'm really fucked."

"No, actually, that's exactly how we should base our assessment," Bill suggested. "Which of the options, yes or no, has the most pros and the least cons to getting Ike tenure. How would you like to proceed, Ike?"

"I'd like to start with yes first, so I can better judge what I'd be getting myself into if I did this."

"Good idea," Tom agreed. "Since you're the most experienced in these things, Bill, why don't you get us started."

"OK, here goes. On the plus side, Ike would get his summer program and surely make a hit with it, likely even get national recognition for it, like that sly old bastard said. As vice-chairman, or whatever Randolph would call this position, Ike would also learn a lot about the inner workings of the institution, and make important friends among the higher-ups in the administration. But that, as far as I can see, is all he would gain from this.

"And the down-side?" I pressed him.

"Where to start. First off, spending a lot of your time in administration will not earn you any points towards tenure. Remember, administration is the least of the three categories they judge you on, and your publishing and teaching could well suffer as a consequence. So unless you really want a career in administration, most likely somewhere else when you ultimately fail to get tenure here, there's not much in this for you. What do you think, Tom?"

"I completely agree, and I'd add a few more negatives. You may make friends among the higher-ups outside the department, but few within. You'd be seen as doing Randolph's bidding and therefore forced to be on the wrong side of many votes in faculty meetings. Doyle, for one, will delight in eating you up, just like she does Randolph. In her eyes, you'll be Randolph's bitch, if you'll pardon the reference."

"I think I'm almost convinced already, guys. But how much do I lose if I tell him no?"

"If you tell him no," Tom offered, "you will surely lose your summer project, but you'd gain, what is it, three more years to publish and get a sterling teaching record to boot. Though Randolph will do what he can to deny you tenure, he'll have a difficult time of it. And once you get tenure, you'll have all the time you need to do the things you want. Come to think of it, I doubt Randolph will even care if you decline the offer. He might actually think more of you for seeing through his ploy."

"I totally agree," Bill chimed in. "But I'm still curious as to why the bastard made the proposition in the first place. What does he have to gain by this? The only thing I can think of is to be able to put the blame on Ike for things that go wrong in the department. Which is, in my opinion, the most compelling reason for Ike not to accept this job."

"Got it," was all I needed to say. I'd gotten the advice I needed and had only to go and face Randolph now with my answer.

CHAPTER 7

I wasn't quite sure how Randolph took my decision to decline his offer. I didn't want to confront him again in his office, on his territory, so I sent him a polite note saying something rather innocuous about needing to commit my remaining years before tenure to publishing and teaching. The response I got back was equally indirect, just a note from his secretary that said, "The chairman appreciates your decision and wishes you well."

I would have to wait another three years to find out what effect my decision actually had.

I spent those remaining three years perfecting my textbook, getting it published, and making an even stronger name for myself as an expert in the field of intensive language training. My student evaluations remained uniformly excellent, so when the time came, I was relatively confident I would get tenure.

There was just one wrinkle.

During my fifth year, the year before I was to come up for tenure, the university announced that Professor Randolph had been selected as the next Dean of the humanities division. The departmental faculty, older and younger ones both, were glad to see him go. It was the only time all eight professors agreed on something. But they were also leery of what Randolph could do now that he was in a position of even greater power than before over the departments in their division. And my tenure decision would ultimately turn out to be the test of that.

The test came in my sixth year, when I had, by the rules of the academic senate, to either be granted or denied tenure. The meeting the department held to decide my fate was a classic example of academic intransigence. The faculty were divided along exactly the same grounds as the day I first entered the university. It was as if I had done absolutely nothing from the day I arrived. As far as the old guard was concerned—Fielding, Higgins and Truesdale—my superlative teaching and publication record meant nothing. They dismissed my teaching, I figured, more out of jealousy, or was it spite, than anything else, since they knew, deep in their own hearts, that their own teaching was anything but worthy of tenure in today's world. As for my publications, even the textbook that had made me a name in my field nationally, they dismissed out of hand.

"These kinds of publications," Fielding claimed with a haughty sense of entitlement, "might be worthy of tenure in a School of Education, but not in a humanities division such as ours."

Tom and Bill, of course, thought my accomplishments were more than sufficient to grant tenure. Jim Taylor couldn't vote because he didn't have tenure himself yet. So it was left to Doyle to cast the deciding vote.

Surprisingly, she had succeeded Randolph as chairperson when he decamped for the deanship. She got the position only because no one else wanted it. True to form, in order to stick it to Randolph one more time, she voted in favor of my tenure, making the departmental vote a tie and daring Randolph, now with the power as dean, to turn me down.

Which of course is just what he did.

He based his decision on exactly what he had claimed from the start, that language teaching does not belong in a university. As far as he was concerned, everything I had done for the past five and a half years had never mattered.

Needless to say, I was not happy with the decision. Truth be told, I was livid, and went around the hallowed halls of the university telling anyone who would listen what I thought about the system, and Aaron Randolph in particular. My younger colleagues, Tom especially, tried to get me to tone it down, so they could work on finding a way to get the decision overturned at a higher level, but I was not in a mood to listen.

"Look, Ike," Tom said the next time he and Bill met with me for drinks, "we'll do what we can here, but you've got to stop mouthing off about Randolph. Your threatening tone could get you in trouble. Instead, since you've already made a name for yourself in the field, why don't you put your energies into lining up a couple of offers from other institutions. There must be plenty who would be more than delighted to have you as a colleague."

To which Bill added, "You know you have a seventh year to work on it, according to the rulebook, before they terminate your employment here for good. Then you can thumb your nose at the whole business and walk away a winner."

I did indeed spend that final seventh year at Macallan securing a couple of job offers, but my heart wasn't in it. I simply couldn't contemplate starting all over again, and was content to use Tom's famous parties as a way to take my mind off things.

It was at ones of those parties that I met a woman who turned out to be much more than the one-night stands I had become accustomed to. Our first meeting would become a story told many times thereafter.

I had been chatting with a group at the party that night when I was introduced to Sarah Blake. Also among the group was someone named Jeremy, whom she seemed to be acquainted with. I had met Jeremy at these parties before but didn't know much about him. Conversations naturally became unguarded when the booze flowed freely, so when I managed to be alone with Sarah later in the evening over by the bar, I casually asked her if she knew Jeremy. Since I was hoping to see more of her after the party, I needed to know if they might already be involved.

"Oh," she replied, sensing exactly why I had asked, "we know each other quite well. Jeremy's my ex."

As I tried to wipe away the part of my drink I spilled on my shirt, I felt my face turning beet red. Sarah laughed so hard watching me, she also spilled part of her drink. Then the two of us toasted with what was left in our glasses.

Far from being awkward, that moment made our first encounter all the more memorable. We spent the rest of that night together at my place. My apartment wasn't anything to brag about, certainly nothing like Tom's, because I hadn't wanted to buy a home of my own until I knew whether or not I was going to get tenure. I'd found an old Victorian building in the center of town that had been divided up into apartments. Then I'd bought some comfortable old furniture to complement the character of the place.

Sarah and I talked the night away, sipping wine and listening to music from my record collection. I learned that she had gotten a position at a law firm up the road in Syracuse shortly after she and Jeremy got married.

As she explained things, "The distance between Syracuse and Oban was too far to commute every day, so my new job kept us apart most weekdays and many weekends as well. Long story short, Jeremy, to put it euphemistically, tended to get lonely. Eventually we both realized living apart wasn't going to work. So we dissolved the marriage and agreed to remain friends. We see each other every once in a while, usually at Tom's parties."

"And what about you," she asked me.

"Well, as everybody knows by now," I told her, "I didn't get tenure, so I'm kind of in limbo these days. I've gotten a couple of feelers to teach at other colleges. Nothing I'm that excited about, though. But I just got my new textbook published, and the royalties from that, together with the advance they gave me earlier, ought to keep me for a while. Oban's a nice place to live, so I think I'll stick around until something better comes up. I certainly have lots of friends here."

"And now you have another one," she added with a smile that said more than I could have hoped for.

For the rest of the night we enjoyed talking with each other so much we hardly realized when the sun started coming up.

Sarah told me she had meetings at her law firm the next day and had to drive back to Syracuse first thing in the morning, when still all we'd done was talk. I wondered what she was thinking when she drove off with the sun peeking through the clouds. I knew what I was thinking, contemplating how a relationship with Sarah Blake would fit in with my future plans for a career.

For the remainder of that seventh year, we saw as much of each other as we could, more than making up for what we hadn't done that first night we met. Sarah occasionally came down to Oban to see me, but I usually traveled to Syracuse to spend long weekends with her at her apartment. Having been denied tenure, I didn't have to attend faculty meetings any more. I still had to teach, of course, but I could spend most of my time working on my own. Sarah, on the other hand, had to be ready at any moment to respond to the demands her job and the court calendar. That accounted for our spending most of our time together at her place, which suited me just fine. That also gave us the opportunity to test the waters, so to speak, to see if we really did want to become a couple.

I have to say we complemented each other nicely, in more ways than one. Where I was relatively tall, with my curly hair and olive skin, she was relatively short, about five foot five with light skin and straight blond hair cut just above the shoulders. Where I could be impulsive, even impetuous at times, she was levelheaded and virtually unflappable, as I assumed she had to be working in a law firm.

The question in my mind was, what to do once my seventh year was up. If I were to accept either of the two job offers that had been dangled in front of me, that would take me away from the ersatz Scottish Highlands of upstate New York I had become so fond of, and from Sarah. On the other hand, now that my textbook was published, I would have a modest income from the royalties, which were quite decent. And being a textbook, it would need to be revised and updated every year or so, which would give me a job to do and a steady income should I stay. It would also leave me time to continue pursuing the research I loved, publishing articles on the side. I wouldn't need a faculty position or a university office for that. And lord knows, I certainly wouldn't miss attending faculty meetings. The Internet was my major source of information and contact with colleagues anyway. I could have my cake and eat it too, doing what I loved, being with the woman I had come to adore, and still be able to see my friends in Oban at Tom's great parties.

By the time my seventh year was up, logic had prevailed and true love had won out. We decided to make a life together in Syracuse, living in unmarried bliss.

CHAPTER 8

This was not by any means all that made my seventh year in Oban eventful, however. Towards the end of that year, sometime in March while I was still teaching classes and living with Sarah on the weekends, the news went out that Dean Randolph was missing. He had not been seen on campus or around town for almost a week. He had not told anyone he would be away, and no one on campus knew of any business he was scheduled to have elsewhere. The Dean's office kept his schedule religiously, and sounded the alarm as soon as he started missing meetings on campus.

The local police got involved right away, but had no idea what sort of issue they might be dealing with. They didn't even know what to call their investigation, they had so little information to go on. It could be nothing more than a missing person case, where they may find him somewhere in the woods behind his home, having tripped over a fallen tree trunk or something. On the other hand, it could have been the result of a murder or a kidnapping, and that made them take the issue rather more seriously. They had been made aware that Randolph had a contentious history, both at the university and in his personal life. Given the number of people he had dealt with in his usual off-putting manner, they were hard pressed to know where to start looking for suspects.

They were aware, of course, that if a missing person is not found within three days, they are more than likely to either be found dead or not found at all. But they were not told of Randolph's disappearance until several days after he stopped showing up at his scheduled meetings. So they needed to spring into action quickly if they were to get anywhere at all.

The first thing they did was search the professor's home for clues, including the woods behind it. Finding nothing out of the ordinary, they nevertheless began to release, in bits and pieces, information about what they did find there. There was no evidence of a struggle. There were dishes in the sink waiting to be washed, an array of books and papers on the desk in his study indicating he seemed to be actively working on something, and his car was still in the garage.

They purposely didn't say anything about what they may have found relating to his personal habits, citing issues of privacy. That was enough, as you might imagine, to set off a robust series of conspiracies about possible peccadillos. Needless to say, the faculty at the university had a field day dreaming up theories. One in particular seemed to strike a chord. Someone came up with the notion that Randolph might have been secretly working for the CIA, though no one could think of what sort of business he'd have with them. Looking for Russian spies in little Oban, New York, didn't seem a likely mission. A possible terrorist cell hiding out in just such an out-of-the-way place, however, did lend itself to a certain degree of credibility. That idea caught on because it gave rise to even more speculation as to whether Randolph was tasked with ferreting out such a cell, or was himself a secret member of one.

What did seem more to the point, however, was the amount of Qanon literature the police reported finding in his study, though no one knew quite what to make of that either.

With nothing more substantial to go on, the authorities decided to bring in the FBI. They immediately started identifying individuals with whom Randolph worked, and scheduled a set of interviews. Naturally, they began with the faculty in our department, since that's where he'd been working most of his time at the university. What they got, from what we learned later, was a pretty good sense of what it's like inside a university faculty, but not much about what might have happened to Aaron Randolph.

I was, of course, not privy to what went on in those interviews, but the transcripts were released some years later once the whole affair was over. It turned out they started with the three oldest professors, apparently on the assumption they would be the least likely to have been involved in anything nefarious, but would by the same token be best suited to tell them what they needed to know about Randolph's history with the institution. As I read the transcript years later, I delighted in substituting their first names with their student-inspired nicknames: Footnote Fielding, Hopeless Higgins, and T-Rex Truesdale. It somehow made the whole thing seem easier to bear.

> *FBI:* Thank you for agreeing to talk with us. We will try not to keep you any longer than we have to.
> *FF:* for the other two: We are only too happy to help.
> *FBI:* What can you tell us about Professor Randolph's time at the university?
> *TT:* Well, he has been here now for about fifteen years. We hired him because of his specialty as a comparativist, which none of us is.
> *FBI:* What is a comparativist?
> *HH:* it's someone who studies the relations among, in this case, the literatures of the various Romance languages. Each of us specializes in either French, Italian, or Spanish. He has the background to look at all three and more.
> *FBI:* And has he been successful?
> *FF:* That's a difficult question. Some would say yes, others no. He has been OK in the classroom but, I

must say, a bit of a disappointment when it comes to his publication history.

FBI: And why is that, do you think?

FF: In my opinion, it has to do with his being more interested in administration than in scholarship these days.

FBI: We understand he chaired the department for about seven years and has just now been elevated to the position of dean in the humanities division. Is that correct?

HH: That's correct.

FBI: Tell us a bit about his style as an administrator please.

TT: Well, to tell the truth, it's a bit more turbulent, shall we say, than we're comfortable with. He has strong personal views on things and can be quite demanding.

FBI: Can you give us an example?

TT: Well, we have a colleague not yet tenured, whom Aaron has made disparaging remarks about recently. It seems he doesn't want him to get tenure, and Aaron can exert a lot of influence in matters like that.

FBI: Which professor is that, if we may ask?

HH: It's Jim Taylor. Aaron thinks his specialty is too narrow and idiosyncratic for a department like ours, when we have so many other more central themes in Romance literature to cover. But Jim teaches plenty of other courses too, so we don't understand his concern.

FBI: Do you think there could be another reason, perhaps? We should tell you we've already heard about Professor Taylor.

HH: Um, you mean, because he's black?

FBI: That could be relevant in a case like this, don't you think?

HH: I guess so, but that's not for us to judge.

FBI: You're absolutely right. So let's broaden this out

a bit more. Is there anyone else you can think of who might have issues with Prof. Randolph?

TT: Well, there is this other young fellow who is also due to come up for tenure, whose work Aaron doesn't approve of. Isaac Bell is a language teaching specialist, and Aaron doesn't think language teaching belongs in any university, let alone this one. For him, and for some of us as well, to be honest, it should be seen as remedial work done somewhere else to prepare for university-level work.

FBI: To your knowledge, has Professor Randolph done anything to keep Professor Bell from doing his work?

TT: Well, yes and no. He has constantly delayed giving the green light for Ike, as everyone calls Professor Bell, to establish either the study abroad program or the summer session program he wants.

HH: But to his credit, Ike has succeeded in getting quite a number of articles published and is already completed a textbook that may well become a standard in his field.

FF: Yes, but publishing textbooks is not necessarily doing university-level work either.

FBI: OK, we get the point. And I think we've already taken up enough of your time. Just one last question: Do any of you have issues with Professor Randolph, personal or professional?

FF: I think I can speak for all of us again that we're too close to retirement to have issues that would matter now anyway.

FBI: Alright. Then thank you for your time.

Apparently what they got out of that interview was nothing more than a suspicion, perhaps purposely laid by those three old geezers, that both Jim Taylor and I were the most likely suspects in Randolph's disappearance. And that was more than bad enough.

CHAPTER 9

For their second round of questioning, we were told, the FBI began with Professor Doyle. She was described as coming to her interview dressed in what others delighted in calling her power suit, replete with everything but a red tie, they said. From the transcript, it was obvious she played the role to the hilt.

> *FBI:* Very nice of you to come, Professor Doyle. We'll try to be brief. May we call you Angela or would you prefer professor.
>
> *AD:* What did you call my male colleagues yesterday?
>
> *FBI:* Well, there were three of them, so we simply said professor each time.
>
> *AD:* Then you have your answer.
>
> *FBI:* Very good. So, Professor, what can you tell us about your relationship with Aaron Randolph?
>
> *AD:* What's to tell? We don't have one. He stays out of my hair and I stay out of his.
>
> *FBI:* And why is that, if we may ask?
>
> *AD:* Very simple. I came here as a tenured full professor before Randolph was made chair. So he has no power over me.
>
> *FBI:* So it's all a power thing, then, right?
>
> *AD:* How much do you boys know about a university? Sounds like not much.
>
> *FBI:* We're learning more every minute, Professor. So we'd like to hear your take.
>
> *AD:* Let me put it this way, since you are both men and seem not to get the power thing. In normal society, men have power over women in all sorts of ways, ways I hope

I don't have to enumerate. But here at the university, a tenured female professor effectively neutralizes that power, even when the male professor is department chair. So again, Randolph stays out of my way and I his. It works out quite nicely.

FBI: OK, but we're looking at a missing person case here, and quite possibly a murder. So it behooves us to ask what kind of a relation you have with Randolph outside the university then.

AD: You're kidding, right?

FBI: I assure you, Professor, we're deadly serious.

AD: Nice pun there, but the answer is the same. Absolutely none.

FBI: OK, let's assume that's true and move on. What kind of a man would you say Professor Randolph is?

AD: He's your classic male academic. Mediocre scholar, power-hungry administrator. Has about as thin a publication record as anyone who has gained tenure, but the moxie to have gotten himself appointed dean, where his power can extend so much farther now. I wouldn't be surprised if he wasn't angling to be president of the university someday.

FBI: You don't say. Do you have any evidence of that, the latter statement, that is?

AD: No, just call it female intuition.

FBI: And you don't have any desires in that direction yourself, by any chance, do you?

AD: None that I'm aware of.

FBI: You know we can check on things like this. So if you have also been lobbying for an administrative position somewhere in the university, we're bound to find out.

AD: Are you calling me a liar?

FBI: Absolutely not. We're just asking a fairly obvious question which could relate directly to our investigation.

AD: And if I lie about this, I become a suspect in his disappearance, I suppose?

FBI: We assume it won't come to that.

AD: Well, if you must know, I did inquire a bit about other positions in the university, but I haven't actually applied for anything yet.

FBI: Thanks for the transparency. One last question. We know you assumed the chairmanship, sorry chairpersonship, of the department when Randolph was appointed dean, but did you seek that position back when Randolph first got it? You can see why we have to ask.

AD: Well, like any good politician, I did put out feelers, but I came away convinced my departmental colleagues would, shall we say, not be happy with me in such a position. I'm only chair now because no one else wanted it.

FBI: Well, then, I guess that does it. Thank you again, Professor, for your cooperation.

After reading this, I could only imagine what the FBI guys thought. Apparently they needed some help sorting through all the bullshit because they next asked to see Tom and Bill, hoping to get some straight talk.

FBI: Thank you professors for giving us some of your time.

BB: No problem. We're here to help in whatever way we can.

FBI: Please tell us about your history with the department.

BB: Well, we were both fortunate enough to have gotten tenure before Randolph assumed the chairmanship. Otherwise, I think he might have tried to block us both, since he is so against language instruction. Thankfully, we have managed over the years to escape the worst of his prejudices.

FBI: So neither of you have issues at the moment that might be relevant to our investigation?

TB: We've learned over the years to avoid conflicts that don't directly affect us and our work.

FBI: May we infer, therefore, that you do know of conflicts that might be germane to our investigation?

BB: We're not the detectives here, so I'm not sure what you are looking for. From your tone, I would assume you think this is a murder investigation rather than a simple disappearance?

FBI: Honestly, we haven't determined that yet. But since the local police are looking into the missing person angle, we are concentrating on the possibility something more sinister might have taken place. Unless you know of something like, say, Randolph's tendency to go off on his own without informing anyone, then we must assume the worst, at least for the time being.

BB: So there must be other people you are looking at, members of the faculty presumably?

FBI: We're not at liberty to say, but just as an example, what would you say about Professor Doyle's relation with Randolph? It seems a bit unique to us.

BB: Does it? Welcome to academe! Beware the woman who has beat the system. They're as cunning as wolves, not to be toyed with. Personally, I think Randolph was afraid of her, and for good reason. She's politically very astute.

FBI: Why should he have been afraid of her when he was the chair?

TB: You have to understand the rituals of academe. The two of them faced off all the time like billy goats in a mating contest—a metaphor I like to use because it makes them both out to be males, by the way. But the drama never took the form of shouting matches in the halls or anything like that.

FBI: So where did it take place?

TB: As often as not in faculty meetings, where she could show her power in an otherwise professional setting without even having to raise her voice.

FBI: Please explain.

BB: Well, let's assume Randolph wanted to get something done and he'd canvassed the faculty to be sure he had enough votes. Then he convenes a faculty meeting to decide the issue, and lo and behold, when it comes time to vote, he discovers that not only she but others she has turned against him on the sly have switched their votes too. Under the circumstances, I would think you should be concerned more about his murdering her than the other way around.

FBI: after looking at each other and making sighing sounds: So what else can you tell us to put us on the right track here?

TB: Well, since you don't want to mention names, let me bring up our two youngest and most vulnerable colleagues, in case you have concerns about them. One is due to come up for tenure in just a few weeks, and the other was denied tenure by Randolph just last year. I'm sure Bill would agree that these are not only two of the most promising scholars in the department, but two of the most decent and trustworthy colleagues as well. I imagine you will be pointing the finger at one or the other of them, if only because of the situations they have found themselves in. And that would be a tragic mistake.

FBI: I presume you are talking about Jim Taylor and Isaac Bell.

BB: Right. And I second what Tom just said in the strongest possible terms.

FBI: We will make a note of that. Thank you for your candor, gentlemen. Just remember, no one is off the hook at this point, present company included.
BB: Of course.

Once these initial interviews were over, some of the agents' conclusions did start to leak. At first we heard that they couldn't find anything to distinguish the nonsense and intrigues in our academic environment from that of any other business or profession. But then they let it be known that they still needed to talk with the two individuals who they thought would have the most likely motive to see Randolph gone, despite, or possibly because of, what Tom and Bill had tried to advise them, namely Jim Taylor and me. Needless to say, it all hinged, in their minds at least, on the issue of tenure. They, no less so than we ourselves, were apparently quite taken by the impact tenure appeared to have on the lives of those in academia. One of them was actually overheard saying to the other, "Aren't you glad you're not in their profession?"

CHAPTER 10

They interviewed Jim Taylor next, and from what I heard, they gave him a rough time. Some said it was because Jim is black. Others thought it more likely had to do with the fact that he was up for tenure right at the time Randolph disappeared, and he hadn't had the opportunity to act on it yet. It was common knowledge that Randolph didn't think the department should devote a permanent faculty position to someone with Jim's unusual specialty. As Randolph often said, "that is not what the department needs." This was apparently motive enough for the FBI to label Jim a person of interest in the case, despite what Tom and Bill had told them.

What I heard about the departmental meeting to decide Jim's fate was a story in itself. Under normal circumstances, one would have assumed the sides would line up the way they usually did, with the older faculty—Fielding, Higgins and Truesdale—voting against, and the younger ones— Bradford and Bransing—voting for. Even if Doyle voted with Tom and Bill, it would still only have been a tie, and the final say would have rested with Randolph. Except that Jim had won the all-university teaching award the previous year, and had received the largest number of positive student evaluations the university had ever seen. One would have thought, therefore, that this would make all the difference, not only for Jim's tenure but also for the credit it brought to the department to have such an honor bestowed upon one of theirs. But such was apparently not the case.

Since I was already on the way out, I no longer was privy to the proceedings at that meeting. But Tom was more than happy to fill me in afterwards. The way he told the story was as realistic as any of the stories he used to tell at his parties. I could just picture myself in the room as he described the scene.

"It quickly became apparent that the vote was destined to end up in a tie no matter what," Tom began. "Fielding spoke first, echoing Randolph's refrain about what the department needed. What we have here, he said in his pompous voice, is a matter of priorities. We have to distinguish between the interests of the candidate and those of the department. It may be in the candidate's interest to become famous for a particular specialty, but what does that do for us? I doubt we want to become a national center for the study of West African literature. It is, after all, more about African culture than French. That may be something students find entertaining, but it's not what we are about.

"Then old Higgins chimed in," Tom went on. "I agree, he squeaked in his high-pitched voice, but I would go further. Are we to let the students tell us what we should be teaching, or give them the training we think they ought to have.

"Seeing the gray heads all nodding in their self-important way, Bill had heard enough. He was sure history was going to repeat itself, leaving Randolph to wield the axe, just as he did with you, Ike. So before Truesdale could add more fuel to the fire, Bill took the floor himself. His soliloquy was one of the finest moments I have ever witnessed in a faculty meeting.

"Bill began with some priceless sarcasm. I can't remember his exact words, but they went something like this. I won't comment, he said, on the racist tone I sense in this because I'm sure it is not intended. But I am disturbed by the way we seem to be defining the department's best interest. If it involves our reputation nationally for research and publishing, then Professor Taylor has more than demonstrated his value in that regard, spear-heading a whole new subfield of French literature. If, on the other hand, it involves our reputation nationally for teaching, Bill continued, glancing ever so subtly at our three ancient colleagues, then we have a problem, as the student evaluations clearly show. What the department needs, Bill said, throwing Randolph's favorite phrase back at them, is better teaching. And this problem certainly does not lie with the person who has just garnered the university's prized teaching award.

"Bill then paused for a moment to let that sink in before continuing. Frankly, he said, I never understood why, as a chairperson obsessed with budgetary matters, Randolph never acknowledged how much money Professor Taylor's classes bring into the department. It's not just his two courses on French African literature that are filled to capacity every semester. His other courses consistently do so as well."

"So what happened after that?" I asked Tom.

"The vote was four to two in favor of granting Jim tenure. And we never found out which of the old farts must have changed his mind."

Given that vote, Randolph as dean would have had to overturn a positive departmental decision in order to deny Jim tenure. But the point was moot then anyway, once Randolph disappeared. The new acting dean made it clear he wasn't about to tamper with such an obvious departmental preference. That made me wonder why, under the circumstances, the FBI had labeled Jim a person of interest and not me. Maybe they were saving the best for last?

Evidently they were because they did eventually ask me to come in for an interview. This time I didn't think I needed to convene my comrades for advice ahead of time. Since I knew I had nothing to hide, I went straight into the interview room with an air of self-confidence that unfortunately for me turned out to be over-confidence.

FBI: Thank you very much, professor, for coming in. You must have been wondering why we hadn't called you yet.

IB: Not really. I figured you'd get around to all of us in due time.

FBI: Are you planning on staying here in town or have you already secured a position at another university?

IB: I am actually in limbo at the moment, not sure what I will do next. But there are several colleagues here who mean a lot to me, so I hope to be not too far away in any case.

FBI: And who are these particular colleagues, if we may ask?

IB: Mostly Tom Bradford, Bill Bransing and Jim Taylor.

FBI: What can you tell us about Jim Taylor, for example?

IB: You mean, aside from the fact you have named him a person of interest? Frankly, I can't think of a less likely person for that honor.

FBI: How so?

IB: He's a brilliant young scholar, well-liked by everyone except maybe some jealous older colleagues, with an excellent academic record that could get him tenure anywhere he wanted. Frankly, I don't know why he wants to stay here at Macallan, except that he loves teaching in a smaller, more intimate environment like this. He'll probably be lured away by some more prestigious school eventually anyway.

FBI: So you don't think he'd have any reason to be concerned about the final decision on his tenure, which was up to Randolph before he disappeared.

IB: Absolutely not, no matter who was in the dean's office.

FBI: OK, then, let's talk about you? What was the nature of your relation with Professor Randolph?

IB: To be honest, from all I have learned since entering

the professorial ranks, it wasn't anything unusual. Before I came here, I would never have expected to be treated the way I was. But once here, it became evident that Randolph was just another example of how the system works. And I learned to deal with that.

FBI: In what ways, if we may ask?

IB: Well, not by killing him, if that's what you think. After all I went through, being denied one thing and then offered another, I understood this was all just a game. A game I really didn't need if I respected myself as a scholar.

FBI: We're not sure what you mean.

IB: Let me put it this way. What I do now without tenure is just what I always wanted to do. I admit that my six years at Macallan gave me the impetus I needed to get where I am, which I may not have been able to do entirely on my own. Be that as it may, I'm better off now than before. That's all I can say.

FBI: So you're saying that Randolph's role with respect to you has had nothing to do with it. Really? That's hard to believe.

IB: You can believe what you want, but the only reason I give a damn about Randolph is that I'm curious to know what may have actually happened with him. Notice I said "with him" not "to him". I'm absolutely certain it has nothing whatever to do with anyone here in this department or the university either for that matter. My hunch is that his disappearance was and is something entirely personal, of his own making.

FBI: If you mean that he just walked away, then with all due respect, professor, this is not a case about a juvenile deciding to run away from home because he hates his parents. Grown men don't do that sort of thing.

IB: Maybe, but on the other hand, have you ever had a case where the kind of petty jealousies and other nonsense that goes on in a university has ever led to murder, or kidnapping either for that matter? Do you know of any such instances?

FBI: None that we're aware of, but we haven't studied the matter from that angle yet. On the other hand, being denied tenure, or even the possibility of being denied tenure, is a pretty good motive, don't you think?

IB: It can be, I suppose, if you let it. But if you're thinking of either Jim Taylor or me, forget it. Neither of us fits the profile of a killer in any way. I'm sure you guys have checked us both out pretty carefully, and I'm sure you've found nothing in either of our backgrounds to suggest such a thing. I know you can't have in mine, and I've gotten to know Jim pretty well too.

FBI: Well, the two of you are not off the hook yet. You're not suspects, to be sure, but we're telling you now that you are both persons of interest as far as we are concerned.

IB: Whatever, but unless you're hiding something, all you've got is a missing person. Nothing more, nothing less.

On this rather touchy note, the meeting ended with my having now assured by my attitude that I would not be rid of Randolph for some time to come. As I left the interview room and got back in my car, however, I couldn't help smiling to myself, realizing the irony of what had just transpired. I had just defended the institution I was being forced to leave, on the grounds that it couldn't be all that bad.

Before starting the engine, I picked up my cellphone and called Tom. I wanted to fill him in on what just happened. Tom reminded me Jim was away, but he'd see if Bill was free for the evening.

We met at Tom's house again. Sitting in the cozy nook by the fireplace, I began to feel nostalgic about having to leave

Oban and the great conversations we'd had. I knew I would be coming back from time to time for the parties, but that wouldn't be quite the same.

This time the Scotch came out in full force, one bottle of Oban 14 and one of Macallan 12, Tom apologizing for not having found the 18. We alternated between the two all night long, me taking mine on the rocks, Tom and Bill neat.

Bill was anxious to know how my interview went. I described it in some detail, ending with the punch line, "so now both Jim and I have the honor of being officially persons of interest. I wonder how Jim is taking his new status, by the way."

"He couldn't care less," Tom answered. "He's in fact off giving a lecture at another university as we speak, one that has been courting him for some time. He's a shoe-in for tenure now, and he'll soon have his choice of universities. But we certainly hope he'll stay with us at least a while longer."

Then we started discussing whether I may have pissed off the FBI guys too much by my behavior at the interview.

"You could be on dangerous ground," Bill advised, "if Randolph should actually be found dead. A zealous prosecutor could build a circumstantial case against you based solely on your past history with Randolph. Innocent people have been convicted on less evidence than that. And there are plenty of prosecutors who would love to make a name for themselves at your expense."

I then tried to turn the conversation to my idea that Randolph's disappearance must have involved something personal, not anything to do with the university.

"Surely," I suggested, "there would have been some indication, some faculty gossip we would have heard circulating, if there was anything as serious as that going on. Randolph was certainly a controversial figure, but no more so than any number of other professors we know. Randolph did have a stormy personal life, however, well documented by his previous divorces and his current estranged wife. There could well be motive there, lots of it just for starters. I thought about saying something like that to the FBI guys, but didn't. I thought it might look like I was just trying to create reasonable doubt, the way lawyers do to get a guilty client off. Maybe just insisting the matter might be of Randolph's own making was already going too far, but I was pissed about their continuing to focus on Jim, not to mention me."

Picking up on that theme, Tom began to recount what evidence the authorities seemed to have about Randolph's personal life.

"They searched his house, but they're not telling us much about what they found. All they'll say is he was last seen exiting a grocery store in town and getting into his car, which is still in his garage. They say there were some dirty dishes in the sink he hadn't gotten around to washing, and some work left unfinished on his desk in the study, as if he were going to come back to it later in the day. They mentioned they found a bunch of materials about Qanon there, but that's only served to create a host of conspiracy theories of its own around the campus, muddying the waters even more. Final point, there was no evidence of a struggle, and everything about the place seemed completely normal."

After chewing on all of this for some time, we all came to the conclusion there was nothing further we could do without getting more information from the police. I felt I had a right to that information, being for all practical purposes a potential suspect.

"I could go to the police and say I need that information to clear my name," I proposed.

"That's probably the worst thing you could do, Ike," Bill responded, almost shouting. "Are you crazy? Do you want to draw more attention to yourself than you already have with the FBI?"

"But you yourself said there could well be some prosecutor anxious to make a career at my expense. Just being at Randolph's mercy these past six years could create enough suspicion. I've read enough to know that people have even been convicted without a body ever having been found."

"Well, we're both strongly against you doing that, Ike. But if you insist, I guess we can't stop you. Just remember Shakespeare's famous words, 'Me thinks he dost protest too much'. It can only make them think you really did do it."

Even with those words ringing in my ears, I still proceeded to follow my own instincts rather than the advice of the friends I had relied on all those years at Macallan.

CHAPTER 11

After staying overnight at Tom's place, I got in my car the next morning to drive to the police station. As revved up as I was, I had to remind myself to watch my driving, or I'd have another reason to talk with the police. Luckily I found a parking spot right next to police headquarters, reserved for visitors. I could only hope my "visit" wouldn't prove that Tom and Bill were right.

Once inside I spotted the desk sergeant and asked to speak with whoever was in charge of the Randolph case. When the sergeant asked me the purpose of my visit, I realized I didn't have a ready answer. If I said I just wanted information about the case, I'd probably get the brush-off. If I said I had information for them about the case, that wouldn't necessarily be true, since all I had were hunches. After an awkward pause, which clearly registered with the sergeant, I decided to just come out with it and admit I was one of the persons of interest in the case. That immediately got the sergeant's attention. He asked me my name, picked up the phone and inquired if Detective Roberts was free. Finally, after several minutes, the detective appeared, introduced himself and ushered me into an office down the hall.

"I understand you told the sergeant you're one of the persons of interest in the Randolph case."

"That's what they say. I'm Isaac Bell, Professor Bell." Then, hoping to set a more informal tone, I added, "But everyone calls me Ike."

"Ah yes, you're the one who had an interview with the FBI yesterday."

"That's correct. That's the reason I'm here, to try to clear my name."

"I see. And how do you propose to do that, Professor? Do you have some information or evidence other than what you told the FBI?"

"My evidence is that there is no evidence to suggest I or anyone else had anything whatsoever to do with Randolph's disappearance. As far as any of us knows, there isn't even any evidence to suggest there was a crime."

"That's exactly why you are a person of interest and not a suspect, Professor. But you are a smart guy, so you must realize that your history with Randolph puts you right up there at the top of the list of persons who might want to see him gone."

"That's what you and the FBI think," I said, losing patience way too early for my own good. "That's because you're fixated on a university connection in all of this, which I and my colleagues are sure doesn't exist."

"Leaving aside what you think we're fixated on, what do you and your colleagues, whoever they are, think is the connection?"

"As I suggested to the FBI, the one that has only to do with his personal life outside the university."

"And you presume we haven't thought of that, I suppose. Well, we have, and we've been working on that angle from the start."

"So what have you found? You've said nothing publicly about it so far."

"I'm afraid I'm not at liberty to divulge that at the moment.

"So you are hiding information that might exonerate me? Please tell me that's not what you're doing."

"Calm down, professor. We're not hiding anything. We're just not divulging anything at the moment that might jeopardize the case."

"And when do you expect to be able to let the rest of us know? There's a whole academic community out there that is left hanging, left to believe the worst. It's a virtual breeding ground for conspiracy theories."

"Let's not get too melodramatic, Professor. There are protocols we must follow that I'm sure you can understand."

"I appreciate that, but you could at least mention that the university is not the sole target of this investigation."

"We could, but then certain individuals outside the university might start to cover their tracks. I've probably already told you too much."

"Not really. I'm by no means the only one who thinks this way. By the way, speaking of conspiracy theories, why did you mention that bit about finding Qanon literature at his house? It's only made things worse."

"I agree, it was a gambit that didn't work. So how can we help you, Professor? Or may I call you Ike?"

"Ike's fine," I answer, sensing the ice may be breaking a bit. "How about we work together to get to the bottom of this? Research is a basic part of my profession, so in my own way I'm a detective too."

"Interesting thought, but you realize, I'm sure, that since you are a person of interest in this case, you would automatically have a conflict of interest if we included you in our work."

"I understand that, but there must be a way. Would there still be a conflict of interest if, say, you let me know what you've found, or more importantly didn't find, inside Randolph's house. What you've already divulged isn't very much. Ideally, I'd like to have access to that house once it's no longer a crime scene. I could be a great help sorting through his papers and such for clues. I would know what to look for that you might not."

"That's a pretty tall order, Ike. We'd have to deputize you and make you a party to the search warrant, which we obviously can't. Neither my superior nor the FBI would go for that. I wouldn't even dare ask them."

"Then tell me how I can clear my name."

"Let me think about it, and I'll get back with you."

We shook hands and I made sure the detective knew how to reach me. Then I headed back to Tom's place to report on the meeting.

If I thought being on a first-name basis with the detective towards the end of our meeting meant I was getting somewhere, I should have known better. Tom told me as much when I got back to his place.

"You know, Ike, both the police and the FBI will play this completely by the book. They'll only divulge the kind of information you need to clear your name when they're good and ready. Which probably means when the case grows so cold they won't care anymore anyway. In the meantime, you, my dear friend, will have to learn how to get on with the rest of your life."

Dejected, I said goodbye and I headed back to Syracuse to be with Sarah. On the way, I tried to put the whole business out of my mind, but found I couldn't. To be honest, being a potential suspect in a murder investigation scared the hell out of me. All I could think of was the number of innocent people who have been convicted with nothing more than circumstantial evidence. Just that past week a 65-year-old man was released from prison thirty-two years after he had been convicted of a crime he never committed. For taking those thirty-two years of his life from him they said they were sorry and gave him a paltry $100,000. To say I was haunted by such thoughts would be putting it mildly.

Once I got back, Sarah could see how upset I was. She tried to calm me down by talking about it, but it didn't work. Even the warm hugs she gave me and the bottle of wine she opened didn't begin to do the trick. So I suggested switching to Scotch and downed a couple of swift drinks.

"This is driving me crazy," I said. "I need to get into Randolph's house, so I can see for myself if there's anything there that might indicate what really happened."

Afraid I might actually do something like that, Sarah tried to steer the conversation in a different direction. "What if," she suggested, thinking in lawyerly terms, "they know something about you, something that has nothing to do with Randolph, but enough to make them think you could be involved?"

That only made matters worse. "What on earth could they possibly have?" I shouted. "I've led an exemplary life, even had the title of Likable Ike throughout the entire time I subjected myself to the fucking system I once thought would provide me the life I wanted. That alone," I yelled at Sarah, "should be enough to exonerate me."

That outburst could only have reminded her just how volatile I can be at times. I realized it proved her point without her having to say another word.

That night, when we finally went to bed, there was no love-making, not even any cuddling. Just a night of fitful sleep.

CHAPTER 12

Just as Tom predicted, I heard nothing from the detective for a long time. I tried to bury myself in my work like Sarah begged me to. I did some final editing on my textbook and finished an article I had started some time ago. I made this happen only because I couldn't sleep at night and needed something to occupy my mind in the wee hours of the morning. Finally, after several more months of this, I had had enough. Despite Sarah's pleas, I insisted on getting in touch with the detective again. I phoned Robert's office and to my surprise, he invited me to come down for another meeting. He even told me to record my mileage so he could reimburse me for the trip. As suspicious as Tom and Bill would have thought that sounded, it nevertheless lifted my spirits considerably.

Two days later, I was in his office. I gladly accepted the coffee he proffered before he began the conversation.

"Sorry I haven't gotten back with you as promised, but there have been some developments I think you should know about."

"Please, I'm anxious to hear."

"I'm sure it will come as no surprise to you that we have been looking into the backgrounds of all the individuals we think, for whatever reason, could have been involved in Randolph's disappearance. Needless to say, there are a fair number of them, both at the university like yourself, and in Randolph's private life. That's what has taken us so long to get back with you."

"I understand. I was hoping you would do that."

"Good. Well, some of these investigations have raised more questions than answers, which is why I have asked to see you."

"Oh, really?" I said, my naively lifted spirits taking a bit of a nosedive.

"I'm afraid so. We know of your interest in intensive language programs and Professor Randolph's lack of interest, shall we say, in supporting them. We have been told you had two projects along those lines which he declined to fund. Is that correct?"

"Not quite. One was a summer program right here on campus and the other a potential study abroad program. I only asked him to support the former, not the latter."

"And why was that?"

"Because the summer program would be simpler to produce and cost him almost nothing. Personally, I would have much preferred the study abroad program."

"I see. Can you say why?"

"Sure. My interest in these programs actually derives from my own experience as a study abroad student myself when I was in college. I thought the program I was on didn't take near enough advantage of the environment in which it was being offered. If I wanted to spend my time in a classroom, like they insisted, I could have done that at home."

"And that upset you, I take it."

"Yes it did. The last straw, if you will, was when they insisted we spend at least an hour a day in what they called a language lab, where you sit in a room with earphones on and engage in interactive learning with the person on a recording. Just imagine, earphones to keep you away from the environment you came to experience, so you can pretend to talk with someone on a tape. I could have done that at home. I wanted to interact with real people out in the community. That's why I was there, after all."

"I can see you are getting a bit worked up right now telling me this. So what did you do about it, if anything?"

"To be honest, I started skipping language class and devising projects on my own in town."

"I'll bet that got you in trouble, no?"

"Yes it did. They threatened to send me home if I didn't abide by the rules of the program."

"And did you? Abide by the rules of the program, I mean?"

"Yes, but only after arguing my case with the director."

"Tell me more about that argument, if you would, please."

After a long pause during which I started fidgeting in my chair, I realized I had just been led into a trap. I stared at the detective and said, "Oh, I see where this is going. You think that because I got upset with that director, I must have done the same with Randolph. Is that it?"

"Well, how far did that altercation go? I mean, what exactly was said and/or done in that director's office?"

At that point I did the absolutely worst thing I could have done. I lost my cool and said snidely to Roberts, "I don't remember, but you seem to know all about this already, so why don't you tell me."

"Did you yell at him?"

"Yes, I did. So what?"

"Did you threaten him?"

"I don't know what you mean."

"Either verbally or otherwise."

"Verbally maybe, physically no."

"And what exactly did you say to him?"

"I really don't remember. Probably the same sort of thing everyone says when they're upset but they don't really mean it."

"I should tell you we have been in contact with Professor Girard, your director back then. He's retired now but he has retained a vivid recollection of what happened that day. He said you were so agitated he was afraid you would do something violent. He said he started to call security when you turned around and stormed out of his office. Does that sound about right?"

"Not really. If it had been that bad, why didn't he throw me off the program? He never did. I went back to language lab after that and everyone forgot about the whole thing. His memory must have taken a few giant leaps since then."

"Did you by any chance tell him you could kill him?"

"Of course not. But even if I did, it would have been entirely rhetorical, I assure you."

"But you would agree, wouldn't you, that at times you become someone other than Likable Ike, as I understand they called you at the university?"

"I can get upset just like any other person, but that does not make me a murderer."

"No, Ike, it doesn't. But it does mean we cannot take you off the person of interest list at this time. I'm sorry."

"So where, if I may ask, are you then with the investigation? I need to know how long I'm going to be held in this limbo, waiting for some prosecutor to make a name for himself at my expense. I need to know how seriously you are looking into the possibility that this has nothing whatsoever to do with me, the department or the university at all."

"I can assure you, Ike, we are looking into all possibilities. We are so far not treating this as a crime, just a missing person case. So I suggest you calm down. I promise to give you a heads-up should anything change."

"I appreciate that, but still, is there no way you can tell me what you did or did not find at Randolph's place? From all you've divulged so far, it certainly looks like he just walked away, as unlikely as that might sound. People like me, who knew his habits pretty well, could be a lot of help here finding things that don't add up."

"All I can say at this point, Ike, is I'll let you know when the time is right. I hope you can understand."

We shook hands, albeit just as a matter of courtesy, and I headed straight back home to Syracuse.

CHAPTER 13

I arrived back in Syracuse determined not to let this latest setback get to me. I resolved to forget about Randolph and try to produce on my own one of the programs I had not been allowed to at Macallan. I would show them all what a real intensive language program should look like. Problem was, which of my two ideas could see the light of day without a university affiliation?

I figured I couldn't put on a summer program unless I started my own summer school. After all, what were the chances of persuading another institution to let me teach one of their summer courses when my own university refused to do so? To launch such a program by myself, however, I'd have to rent facilities, hire teachers, and develop a curriculum. I'd have no trouble devising the curriculum, of course, but I'd then have to get it accredited. It wouldn't be like offering courses at an already accredited institution, and it would take a long time. Finding a facility to rent and hiring teachers wouldn't be much easier either.

After mulling this idea over for a few weeks, I decided this was not the way to go. So I turned my attention to what I had always preferred to do anyway, start my own program abroad. I wouldn't need a university affiliation to take a group of students abroad in the summer when they're not normally in school. If they wanted academic credit, they could have their home institution approve it. Most students, I knew, aren't interested in the credit anyway. They're there for the experience.

I would still have to rent facilities abroad, however, and most importantly with a program for American students outside the U.S., become in effect my own risk management officer. I would be personally responsible for the students' health and safety for the entire time they were abroad. They would essentially, legally in fact, as Sarah reminded me, be under my care. Having already heard stories of students getting into serious trouble on these programs before was enough to give me pause. Students getting drunk and running afoul of the local police happened all too often. I particularly remembered reading about the time a bus taking a group of students on an outing crashed, killing one student and injuring several others. The program director and the home institution that certified the program were held liable when it was determined they hadn't checked out the safety record of the bus company thoroughly enough. It cost them millions of dollars to settle the lawsuits.

Sarah and I spent several evenings for the next week or so thinking this option through together. In the end it was she who brought up the one other obstacle I hadn't thought of, being so immersed in my own thinking.

"You realize," she said, "what this would mean for us? We'd have to be apart for months at a time, far longer than Jeremy and I ever were. And you know what that did to our marriage."

"I did think of that, actually," I responded, "but we're only talking about a summer abroad, three months at the most. I was hoping you might be able to take a leave of absence for at least part of that time and be with me. You work so hard, you deserve a break like that."

"I work so hard, Ike, because I want to become a partner in the firm. Instead of taking time off, I need to work overtime if I want to achieve my goal."

So it came down to this: which to put first, Sarah's future or mine, a career or a relationship. And as if to put an even finer point on things, Sarah came home one evening with the news that she had just received a promotion at her law firm, giving her the leg up towards becoming a partner she had been hoping for all along.

As happy as I was for her, the irony of the situation was not lost on me. I couldn't help thinking she was on a kind of tenure track to a partnership for as long as it would take, and she'd still have her job if she failed to get one. I, on the other hand, had had just six years to obtain a partnership in the university, so to speak, or lose my job entirely.

Irony can certainly be appreciated without bitterness, so I insisted on celebrating Sarah's promotion. I suggested either a special dinner out or I would cook her one of my special ones at home. Sarah opted for the latter, saying how much she envied my culinary skills and couldn't wait to see what I'd come up with next.

Glad to have something to distract me from my problems, I began making a production out of preparing one of my favorite dishes, the French stew I learned how to make in Paris, called the *coq-au-vin*. I decided to make it the traditional way, taking all three days so I could bask in memories of my beloved Paris, listening to French music from my record collection. What could be more romantic than creating a Parisian setting with Sarah right there in the apartment over a three-day weekend.

Fortunately, we found such a weekend when Sarah could be away from the office and the courtroom. We went out together and bought a whole roast chicken, which we soaked in a pot with two bottles of French burgundy for the rest of that day and the next. While the bird was relaxing in its bath, we relaxed together in ways we hadn't for a long time, with no court briefs to write up and, most importantly, no thoughts of missing persons and threats of incarceration.

On the third day, I made a joke about the resurrection of Christ as I dramatically raised the chicken from its bath. Then we went to work preparing the meal, keeping with the spirit of the process by opening a third bottle of burgundy to drink while we worked. Sarah happily agreed to be my sous-chef, chopping the trio of celery, carrots and onions I told her was called a *mirepoix*, relishing the occasion to give everything its proper French name. The prepping process itself, I told her, was called the *mise-en-place*, putting things in place ahead of time. Meanwhile, I cut the chicken into ten pieces, each of which was now a rosy pink from its bath. I then dredged them in flour seasoned with salt, pepper, and *herbes-de-Provence*, the latter being a little added touch of my own.

With the prep work completed, I sautéed a healthy amount of bacon to render its fat, took out the bacon when crisp and browned the chicken in the fat. Then I removed the chicken and put in the vegetables, loosening the fond left from the browning process at the bottom of the pot to add more flavor. Once the vegetables were softened, I put the chicken back in the pot, added a generous amount of chicken stock, the crispy bacon pieces and rest of the burgundy we hadn't already consumed.

All that was left was to let the stew simmer, providing the perfect time to retire to the bedroom to wait. Our love-making was so prolonged and sensual we almost forgot there was a stew that still needed some final touches in the kitchen. That required sautéing some mushrooms in lots of butter and a little cognac, then adding them and a package of frozen pearl onions to the pot. As a final touch, I insisted on completing the stew with the process called *monter au beurre*, adding a few more pats of butter to give the sauce a nice sheen. When Sarah commented on how much butter was being used, I asked her with big grin which country's cuisine she thought we were creating here?

Then we sat down to savor the scrumptious stew by candlelight, with me telling more stories of my time in Paris and Sarah making me promise to take her there sometime.

No matter how perfect the mood was that evening, however, it didn't last for long. Though I certainly tried, I couldn't take my mind off my precarious position with the Randolph affair. As the days grew into weeks and the weeks into months, I became increasingly frustrated, not having heard anything further from Detective Roberts. Eventually I decided to go back to Oban to talk with Tom and see for myself what progress, if any, had been made on the case.

"I'm afraid there isn't much news," Tom began. "Things are pretty much where they were when you were here the last time."

"What about Randolph's house?" I asked. "If the police are still refusing to release any information about what they found there, I really need to see for myself."

"Well, I'm afraid the place is still cordoned off as a crime scene, so we can't get in there. If it weren't, I would have gone there myself."

"Then I need to talk with that Detective Roberts again and shake his cage a bit."

"That would be even more serious a mistake than the last time you did that, Ike. Keep pestering them and they'll be convinced there's still more about you than what they've already discovered. I promise you, I'll keep my eyes and ears open and let you know the moment anything develops."

Seeing how distraught I still was, Tom offered to organize another of his famous parties, to take my mind off things. But I declined the offer and returned to Syracuse in even more of a funk than before.

After a while, my frustration turned into depression and the depression into anger. On more than one occasion I took my anger out on Sarah, and that began to take a serious toll on our relationship.

"You know, Ike," she told me after one such outburst, "I've been thinking. Maybe starting a program abroad is not such a bad idea after all. Spending some time apart might be just what we both need at the moment."

"Maybe," I responded, "but the liability issue still troubles me. I promise I'll try to keep it together until something good happens."

Then something good finally did happen, but not quite in the way either of us could have anticipated.

CHAPTER 14

Three weeks later, I spotted an advertisement for the directorship of an existing summer program in Italy. The current director was retiring and they were looking for his replacement. The program was sponsored by a consortium of American universities that had been operating for about five years. I happened to see the notice because one of the sponsoring institutions was a small, liberal arts college right there in Syracuse. I did some research and learned they had a cadre of local Italian instructors and a small staff that handled day-to-day administration of the program. I noticed in particular that they had a well-established student health and safety regimen which met all the requirements set forth by the study abroad profession. Best of all, the program was located in the charming town of Siena in the Tuscan hills above Florence, an ideal location for developing the kinds of extra-curricular projects that were at the heart of my theory of intensive language training. Since I spoke Italian as well as French, I thought this could well be the answer to my problems.

With Sarah's encouragement, I made an appointment for an interview and filled my briefcase with material establishing my credentials for the job. The college turned out to be what I imagined Macallan must have been before it became a university. I received a warm welcome and was ushered into a small but tastefully furnished conference room, replete with a fireplace at one end. Far from the dreadful room where we held faculty meetings at Macallan, this one felt more like someone's living room, an inviting place to have civilized conversations that might actually produce something more than political drama.

Once seated and the customary introductions out of the way, I learned that I was anything but an unknown quantity to the assembled group of faculty and administrators. The person who seemed to be the head of the consortium began the interview.

"Thank you so much for coming, professor. We're happy to find someone with your specialty and your qualifications considering this position. We would have invited you to apply ourselves if we had known you were available. We are familiar with your publications and think you could be just the person we have been looking for."

I was reluctant to tell them why I was available, but when I did, they didn't seem the slightest bit concerned.

"That can only mean," one of them said with a smile, "you can now devote your full attention to our program!"

"Indeed," I replied. "I am anxious to put into practice my ideas about learning a foreign language abroad rather than in a U.S. classroom. I hope they will fit with what you have in mind about your own program."

"In fact," the lead administrator continued, "they are exactly what we need at the moment. While we have an excellent staff running the administrative side of things, and a small cadre of well-qualified local instructors, it is the curriculum that needs to be revamped to insure we achieve the outcomes necessary for the program to succeed."

At this point one of the others intervened.

"We should tell you professor, in the strictest confidence of course, that while the current director is a highly respected colleague of ours right here at this college, he will be the first to admit he was not a good fit for the job. For several years now students on this program have returned to their home campuses having made less progress than expected by their own faculties. We advertise that students' proficiency will improve in one summer with us equivalent to a year's worth of instruction at home. Unfortunately, we have fallen short of that goal, enough to threaten the program's very reputation."

Hearing this, I asked for more specifics. "What exactly has been the nature of the problem?"

What they told me did not surprise me at all. "While our students do return able to speak Italian reasonably well, certainly better than their peers who stayed home, when asked to write a grammatically acceptable essay in the language, they lag significantly behind. For this reason, too many of them have had to repeat courses they assumed they had just taken."

This discrepancy between written and oral skills was precisely the criticism I had heard from the classical grammarians back at Macallan. It was something I had written at length about in my publications, and had been waiting years to address with a program of my own. I told the assembled group as much, and was assured I would have carte blanche to redesign their program any way I saw fit.

As I left the interview, I felt confident I would get the job.

Sure enough, a week later I received a contract, which I was more than happy to sign. The celebration Sarah and I had, however, was not quite the same as the one we had when she got her promotion. To say it was a bitter-sweet moment would be an understatement. We spent a quiet evening together, trying to sort through what was about to happen.

Could our relationship outlast this separation? Just how much did it really mean to each of us?

I was certain I would come back in the fall, all fired up about my success with the program and be more than happy to see her. Sarah wasn't so sure.

"Spending three months in the company of some of the most beautiful women in the world, eating sophisticated

Italian cuisine and indulging in the famous wines of Tuscany, what could possibly go wrong?"

There was again, to be sure, candlelight and wine that evening, but nothing as elaborate as a *coq-au-vin* this time. I did prepare a simple French salad, with butter lettuce and the traditional dressing of red wine vinegar, minced garlic, Dijon mustard and extra-virgin olive oil. Then I grilled a rib-eye steak and some French fries, recreating the *steak-frites* I loved so much during my student days in Paris, pretending in my own mind that I was already abroad again.

Our love-making was very slow and quiet that night, like grasping a flower that might wilt at any time. The next day I was on an Alitalia flight to Malpensa airport in Milan, sipping the last drops of vin santo before falling asleep to some gentle turbulence over the Atlantic.

CHAPTER 15

Having been to Italy before, I knew that once my plane landed in Milan I would still have quite a journey ahead of me getting to Siena. I could rent a car but I didn't want to contend with the likes of Italian drivers in my jet-lagged state. So I settled for taking the train to Florence and then the bus on up to Siena.

I had purposely not packed anything more than I absolutely needed, knowing how complicated surface travel in Italy can be. I knew, for example, that most Italian train stations have only stairs to the platforms, and getting there can be an exercise in itself if you have too much luggage. Plus they give you only a few short minutes to board a through train from the time it arrives to the time it departs. Once you get from the airport to the train station, you have to buy a ticket and then remember that they don't punch your ticket on the train. You have to punch it yourself in one of those machines on the way to the platform. Forgetting to do so will cost you at least a scolding when they ask to check it again on the train. The last time I forgot that, I pretended not to speak Italian, and the agent gave me one of those classic dumb-foreigner looks as he punched it for me.

Fortunately, I navigated the situation fairly smoothly this time, despite the jetlag. Once in Florence, though, I discovered that the next bus to Siena was not one of those new tourist ones but an older local one and it was packed, so packed I had to throw my luggage up on the roof like everyone else and hope it would still be there when I got to Siena. Luckily, it wasn't raining. Even luckier, I found one vacant seat so I didn't have to stand the whole way. I could ignore the bumping and swaying of the bus and enjoy the charming villages we drove through on the way. I spent the time thinking of the trips I would soon be taking the students on, to teach them how to properly appreciate Tuscany's most famous beverage.

I used my cellphone to let the program people—soon to be *my* program people—know when I'd be arriving. I was more than happy to see them there to greet me when the bus pulled in.

They had made all the necessary arrangements ahead of time in Siena so I could settle in a month before the students arrived. They had secured a nice apartment for me at the top of the hill in town near the *duomo*, the ancient cathedral of Siena. It would be a bit of a walk from there back down to the study center just off the main square or *campo*, but I told them that should be no problem. I needed the exercise, and the view from above the city would be more than worth it.

They accompanied me up the hill on foot through the ancient streets to a delightful old building just a block or two from the *duomo*. We agreed to meet again down at the center early the next morning.

Once alone, I took some time before unpacking to admire the gorgeous view over the city from my window. I had noticed when I first entered the apartment how much cooler it was than outside in the summer heat. Looking out the window told me why: the stone walls of the old building were nearly a foot thick. The apartment itself was rather small, but it was all I needed. I wasn't going to spend much time there anyway, and it would be a nice place to cool down after a hot summer day. There was a comfortable bed and a table to spread my work out on. The kitchen was just a small alcove with a stove and a refrigerator which the staff had thoughtfully stocked with some basic items to help me settle in.

After unpacking, I showered and laid down for a nap to help stave off the jet-lag.

I found the study center the next morning without any trouble. The staff made me feel more than welcome. They filled me in on how the program had been operating in the past. As evening approached, they suggested going to dinner so they could hear about my ideas for revamping things. They chose a restaurant at the *campo* where, they told me, the students usually hang out when not in class.

Hearing this, I said with a smile, "Oh, I don't think the students will be hanging out around the *campo* very much this summer. They will be far too busy working on their projects when not in class." Then I launched into a general description of what the new program will look like, how the students' outside activities will be fully integrated with classroom teaching.

It wasn't until the following day that I got to meet the instructors themselves. I was a bit nervous because I needed to get their buy-in if the program was to succeed. Much to my delight, they seemed eager to adopt my ideas, even though they would have to alter their own teaching methods to accommodate the changes. They understood right away they would have more of the students' attention once their time outside class became integrated with the class time itself.

On the third day I sat down again with the staff to work out in detail what I needed to accomplish in the month before the students arrived.

"I will need to organize two kinds of activities," I began. "On the one hand each student will have a project to work on as their summer thesis, and in addition, they will all partake in weekly excursions to the nearby medieval towns and wineries."

"What can we do to help?" Was the first question they asked.

"Well, for the projects, I'd appreciate your input as to which kinds of enterprises in town might like having a student working as an unpaid intern at their place of business. I suspect most of these would be in town, but some could just as well be out in the countryside, like at a winery, on a farm, or in one of the other nearby hillside towns."

That was when I realized the initial enthusiasm the staff displayed was going to be tempered with a certain amount of realism.

"That might be difficult," one of them exclaimed. "Except for those accustomed to working with tourists, not many of our local people speak English."

"Ah," I eagerly responded, "that's exactly the point. All of these activities should be of a kind that require the students to use Italian in order to perform their duties. What better way to speed up the learning process? You'd be surprised how quickly they will stop cruising the bars speaking English and start using Italian on a daily basis. Don't worry. All of them will have learned enough Italian before they come. So it will just be a matter of putting them in a position where they have to use what they already know right from the start."

Seeing everyone suitably mollified, I continued, "For the projects in town I envision things like helping at the public library, working as a docent at an art museum, as an orderly in a hospital or clinic, that sort of thing."

Then came another dose of realism. "Maybe we should inform you professor," one of them said, "that not everyone here in town has been happy to have the American students here. Many of them see our students as what you call ugly Americans. They may be reluctant to take one of them on."

Hearing this, I was inclined to ask how serious this issue might be, but decided to sidestep it for the time being, feeling pretty sure I had a way to deal with it.

"I can imagine," I said, "that there have been behavioral issues, if that's what you are referring to, but the very idea of the new program is to deal with such things in a positive manner. Again, please don't worry, I will take it upon myself to work with any towns person you suggest, even those who may have previously expressed their concern about the students."

Hoping to have put the issue aside for the moment, I continued, "As for the weekly excursions out of town, I need to organize a number of day trips. I envision a "wine as food" series where the students will learn how to treat wine the way it is meant to be appreciated, paired with food rather than just a drink. They will also learn about wine-making and the history of the various medieval towns they visit. But for that, I will need a car. I assume I can rent one somewhere here in town, no?"

"Please, professor," one of the staff responded, "that won't be necessary. We can loan you one of ours during the week while we are working at the center. Since we walk wherever we need to in town anyway, that won't be a problem. And if you like, one of us can accompany you out of town, since we have connections at some of the best wineries."

"That would be splendid," I exclaimed.

Then we all set to work organizing the next few weeks.

Before any of this actually got set in motion, I asked to pay a visit to the mayor. I wanted to present my credentials, but more than anything I needed to find out just how serious a problem I may have with the town's view of the students in their midst. What the staff had said worried me, and what I learned from the mayor turned out to be even worse than I feared.

Once I arrived at the *Officio del Sindaco* and the usual introductions and pleasantries were out of the way, I was ushered into his office for a private conversation. It was a beautiful, high-ceilinged room, decorated in a way that showed appreciation for the centuries-old building it was in.

Portraits of former dignitaries adorned the walls, and the furniture appeared to be replicas of pieces from bygone eras as well. There was also a beautiful old tapestry on the wall behind his desk. The mayor indicated one of the elegant chairs for me to sit in, while he chose another for himself. I was rather surprised how comfortable it was. He then asked if I would prefer to speak English, but I assured him Italian would be fine.

If I thought speaking Italian would make for a more congenial conversation, I soon found out otherwise. Right away, being on his own turf, both physically and linguistically, the mayor didn't waste any time describing the city's past experience with *my* program.

"You'll forgive me, professor, but I won't beat around the bush regarding the town's attitude towards your students, an attitude with which I totally agree, by the way. Since your students are here for the better part of the summer each year, the townspeople expect them to act less like tourists and more like members of the community. Instead, they often behave worse than tourists, taking what they can from the town and giving nothing in return. Of course, we appreciate the money the students contribute to our economy, but it comes at a certain unwelcome cost."

"Tell me, *vostro honore*, just how bad has it been?" I asked, intentionally adopting a formal tone.

"To put it bluntly, professor, the townspeople dread the arrival of your group each summer. The worst time is right at the start, when the students first arrive. For those first few weeks, they are regularly seen around town drinking and generally making a spectacle of themselves. We understand the reason of course. For many of them, this is the first time they have been able to drink alcohol legally, being under the age of twenty-one and no longer in the U.S. It usually takes them some time to settle down to their studies, but many of them carry on like this throughout the summer as well."

Hearing this, I wondered why the consortium never informed me how bad the reputation of the program actually was in this respect. They had told me about the language problems but not the behavioral ones. Maybe the former director had kept it to himself. But I had an answer to this problem in the very structure I was about to implement. And this was my one chance to prove my system works. I had spent my whole life trying to get to this point, and I couldn't afford to fail now.

"I can only apologize for the past reputation of the program," I began, "which I must admit seems worse than I was led to believe. But I can assure you that the structure I am putting in place now will go a long way towards addressing the problem."

I then proceeded to explain how the projects the students will be required to complete will make them good citizens of the community.

"However," I added, anticipating the mayor's reaction to be much the same as that of my own office staff earlier, "I can see I may not have an easy time convincing your townspeople to welcome our students into their establishments. I can only assure you, and them, that we are serious about this and try to gain their trust."

"Well," the mayor responded, "I am glad to hear that. You can count on my help in that regard. Feel free to call on me any time."

We shook hands and I got the feeling maybe I was off to a good start after all.

It took me the better part of the rest of my time before the students arrived to visit a number of establishments in town. I asked each one if they could use an extra employee, free of charge, to help them out during the summer when the tourist traffic is the heaviest. Following the suggestions of my staff, I spoke with people at both the history and art museums, the local library, the city market, the local hospital, a couple of nursing homes, and even one of the local ambulance services. Many of them hesitated at first, but I won most of them over and assured them they would not be sorry.

Then, on five different days I drove out of town to set up the excursions, often accompanied by one of the staff. We went just down the road to the ancient town of Montepulciano the first day, to Montalcino, home of the famous Brunello wines, the next, and so on, to Montafollonico, known for its vin santo, to Pienza, so-called capital of pecorino cheese, and finally to San Gimignano with its famous twelve towers. In each place we arranged for a midday meal at a winery, where the students would learn how to drink wine responsibly and pair it with food.

When the time finally came for the students to arrive, the staff spent the entire day meeting them and bringing them to the study center. They first registered them with the local police, so they would have the required legal status to live in the city for the duration of the summer. Then they escorted them to their housing and told them to meet up first thing the next morning back at the center.

They also told them, in a surprisingly stern tone of voice, that they were not to spend their first night in town partying in their current jet-lagged state.

"Remember that you are now guests of the city, and anyone who is found to have behaved improperly will be sent home immediately."

I was a bit taken aback hearing them talk to the students like that, certain it would be counter-productive. But I didn't interrupt. This must be the way, I thought, they have dealt with behavioral issues in the past. Obviously, from what the mayor told me, it hadn't worked. Tell students not to do something and they'll be inclined to do just that. No matter, I had already set in motion the means to address this sort of thing and wasn't particularly worried.

Of course there were a few students who didn't heed the warning that first night, but fortunately morning came and there were no incidents, at least none that ever came to our attention.

Once the students reassembled at the center the next morning, I explained how they would be spending their summer.

"Success on this program," I began, "will depend on how seriously you take the internship you will be asked to pursue outside of class. Each of you will select a service-learning project to work on as a resident of the Siena community. The work you do will constitute an integral part of the course and a significant part of your final grade. You will be required to write weekly progress reports and make oral presentations in class about what you are learning from your internship. You will be graded on how well you use the language, not only in speaking but also in your written reports. Class time will be used to teach proper usage and to correct grammatical mistakes, but the bulk of the learning process will occur outside in the community, where you will become partners with the local population."

Having got their attention, I then presented the various internships I had procured so far, explaining the concept of service-learning. I purposely presented those projects first, saving the excursions to the various towns and wineries for last, knowing that once I mentioned the latter, their attention was bound to wander. When I finished, I got the sense I had them hooked.

I went back to my apartment later that evening, pleased that things seemed to have gotten off to a good start. It had been a long and somewhat stressful day, not knowing what kind of reception I would get from the students. The walk up the hill didn't seem nearly as steep this time, having that weight taken off my shoulders, not to mention the other weight I was beginning to lose walking up and down the hill for a month now.

Once inside my delightfully cool apartment, I opened a bottle of Chianti Reserva, poured myself a glass and phoned Sarah. It was late enough at night that I figured the time difference would mean she would just be home from work. I could picture her sitting on our couch in the living room with the stack of legal briefs she brought home with her, while I was looking out at the lights of the city from my hilltop perch. I suggested she put away her yellow legal pad, pour herself a Scotch and retire early with the phone to the bedroom. We imagined ourselves together in bed before ending the call, assured our relationship was still intact.

CHAPTER 16

Neither Sarah nor I knew what had transpired in the meantime with the search for Randolph. She was in her world and I in my new one. We hadn't been told yet that there were several reports of people thinking they had seen Randolph since he disappeared. Trouble was, I learned later, the sightings came from such disparate places, the Oban police didn't bother verifying them, didn't take them seriously.

What they did take seriously, apparently, was my having left the country soon after being informed I was a person of interest and possible suspect in the case. But since they never told me I couldn't leave the country, and they didn't even have any evidence of a crime having been committed, they let it go. They still had nothing more than a missing person case.

Tom Bradford had been keeping in touch with the police all this time on my behalf, as he promised he would. He phoned me in Siena and told me what he'd been up to. It was a long and dramatic tale, as only Tom could tell it. I wondered afterward how much that phone call must have cost him.

"Guess what," he began, "I recently found out that Randolph's house is no longer a crime scene, so knowing how anxious you were to get in there and look around, I took it upon myself to see what I could find. Since the house was still a private residence, however, I still needed to get permission to enter.

"When I asked who could give that permission, I was told the property was now legally in the hands of Randolph's estranged wife. That was no surprise, but it did pose a problem. Since Mrs. Randolph was bound to also be a person of interest, if not a suspect, in her husband's disappearance, I figured she might well be suspicious of my coming to her about the case, wanting to snoop around in her house no less.

"I found out she still lived in town and called her on the phone. I tried to keep my request as neutral as possible, telling her only that I was a colleague of Randolph's and would like to come and see her. Her response was classic. 'Whatever for? I want nothing to do with him or this whole affair. For all I know he's run off with another bimbo he expects to make wife number four.'

"With that kind of reaction, I had no other choice but to bite the bullet and tell her exactly what I needed from her, permission to access the house, I told her, so I could clear my good friend's name.

"Her answer this time was just as good, but it took me by surprise. 'Sure, why not. Maybe you can start getting rid of some of that crap of his that I'll eventually have to dispose of anyway. The cops still have the keys though, so I'll have to call and tell them it's OK to give them to you. Lots of luck finding what you need in all that stuff.'

"I didn't even have a chance to thank her before she hung up. But she was true to her word. Once I got the keys, I unlocked the front door and went in search of the holy grail. The house was remarkably neat for someone having lived there as a bachelor for so long. It was almost as if wifey number three had never left. Right away I wondered why, if the police had supposedly done a thorough search, the place wasn't turned upside down. Maybe they thought the very tidiness of the house was evidence enough that no struggle, no abduction could have taken place. Besides, they didn't seem to have a clue what to look for anyway.

"Then I remembered the police saying Randolph was last seen leaving the grocery store and apparently driving home, since his car was still in the garage. Out of curiosity

I went to the kitchen to see what groceries he must have bought that day, and to my surprise found the refrigerator nearly empty. That struck me as odd, but I still can't think of any reason why.

"So I made a beeline for Randolph's study. The holy grail had to be in there somewhere. I went through the papers on, in, and around the big ugly desk in the center of the room. They all had to do with his academic work except for a bunch of material about Qanon, just as the police had reported. What seemed odd, though, was what was not there. Just like there being hardly any groceries in the fridge, there were no papers of a personal nature in the study either, no tax returns, no insurance policies, no medical reports, nothing. Plus his phone and the laptop were gone as well. It was as if his very personhood had disappeared.

"That made me think maybe you were right, Ike, that he did just walk away, taking everything personal with him. All I could find was his academic work, which I knew all about anyway, and that stuff about crazy conspiracy theories the police mentioned.

"Just as I was about to give up and leave, I remembered what the ex said about 'getting rid of all that crap', so I gathered up the Qanon papers just to have something to take home and justify my search. I thought maybe he collected the stuff in order to write a book about the movement. Lord knows, his academic research never got him very far. Maybe this would?

"To make a long story just a bit longer, Ike, I have to admit those Qanon materials sat in a pile in my study for several weeks before my conscience got the better of me. As I started looking through them, I felt increasingly disgusted and started drinking more of old man Macallister's Scotches than I usually do just to keep at it. After a while, though, I actually began to see a pattern of sorts. I noticed there was one name among all the authors there that kept cropping up. And it wasn't one I remembered ever having seen or heard before, on line or on TV. It was someone named Jacques Perveux, evidently a Frenchman, I figured, judging by the name. Just to make the job bearable, and keep up the Macallan tradition, I started calling him Jack the Pervert.

"Now, dear friend, if you've finally come to your senses and don't care about this anymore, I'll be more than happy to have spent this time on your behalf. But if you're still inclined to follow down this rabbit hole, then see what you can find over there about this guy Perveux. I figure there are fewer crazies over there in Europe than back here, so maybe the cohort is small enough they will have heard about a guy with a French name."

I would have felt awful guilty after all Tom had done for me if I didn't follow through with the Perveux name, even if, or maybe because, it may have been a pseudonym for someone else. But I didn't find anyone who had heard of the name for quite a while.

Meanwhile, I heard from Sarah that she was enjoying a rather successful time with her law firm. She had been made lead counsel on a case involving, of all things, a missing person. The individual was eventually found dead and the D.A. indicted one of the suspects with barely enough circumstantial evidence to make a case. All Sarah could think of throughout the proceedings, she told me on one of our nightly phone calls, was what if this were me and they eventually found Randolph's body? She said she'd move heaven and earth to clear my name. Which is exactly what she said she did in this case. She got the defendant acquitted by planting so much uncertainty in the minds of the jury, they couldn't convict "beyond a reasonable doubt."

That call ended with the two of us counting the number of weeks left before I would come home.

CHAPTER 17

I had every reason to be pleased with how quickly the students took to my new program. There had been only a few minor incidents of them acting inappropriately in town. As I suspected, the culprits were the same two who defied the self-curfew the staff tried to establish that first night when they arrived. It took the group a week to settle down, just as the mayor had predicted, but now all, even those two, were preoccupied with their projects.

The service-learning program was already a big hit with the students and the townspeople as well. I found jobs for everyone. A student getting her degree in library science was a welcome addition to the staff at the city library. A pre-med student was working as a much-needed orderly in the city hospital. Another was riding as a paramedic with the local ambulance service. One who wanted to be a veterinarian was working on a local farm just outside town. Two art majors found jobs as docents in two of the city's many art museums, staying one step ahead of the tourists with what they were learning about the treasure-trove of medieval art that made Siena such a historical landmark.

One student in particular was having a truly unique experience. He was invited to participate with one of the *contradas* as it prepared for the *palio*, the horse race Siena is famous for. Each summer ten of the city's seventeen *contradas*, or neighborhoods, compete with one another in a horse race that takes place twice, once in July and again in August, right in the *campo* itself. If I thought converting the L.A. Coliseum into a NASCAR race track once a year was weird, converting the *campo* into a race track by carting in tons of sand and dirt seemed almost tame by comparison.

Preparations for the race begin months in advance and the competition is fierce, so being embedded with a *contrada* during this time was something the student will never forget. Naturally, the rest of the students adopted this *contrada*, the one called Chiocciola, as theirs to cheer for during the race. They even learned how to pronounce the name!

By the time the first palio arrived, everyone was hyped up. The mayor, who had now become a big fan of my program, arranged for the entire group to get seating at the *campo*, a very special privilege. When the race was over, only two horses had fallen this time trying to negotiate the turns around the inside of the square. Chiocciola hadn't won, but they did come in second.

Next to the palio the experiences the students liked most, not surprisingly, were the trips every other week to the wineries near each of the medieval hill-top towns. The very first trip they took, to Montepulciano, was so successful two of the students decided on the spot to make the histories of this and the other ancient towns they would be visiting throughout the summer their projects.

As for the rest of the group, it was the wineries themselves that tended to dominate their interest, but not for the reason you might suppose. Thanks to the way I structured the visits around sit-down meals rather than just tastings, the students learned to appreciate the wines for their distinctiveness from one another, and how those differences paired with food. Even though the wines of the region are predominantly of the Sangiovese variety, being able to distinguish one from another became a game they played at each location. Seeing how seriously they seemed to be taking these outings, I arranged for another two students to learn about wine making first hand as their projects.

As for me, I was so busy with the program I had hardly any time for myself. The most I managed was dinner occasionally with one or another of the instructors teaching the program courses. But even these could hardly be considered social gatherings, as they inevitably turned into discussions about the program itself.

One day towards the middle of the summer, however, the mayor invited me to dinner at his official residence. He had arranged the guest list to include individuals from different walks of life in the city. There was a city official, a businessman in town, the owner of a vineyard nearby, and a professor from the University of Siena. From the very start the evening was more than congenial, all the more so because my fluency in Italian made everyone else feel comfortable using their own language. Over the course of the evening I learned a lot about the community I had adopted on behalf of my students.

Naturally, I was especially interested in what the university professor had to say, though I tried not to steer the conversation in that one direction. I already knew about the famous universities of Italy and their incredible histories, dating back to the Middle Ages, but not much about the one in Siena. I was surprised to learn it was the fourth oldest, having been founded in the year 1240. Only the universities of Bologna, Padova and Naples were older. We had a good joke about my beloved Sorbonne in Paris being younger even than the one in Siena, but still older than either Oxford or Cambridge. There were gales of laughter when the mayor made me admit that America's oldest university, Harvard, was founded four hundred years later. My mock protest that the U.S. wasn't even a country in the thirteenth century met with even more laughter.

Aside from the university talk, it was the university professor herself who I must admit attracted my attention. She was introduced as Claudia, and she looked to be about my own age. She had that classic Italian look, strong and attractive in a way I found hard to ignore. When I learned she was not married, warning signals went up almost immediately. I wondered if the mayor may have invited her for other than purely professional reasons. I tried hard not to seem to be paying more attention to her than to the other guests. But as the evening came to a close and everyone was saying good-byes at the door, my efforts were thwarted when Claudia took me aside.

"We should get together again," she said, "while you are here in Siena."

I hesitated before responding but found no polite way to say no.

"I would love to," I said, "when I can get away from work. I have found out that being responsible for a group of young Americans who have never been abroad before is a full-time job, one that requires my attention twenty-four hours a day."

What I didn't mention, of course, was that I had a wonderful staff who would be happy to cover for me if I really needed them to. But Claudia was not fazed. She insisted we exchange business cards and said she hoped to hear from me again soon.

To ease my conscience, I called Sarah later that night. She said something about how upbeat I seemed to be about the program and hoped that was the only reason why. I assured her I'd had virtually no social life since I arrived in Siena, so she needn't worry. I was tempted to turn the tables and ask her how her social life had been going, but thought the better of it. If I was busy, her life in the U.S. court system couldn't be less so. We ended the call assuring each other that all was well between us.

Nevertheless, I couldn't get Claudia out of my mind, especially when I tried to fall asleep. When she was introduced at the dinner, the image that immediately sprang to my mind was of the gorgeous Claudia Cardinale in one of my favorite films, "Once Upon a Time in the West".

Now, lying in bed, all I could think of was that scene between her and Jason Robards just before he bids her goodbye at the end of the film. I have never forgotten the words Robards uttered about how the workers laboring on her behalf lusted after her:

"You can't imagine how happy it makes a man to see a woman like you," Robards' character Cheyenne says. "If one of them should pat your behind, just make believe it's nothing. They earned it."

If only I had Sarah's behind to appreciate at that moment, I thought, all would be well. But I still had half the program left to keep temptation at bay.

CHAPTER 18

My professional duties brought me abruptly back to reality the very next morning when I arrived at the center. The staff informed me that one of the students, Trisha, had begun acting strangely. Up until then she had been a model student, one of the most positive, always going above and beyond what was expected. But in the past few days her mood had suddenly changed to one that could only be described as serious depression. When I asked to see her later that morning, she was at a loss to explain what was going on. She said she'd been having violent mood swings she'd never experienced before.

I was at a loss to know what to do in a situation like that. Fortunately I had a well-trained staff accustomed to dealing with the sorts of mental and physical conditions that were likely to happen on a program like this. One of them suggested Trisha could be suffering from what was called *disordine bipolare* in Italian. She knew about such things because she had a sister who was diagnosed as manic-depressive when she was in her late teens, she told me, just as Trisha was now. This staff person had been keeping an eye on Trisha since the start of the program because her exaggerated enthusiasm struck her as rather manic, just as her sister had been before she had her first serious depressive incident.

I had, of course, heard of bipolar disorder, but I'd never witnessed it or had to deal with it before myself. This was precisely why I had opted to direct this program rather than try to run one of my own. My staff suggested Trisha be evaluated at the university's first-rate medical school, which thankfully Trisha agreed to do. The doctors there did indeed make a preliminary diagnosis of bipolar disorder, and prescribed medication to stabilize her for the time being. But they recommended she return home and obtain more permanent treatment as soon as possible. They made sure Trisha understood that people with this disorder lead perfectly normal lives once they are on a proper long-term regimen. For my benefit, they explained that this kind of disorder often does not fully manifest itself until people, around her age, find themselves for the first time in an unfamiliar and stressful environment. Being away from home without the support mechanisms one normally relies on, as in a study abroad program, can certainly be such a catalyst, they said. They assured Trisha and me there was nothing to worry about, but she would need to have her parents come to collect her so she would not be alone on the plane home.

Although she was devastated to have to leave, she understood she had no choice. The students were just as sad to see her go. They organized a special dinner for her at their favorite restaurant on the *campo* her last night there. Needless to say, I was deeply touched by such a show of affection for someone the students had known for only a few weeks.

The incident was still very much on my mind when I got a call from Claudia a week later. She invited me to spend an afternoon viewing some of the marvelous works of art that are not in the museums but in the various ancient churches in the city. Needing an emotional break from my first serious incident of the summer, I couldn't say no.

"Much of the art in early Siena," Claudia informed me, trying not to sound too professorial, "was inspired by the rise of Christianity, and many famous artists lent their talents at the time to the adornment of the churches that sprang up in this city and hundreds of others throughout the new Christendom."

Since my apartment was at the top of the hill near the *duomo*, we agreed to spend some time in the cathedral itself first. Claudia arrived at my apartment dressed casually but elegantly, as only an Italian woman can. I had to tell myself to concentrate on the art inside the church and not the work of art I was with now.

We walked the two blocks to the *duomo*, which Claudia described as a veritable treasure-trove of medieval and early Renaissance art. I already knew that the building itself is one of the best examples of Italian Romanesque-Gothic architecture. I didn't know much, however, about the art inside. Upon entering, Claudia first pointed out the cathedral's famous marble mosaic floor, one of the most elaborate in all of Italy. Then she turned to the cathedral's pulpit, the thirteenth century masterpiece sculpted by Nicolai Pisano, famous for having instigated the classical revival in Italian renaissance art. Afterwards she took me to the church's *Pinacoteca*, the gallery that housed some of the best-preserved thirteenth century paintings by Sienese artists.

We spent so long in the *duomo*, there was only time for one more church before evening. Claudia suggested the famous Basilico of San Domenico. It contained so many more notable works of art that after a while my eyes begin to glaze over. Noticing this, Claudia suggested we'd seen enough for one day.

"But you must come to dinner at my place this evening," she insisted, "so you can see the artwork I have there."

Trying my best to avoid getting involved in anything so intimate, all I could think of to say was, "Please, Claudia, let me invite you to dinner at one of the nice restaurants in town. That's the least I can do to thank you for being my guide on such a perfect afternoon."

Having none of that, she responded with mock seriousness, "You can thank me by coming and appreciating *my* cooking."

Before I could say anything more, she explained where she lived and said she hoped to see me around eight o'clock.

To say I felt at odds with myself back at my apartment getting showered and dressed would be an understatement. I hadn't been alone with a woman for two months now and didn't trust myself. I had visions of my one-night stands after Tom's great parties. I could only hope that the intellectual side of the evening might prevail over the romantic this time. But with a woman as self-assured as Claudia, and on her territory no less, I didn't think it would necessarily be up to me.

My fears were realized the moment I entered her home, at the appropriate half-hour later than the suggested time. Claudia was dressed more casually than before but as elegantly as ever, highlighting every seductive curve of her figure. The customary two-cheek greeting at the door only served to heighten my concern. I was immediately struck by the intoxicating aromas emanating from the kitchen. Then I noticed the bottle of wine and two glasses on the sideboard in the dining area, and candles seductively flickering on the table.

Right off the bat she joked, "I could still show you the artwork here in the apartment, professor, but I suppose you've had enough of that for one day!"

Before I could stop myself, I heard myself say, "I think the work of art I'm looking at right now will more than suffice."

If I was embarrassed for having blurted that out, Claudia wasn't the slightest bit fazed. She graciously accepted the compliment and said, "Why don't you open the wine and join me in the kitchen."

Then she added, "You can be my *sous-chef* for the evening."

At that point I no longer had any doubts about who was going to be in control. I tried to keep the conversation in the kitchen focused on my work with the program and hers at the university, but that didn't last very long. It was a pretty feeble attempt anyway, given that we'd gone over much of that territory already at the mayor's dinner. So by the time we sat down to eat, we had already begun sharing more personal information.

Claudia wasn't the slightest bit shy talking about herself.

"I was previously married," she told me. "My husband was also a professor, not here but at the University of Florence where we met. We had only a few years together before he died suddenly of a heart attack."

"I'm so sorry," was all I could think to say.

"Technically that makes me a widow," she continued, "but I don't think of myself that way. I left Florence and that life behind and got another position here in Siena. Still being in Tuscany, I can visit my past whenever I feel the need. Because we never had children, I dedicate myself almost exclusively now to the other love of my life, the study of art."

Then she added, "Meeting you is a welcome change for me, all the more so because you are the first American I have had the occasion to spend time with. So tell me more about this American I am spending time with."

I seized the moment to describe my relationship with Sarah, hoping that would protect me from myself later on. Then I segued into my time at Macallan, trying to shift the discussion to mutual academic interests. As I described my tenure situation, Claudia's demeanor showed more and more signs of surprise and disbelief.

When I finished, she exclaimed, "I can't believe how open to subjectivity and manipulation your system is. That would never happen here at an Italian university, or any other European university either, for that matter."

"How so?" I responded, eager to learn something new.

"Well, for starters, all but a few specialized institutions of higher education in Italy are public, governed according to policies and procedures set down by the European Union, the state governments, and only to a lesser degree, the individual universities themselves. To earn a tenured position you have to enter a national competition along with everyone else in the country, based largely on how your publications compare with others in your discipline at that stage in your career."

"That sounds more like the way our legal system works," I remarked, thinking of the comparison Bill Bransing had made between the academic and legal systems in the U.S. "To practice law, you have to pass the bar exam, which puts everyone on a level playing field. Then you just have to find a law firm willing to take you on."

"That does sound like our academic system here too," Claudia went on. "Once you obtain the tenure certification, you have to find a university where your particular specialization is desired."

We became so engrossed in this conversation I didn't realize it was already past midnight. That gave me the cover I needed to insist I had things to attend to first thing in the morning, and needed to get some sleep. Reluctantly, Claudia let me go, but not before she said something in colloquial Italian that sounded to me suspiciously like, "You won't get away so easily next time!"

Back in my apartment afterwards, I felt good about not having succumbed to temptation. What I didn't know at the time, however, was that Sarah had accepted one of Tom's invitations to party again with friends in Oban. Not surprisingly, Jeremy was there too. The two of them ended up spending most of the evening talking with one another rather than circulating. And of course the drinks were flowing. Now in a situation like this, I could only assume that she, as concerned as she was about my ability to remain faithful, would have redoubled her own efforts in that regard. Except that she and Jeremy had known each other intimately for years and had apparently never lost the sense of urgency when they were together.

Long story short, unbeknownst to me that night, Sarah was sleeping at Jeremy's place in Oban while I was alone back in my little apartment in Siena, priding myself on my self-control.

CHAPTER 19

A few weeks later, my program ended and I was on the plane home. The program's grand finale was indeed grand. The mayor invited everyone associated with the program, the students, the teachers, the staff and as many people who had hosted the students' projects as were available, to the town hall for a celebratory dinner. The first thing the mayor said in his opening remarks was how, in contrast to previous years, "the city can't wait for the next group of Professor Bell's students to return."

One of the students acted as sommelier for the evening, demonstrating all he had learned from his summer project at a winery. Another wore the badge he had been given as an honorary member of the city ambulance corps. The student who was embedded with the Chiocciola contrada wore its insignia proudly on his jacket. Still another spoke briefly about a certain Sienese artist whose works she had studied first hand in various churches in town. Everyone burst out laughing when the mayor had to admit this was an artist he himself had never heard of. The program staff got several rounds of applause from the students for all the help they'd provided throughout the summer. Perhaps the most touching moment came when one of the students got up and asked everyone to raise a glass of Sangiovese to Trisha, who never got the chance to finish her thesis on the Roman origins of Siena.

I never did have another rendezvous with Claudia before I left. I was busy wrapping up the program and she had to go out of town for a conference that final week. But she did leave me a note saying she was looking forward to seeing me again when I returned the following summer.

There were two things on my mind when I got home late in the afternoon from my flight. First of course was settling back in with Sarah. I was so anxious to be in bed with her again, she had to tell me to slow down. I thought nothing of it at the time. I knew I was being too impatient, having daydreamed of nothing but that during the entire flight back. Instead, I used the time to raise the second thing on my mind, asking her what had transpired in the meantime with the Randolph business. Unfortunately, she had to tell me there were no new developments. I'd have to talk with Tom about that.

We spent the rest of the time catching up on things we hadn't had a chance to talk about during our various phone calls. When we finally did go to bed, I sensed something different about our lovemaking, but put it down to my being too eager after the long hiatus.

I spent the next week or so writing a lengthy final report on the program for the consortium. Then I met with them personally at the college to review things and plan for next summer. They were so pleased with what I had been able to accomplish in just one summer, they offered to double my salary next year. They noted in particular that more students had been granted credit at their home institutions for their work on the program this year than ever before. Once the meeting was over, we all went to dinner to celebrate the success.

At home again the next day, I tried to get back to my research, but found I couldn't concentrate. I was still obsessed with where I stood in relation to the Randolph case. The last communication I had had with Tom was that long phone call which ended with the query about the guy with the French sounding name. And that had led nowhere. I called Tom again only to find he also had nothing new to report.

"The whole business is fast becoming a cold case," Tom told me, "which is a good thing since it means you'll soon be off the hook. Whatever you do, Ike," he said, "don't for God's sake go back to the police and put yourself in the spotlight again. Just let it go."

If I was looking for something else to take my mind off Randolph, my relationship with Sarah ultimately provided it. Our lovemaking became less satisfying with each passing week, and noticeably less frequent. When it got down to only once a week, I couldn't remain silent anymore. I sensed something was wrong and tried to speak with Sarah about it. At first she was reluctant to even talk about it, but eventually, to keep me from badgering her, she relented. And what she told me about the time she had spent with Jeremy after Tom's party was devastating. I couldn't decide which was worse, being a person of major interest to the police in a murder investigation or being a person of less interest to Sarah than her ex-husband.

At first she insisted it was just a one-off thing. Then, when I wouldn't let it go, she had to admit she still had feelings for Jeremy. That, needless to say, got me pretty worked up.

"What are you telling me?" I demanded. "Do you mean to say you have more feelings for the guy who cheated on you and your marriage than the one who spent a whole summer being faithful to you?"

"No," she answered. "I'm just saying I'm confused and don't know what I feel."

"So where does that leave me?"

"I don't know, Ike. I don't even know how you could have remained faithful with all those gorgeous Italian women around you all summer."

"So you think I've been lying, is that it?"

"No, I didn't say that. But you did have a reputation in Oban as the guy who never went home alone from Tom's parties."

"That was then, Sarah, but we're talking about now. I think I've proven I'm a different person now. I did meet a number of beautiful women in Siena, one in particular, a professor at the university. But the relation remained professional. What really upsets me now is your having asked me on the phone all the time if I was being faithful."

"I don't remember ever asking you that."

"Well then it was my conscience telling me that's what you were thinking. The irony of the whole thing, now that I think of it, is that I never asked if you were being faithful. And you were the one who wasn't. What a schmuck I must be."

"You're nothing of the kind, Ike. You're a terrific guy I happen to have fallen in love with."

"So where does that leave me now? I thought I was in enough limbo with the Randolph affair. Am I in limbo with you now too?"

"I don't know, Ike. I really don't. And I feel terrible about it. I just don't know what to say."

"Well, maybe we should sleep on it, if you'll pardon the bad joke."

"Maybe we should. We can at least cuddle."

Cuddling may have gotten us through that night, but it didn't last long. Over the course of the next few months, well into the new year, we grew further and further apart. The next time Tom invited us to come down for another party, I suggested Sarah go alone to see Jeremy and find out, once and for all, who it was she wanted.

The visit to Oban did indeed turn the tide. She and Jeremy spent the weekend together and realized they had never stopped longing for one another. In the end, apparently, it was the sex that did it. Sarah admitted there was something about it with him that she couldn't explain, and evidently Jeremy confessed his affairs always left him unsatisfied as well.

Though they didn't talk about getting remarried, they did decide to get back together again. Jeremy was due to have a sabbatical the following year, and I would be gone by the summer anyway. Despite the fact that I had just lost the love of my life, I had all but resigned myself to this outcome and had been planning my future accordingly. How I was able to manage this, however, I never understood. Tom would tell me later that it foretold an extraordinary strength of character. I wasn't quite so sure. I couldn't avoid thinking how ironic it was that I had now been jilted twice, once by the university and now by Sarah. So much for the guy who never went home alone!

Sarah and I continued living together for the few months left before I had to take off again for my second summer in Siena. It was a bitter-sweet time, made bearable by the gentle hugging we allowed each other sometimes at night. We never discussed where I would be once the summer was over, since that would be none of Sarah's business anyway at that point. For all I knew, I might be staying on in Siena with Claudia. What with the increased salary I'd be getting and the royalties from my textbook, which was already selling quite well, I figured I'd be able to manage for a while financially.

I had one more thing I wanted to do, however, before I left. I was still determined to find out whatever I could about Randolph's disappearance. Despite what Tom told me over and over, I just couldn't let it go. I couldn't stand the thought of having such a threat hanging over my head indefinitely. I phoned Tom again and asked him if he would please get back in touch with Detective Roberts for an update.

"I understand I can't do that now myself," I said, "but you can do it innocently enough."

Somewhat reluctantly, Tom obliged. The response he got from the detective was both encouraging and disappointing at the same time. Disappointing because there had not been any progress on the case in the meantime, but encouraging because they were indeed treating it now as a cold case. Randolph had been missing for so long, they were no longer actively working on it. They had not received any new reports from people claiming to have recognized him somewhere. Even the university seemed to have put the whole affair behind them. No one but me had been bugging people for more information, not the university and certainly not Randolph's wife.

Hearing this news, I asked Tom for one last favor.

"Would you please send me the Qanon materials you collected from Randolph's house that day? I need to satisfy myself there is nothing in there that might provide a clue."

Tom agreed and I added the stack of papers Tom sent me to my luggage, trying not to think of what that would mean when I had to climb the stairs to the platform at the train station in Milan.

CHAPTER 20

The reception I got back in Siena was more than I could have wished for. I was treated like the conquering hero, the person who turned the program around in just one summer. As before, the consortium provided me with a nice little apartment in the same neighborhood at the top of the hill by the *duomo*. After a long sleep to get over jet lag, I spent the following day with the instructors and staff. For the next two days I held meetings with the local people who wanted to host the students' service-learning projects. To my surprise, the number that actually showed up was about twice the size of the original group. That made the month before the students were to arrive flow so smoothly, I found I had finished all I needed to do in the first two weeks.

Consequently, towards the end of the second week, I started thinking about getting in touch with Claudia again. We had not communicated with each other the entire time I was back in the States. Unbeknownst to me, however, the staff had already been conspiring behind my back to let her know when I returned and when the preliminary arrangements for the new group were completed. So at the end of that second week, right on schedule, the word went out like a smoke signal in an old Western and I received the phone call that would alter my life one more time.

Claudia arranged for us to meet at the *campo*, in front of her favorite restaurant on Friday evening. Our initial meeting could have been embarrassing, had anyone recognized the professor from the university displaying such affection for what looked like a tourist right out in the open on the *campo*. No mere two-cheek greeting this time. Something far more exuberant, like what you might see in the States. I could only imagine what that would portend.

The restaurant she chose was one where the chef prepares special meals for the local cognoscenti, meals the tourists never realize exist. Rather like a Chinese restaurant in America, I thought once the ritual began, where the Chinese themselves seem to be eating something different from everyone else.

And quite a ritual it was. Once we were seated Claudia didn't even look at the menu. She waved it off and told the waiter, "Just bring whatever the chef recommends for tonight."

Then, when I started to peruse the wine list, she waved me off as well, signaled for the sommelier and asked, "Please bring whatever goes best with the meal the chef is preparing."

"Now just relax and enjoy the show," she said.

The "show" consisted of the traditional five courses: *aperitivo* (cocktail), *antipasto* (appetizer), *primo* (pasta dish), *secondo* (main course), and *dolci* (dessert), followed by a *digestivo* (after dinner liqueur). The establishment even offered me a cigar to enjoy at the end of the meal with their homemade herb-infused grappa. Being the modern American I was, however, I couldn't countenance blowing cigar smoke in other people's faces while they were still eating their dinners. I politely declined, but I did accept the one they gave me to take home.

The length of the meal provided plenty of time to catch up on what each of us had been doing the previous nine months. At one point I used the occasion to mention that Sarah and I were no longer together, assuming that would remove any obstacles to a potential relationship with Claudia. Surprisingly, or maybe not so surprisingly, she let that pass without even commenting, as if it made no difference. I should have known better, having lived in France before.

Europeans can have different attitudes towards things like that, so I needn't have said anything at all.

The length of the meal and our conversation brought the clock past midnight, much like the first time we dined together, and this time Claudia was true to her word. I was not going to get off easy. She proposed we meet up again the next morning.

"I have a special weekend planned," she said. "Two days in the glorious Tuscan countryside, if that appeals to you."

Naturally, I was only too happy to oblige, to put myself in this beautiful and assertive woman's hands. It felt good to know I would no longer have to make decisions, of whatever kind.

"No more lectures on art," she promised when she came to pick me up the next morning. I got into her spiffy little Italian convertible and we headed off out of town with the top down. I realized where we were heading once I recognized the road to Montalcino. But I was still curious to know exactly what she had in mind. She didn't say a word until we got to the town and pulled up in front of a charming guesthouse at the end of a narrow street.

While the building must have been hundreds of years old, the inside was as modern as any contemporary inn. Though small, as most rooms in those days were, ours was absolutely charming, overlooking part of the city and a large expanse of the countryside. Claudia suggested we spend the rest of the day in town and reserve the second day for a visit to a very special winery whose proprietors she knew well. We grabbed a bite to eat at the café next door and began to walk through the winding cobblestone streets.

"Maybe no more lectures on art today," she said with an evocative smile, "but lots on architecture."

Though I had been to Montalcino before, I had never toured the city with a guide like Claudia. We started by walking up to the fourteenth century fortress at the top of the hill that dominated the town, then proceeded down to the thirteenth century Saint Agostino church and adjacent art museum.

"Are you sure you don't want to look inside the museum?" Claudia asked with that smile again. "Lots of art history in there."

"No," I answered, faking a pause as if to consider it, "I think I'll pass."

Next was the fourteenth century *duomo* of Montalcino, with its "mere nineteenth century façade," as Claudia put it.

Finally we arrived at the main square, here called simply a piazza, as in most Italian towns.

"Why is this called a *piazza*," I asked her, "whereas the one in Siena is a *campo*. I know that *campo* means 'field' and *piazza* means plaza or square, but what's the difference? One square looks more or less like any other."

"The difference is not so much in the way they look, but in their history," she explained. "When a town square is called a *campo*, it usually means it was once a field. Take the famous *Campo de' Fiori* in Rome, which I'm sure you're familiar with. It was once a field of flowers, exactly as the name says. Now it's one of the most beautiful squares in all of Rome. The *campo* in Siena used to be a marketplace in the countryside midway between three communities. When those communities coalesced into what is now the city of Siena, the *campo* became the natural site of the town square."

"And that crazy horse race twice a year," I added, "as if they still think it's a field."

"Exactly. You know," she went on, "many of the medieval towns in Tuscany have similar traditions to this day. Montalcino is also divided into *contradas*, like Siena, and they too engage in a competition every year. Only theirs is an archery contest held back up where we began the tour, by the fortress at the top of the hill."

As the sun began to set, we started making our way back to the inn. At one point we had to step aside as an enormous tourist bus squeezed its way down the narrow street between buildings, with its side mirrors folded in so they wouldn't get torn off. Then we found a nice little restaurant where only the locals ate, so we could enjoy a simple but traditional Italian supper.

What transpired once we arrived back at the room and spent our first night alone together was everything I had dreamed it would be, and more. The vision of Claudia's raven-black hair and godlike body made the Claudia of Sergio Leone's western vanish from my mind. I now had my own Claudia, in the flesh, and the sensation was nothing short of divine. It was as if heaven and earth had met.

The next day we drove to one of the two hundred or so vineyards that make the famous Brunello wine in the countryside around Montalcino. The property Claudia chose had been in the same family for more than a hundred years. The proprietors were a husband-and-wife team, surprisingly named Antonio and Antonia, who specialized in organic farming. They grew only the Brunello grape, the queen of the Sangioveses, famous for its complex flavor and structure.

When we arrived, we found a table already set for four in a grove of olive trees. On the tablecloth were china plates and silverware plus a line of fine wine glasses at each place. Our hosts had planned a flight of the winery's Brunellos, six vintages in all, and various cheeses and charcuterie to sample them with. The oldest bottle in the flight was some thirty years old. When I expressed surprise that it was still in perfect condition, Antonio explained that one of the things that make Brunello wines so famous is their unique aging properties.

Although we stayed for quite a long time talking and sampling the wines, our hosts insisted we stay for a while longer and tour the winery itself before driving back to town. They didn't want us taking any chances with Italy's strict rules about drinking and driving. I knew that drinking more than one glass of wine can get you a DUI in Italy.

"Not only that", Antonia explained, "we don't fill a glass near as full as Americans do. You should fill the glass only half-way so you can appreciate the aroma, the nose, that permeates the rest of the glass."

"That is," Claudia added with a nod to the proprietors, "when you are savoring a fine wine like theirs out of a proper glass. If you're drinking ordinary table wine in a bar or café, on the other hand, it will be served in those little glasses you see everywhere here that don't leave much room for the aroma that may or may not be there anyway."

Two hours later, safe for the road with our systems appropriately cleansed by time, we got back in the convertible for a leisurely drive around the Montalcino countryside. As evening approached, we headed back to town, parked the car and found a table in the café next to the guesthouse. We ate while watching the sun disappear behind the hills and vineyards, casting shadows that changed the color of the landscape every few minutes. It made me think of my time in the Monet Museum in Paris, observing how he would paint the same scene over and over again, showing how the colors changed depending on the time of day.

It was a truly romantic setting, surpassed only by the lovemaking that made our second night together seem even more special than the first.

Back at the study center, it wasn't long before the students arrived and the summer got in full swing. There were, of course, a few students who ignored the advice I gave them, rather less sternly than the previous summer, not to party while they were still jet-lagged. But thankfully there were no incidents this time either. The mayor himself came to the study center to greet the new group. He informed them he would be hosting a welcoming party at the town hall later in the week. Needless to say, I was pleased to see how well my efforts the previous summer had succeeded.

Claudia and I continued to see each other when our schedules allowed, occasionally spending weekend nights together. Other evenings I might join some of my students when I was out alone and spotted a group of them at a café. I didn't have to look very hard to find them, but not because they were speaking English. I was gratified to see them speaking Italian most of the time, even amongst themselves. Nor was it their American accents that gave them away. The difference was, they were the ones talking loudly while the Italians were the ones talking with their hands. Smiling to myself, I wondered if I should ask the teachers to give instruction on the use of gestural in addition to oral and written language.

I was especially pleased to see how often the students' conversations were focused on their projects, comparing experiences and offering advice to one another without my having to intervene. When the subject changed to other things, it was usually about what was happening back in the States, since their iPhones were never turned off.

On one particular evening the group I joined started discussing the political situation and how polarized discourse in America had gotten. When one of them mentioned Qanon, my ears perked up. I used the occasion to ask if they had ever heard of the name Jacques Perveux.

"Oh yes," one of them answered. "he's some obscure guy who has his own theories. No one really knows who or where he is. Kind of like Q himself, I guess. He might be French, but no one knows for sure. I got interested in him," this student went on, "because he's different from the other whackos. His conspiracy theories are not that crazy, almost believable."

"How so?" I asked, eager to hear more.

"One of his theories, for example, suggests that Fauci's involvement with the lab in Wuhan had an ulterior purpose no one will acknowledge. Fauci, the story goes, was part of a plot to let the virus escape from that lab so it could infect and ultimately decimate the Chinese population. The assumption was that their government would keep it a secret and immediately seal the borders. They'd try to deal with it themselves and ultimately fail, killing hundreds of millions of people. Only it was Fauci's plot that failed, the theory goes, since as we know the Chinese pretended the virus didn't exist for quite some time and left their borders open. And we know what happened then."

Hearing this, I vowed to spend my leisure time while still in Italy finding out more about the guy Tom had dubbed Jack the Pervert.

CHAPTER 21

Unfortunately, I didn't get that leisure time for quite a while. I had a feeling the program was going too smoothly. Something was bound to happen. It was about halfway through the summer when I got a phone call in the middle of the night. One of the students had been arrested by the Carabinieri of all things, not the local police but the national military police. Needless to say, I assumed something really terrible must have happened. When I got to the police station at three that morning, I was told the student was Alex Cardona, but he'd already been transported to the regional police headquarters in Florence. The charge, they told him, was *furto d'auto*, or grand theft auto.

Instinctively, I thought of going right away to Florence to find out what was going on. But my staff advised me in the strongest terms not to go there alone, and certainly not in the middle of the night. I would need a lawyer to help me navigate the Italian judicial system, they said. The program did have a lawyer on retainer, but he was not a criminal lawyer. He only handled civil issues having to do with the functioning of our program in Italy, its financial and other organizational matters.

That's when I turned to Claudia, phoning her first thing in the morning, as soon as I figured she'd be up. She said she knew exactly the lawyer to call in Florence, and hoped he would be available. Luckily he was, and we took off right away in her car. Even though she knew the city well, it took her a while to find the correct police station. When we did, we asked for information regarding an American student named Alex who was arrested near Siena the day before. We were told he had been pulled over for making an illegal turn, and when they stopped him they found he was driving a car that wasn't his own.

From the way the police described the situation, it was obvious they didn't believe whatever explanation Alex must have given them. That's when the lawyer demanded to speak with Alex in person.

We were led down a long corridor to a holding cell, where we found Alex sitting half slumped over from lack of sleep on a bench with several other men. We asked to talk with him in private and after a bit of back and forth were allowed to do so. Alex was clearly distraught, but was overjoyed to see us.

"I don't get why they wouldn't believe me when I explained why I was driving that car. My Italian is more than adequate, so I know they understood me."

"Don't worry," the lawyer told him, "We'll sort this out. So tell us what happened."

Looking at Ike, Alex began, "You know I work on a farm for my project, right? Well, last week the owners, husband and wife both, had to leave for a week on some personal business. They asked me to drive them to the train station and pick them up again when they returned. They offered to let me keep their car in the meantime rather than continue taking the bus to get there every day, like I normally do. That's why I was driving their car."

"OK, so why did the Carabinieri stop you?" the lawyer asked.

"I was driving back to Siena after work and got lost. It was already getting dark and I guess I took a wrong turn. When I realized what I must have done, I made a U-turn to get back on the right road. That's when they stopped me and told me I'd made an illegal turn. Then they asked to see my license and registration for the car. I tried to explain why I was driving that car but they wouldn't believe me. I tried calling the owners on their cell phone so they could confirm my story, but I couldn't reach them. I've been trying their phone ever since I got here, but they still don't answer. They must have turned it off."

"Problem is," the lawyer said, "the police won't take the word of someone over the phone anyway. They'll insist on speaking with them in person. So Alex, I'm afraid you'll have to remain in custody until they can be reached and asked to come to Florence to vouch for you. Unless, that is, I can get them to release you into my custody for the time being, but I doubt it. They might do that for an Italian but never for a foreigner. Let me see what I can do."

As he suspected, they refused. Worse still, they insisted on booking Alex into the general population at the jail. I promised I'd stay right there in Florence and visit him every day until things got sorted out.

My next thought was to contact the American consulate in Florence. They are responsible for the welfare of US citizens abroad, and the staff at the study center registered the students with them every summer. I decided to go there personally. I thanked Claudia and the lawyer profusely and told them I'd take it from there.

I had had some experience with a US consulate abroad before, so I knew that the degree of help they provide can vary. I was in Marseilles once with two other students during my junior year when one of them was mugged and robbed. The local police said there was nothing they could do about it since we were in an area we should have known was unsafe. The consulate told us exactly the same thing and said we should just chalk it up to experience.

The reception I got at the consulate in Florence this time was not much different. The place was packed with Italians applying for visas to the US and Americans complaining about every imaginable thing under the sun. It took me a while just to find someone to talk to. When I did, the answer I got was just what I feared.

"I'm sorry," the consular officer said, "but it'll be a while before I can get to the kid's case."

Waving his hand around the packed room, he added, "See what we're dealing with here? All this and Washington has just cut our budget for the second year in a row."

Not satisfied with this excuse, I asked, "Can't you just take a moment to call the police and insist they release Alex into your custody, as an official of the U.S. government?"

I should have guessed the answer. "The police won't deal with anyone over the phone in a case like this, not even us," the officer said.

Out of ideas, I decided to get a hotel room, something to eat, and some much-needed sleep. I got lucky finding a hotel room but it took me a while to find a restaurant that wasn't full of loud and obnoxious American tourists. I was in Florence, after all, and the scene in the restaurants was classic. If they weren't squabbling among themselves, they were grousing about why they couldn't get the food they like in the States. I wondered why they even come here in the first place.

Eventually I found a little restaurant down a narrow street where I heard nothing but Italian being spoken, spied a table in the corner and relaxed for the first time that day.

It wasn't until several days later that I finally got Alex out. I could only imagine how trying it must have been for him, being in limbo like that, waiting to find out whether or not he would be found guilty of something he didn't do. I couldn't help thinking of my own situation, still being in limbo myself, not knowing what will eventually transpire with the Randolph business.

What ultimately happened in Alex's case was this. The proprietors of the farm wanted to get away for a week, knowing the property would be in good hands with Alex. He had proven himself such a reliable and conscientious worker, they entrusted him with both the farm and their car. Consequently, they turned their cellphone off and didn't turn it back on until they were on the train returning to Siena. When they tried calling Alex to come pick them up, he never answered because the police had confiscated his phone when he was put in with the general population at the jail. So they hired an Uber to get back to the farm. Finding neither Alex nor their car, they immediately called the study center and were told the story. They agreed to go to Florence right away to clear up the situation. Once they told their story, the police had no choice but to release Alex. No apologies, no regrets, just a terse three-word statement in English, "you may go".

Fortunately, Alex was as strong a kid as he was trustworthy, so it didn't take long for him to put the whole business behind him. In fact, he rather enjoyed telling his story to anyone who would listen for the remainder of the summer.

"My out-of-class experiences," he would say, "now include intimate knowledge of the Italian police and jail system. Not to mention getting to know the colorful lot of people I met behind bars. Maybe I can get extra credit for my vastly expanded Italian vocabulary!"

The rest of the summer passed rather quickly and without further incidents. The *palio* was a great hit, even more than the previous summer because the *contrada* one of the students was embedded with this time actually won the race. The celebration afterwards proved that Italians can be just as loud and boisterous as Americans when the situation warrants.

As the end of the program neared, I had an important decision to make. I would need to go back to New York for my post-program interview with the consortium, of course, but I no longer had any need to stay there. I could do my research and finalize the second edition of my textbook anywhere. There being no reason not to assume I'd be directing the program again next year, I could come back to Italy and enjoy the company of Claudia.

It could not, however, be the same kind of relationship I had with Sarah. Claudia and I had a lovely but only limited time together throughout the summer. She was completing research and writing a major book on "Tuscan Art Through the Ages" which, in addition to her other duties as a professor, took virtually all of her time. We only saw each other on occasional weekends, and it became evident that a closer relationship was not in the cards. Not that I was necessarily looking for one.

To enjoy a bachelor existence in Italy and be intimate with such a sophisticated European intellectual from time to time, how bad could that be?

I would, however, need to apply for a permanent residency permit if I were to stay in Italy longer than my temporary three-month visa currently allowed. And that would involve dealing with the Italian bureaucracy on my own, something you wouldn't wish on your worst enemy. It being a personal matter at that point, I could no longer have the consortium handle it for me.

On the other hand, if I were to stay in the States, I would definitely want to find some kind of closure with the Randolph affair. It would be more out of curiosity now, though, since the authorities didn't seem interested in the case anymore anyway.

With that in mind, I used what little free time I had left in Siena to look once more through the Qanon materials Tom gave me. I couldn't countenance having schlepped them all the way over from the States for nothing. I was convinced there had to be a reason why Randolph was collecting them.

By the time the program ended, however, I still hadn't found anything new. But I was determined to keep trying.

CHAPTER 22

It was in this frame of mind that I got on the plane back home, having basked in the pleasure of the farewell dinner the mayor, once again, graciously offered to host at the town hall. I'd made arrangements with Tom to stay temporarily at his place in Oban, not having a home of my own anymore, while I decided what to do with my life.

To celebrate my return, Tom arranged a quiet party with just our mutual friends Bill and Jim. I asked Tom to invite my other friend from those days, Phil Cranston, as well. I was anxious to hear how he was doing, remembering how despondent he had been about not being able to get his work published. I figured Phil's tenure decision would have had to come up by now.

Tom hesitated before answering, unsure how to break the news.

"I'm sorry to have to tell you this," he said, "but Phil's tenure decision never came up."

"What do you mean, never came up?" I responded incredulously. "It's been six years, so by rule it had to, no?"

"Well, despite all the encouragement he got from his colleagues to keep at it, he was convinced he would never make it."

"So what did he do? Just quit?"

"I don't know any other way to say it, Ike, but Phil committed suicide last year. The funeral was private and the family honored Phil's request that there be no memorial service, no remembrance of any kind."

I must have said something like "Oh my God," but I don't remember exactly. I do remember shouting in anger, "Damn the system. Damn this fucking system."

Then, once I calmed down, all I could think of was, "Maybe if I hadn't given Phil false hope of eventually getting tenure, I could have used my own experience to show him how little meaning tenure has anyway. But it's too late now."

It took a while and several rounds of Scotch once we got together to take the pall off after that. Tom saluted me for having achieved such success doing, as he put it, "what old man Randolph refused to let you do at Macallan."

"I'm amazed at how you were able to mobilize the entire community of Siena in such a short time," Bill chimed in.

"It wasn't so much me," I countered. "The students are great kids once you get them to focus on what really matters. It was they who earned the community's respect, and the community responded in kind."

To which Jim added sarcastically, "If only Macallan University had shown you the same respect."

Thanking them all for the compliments, I tried to change the subject. I couldn't help myself, but I just had to know more about the Randolph affair.

"Tell me," I began, trying not to sound too obsessed, "have there been any new sightings of him that would suggest he's still alive somewhere, living incognito like a ghost waiting to haunt us and torture us some more?"

Smiling at the overwrought simile, Tom merely responded, "Not that we've heard."

"OK, then, what about Jack the Pervert?" I asked. "Anything new about *him*?"

That got a confused look from Bill and Jim, who had no idea what I was talking about. Tom told them about finding things with the Jacques Perveux name among Randolph's Qanon papers, and how, in the true Macallan tradition, he'd given him an appropriate nickname.

"Nice touch," Jim responded appreciatively. "But who the hell is this guy?"

"That's the point. We don't really know," I cut in. "I did ask about him in Siena, but all I learned was he's apparently some obscure guy no one seems to know much about, except that his theories are not quite as crazy as the others. I read through some of them while I was in Siena, and that does seem to be the case."

Then, against my and everyone else's better judgment, I reiterated my desire to have another meeting with Detective Roberts.

"Not again," Tom said in exasperation. "Whatever for? The case is dead, Ike, so there's nothing more to know."

"Not necessarily," I responded. "I need to put some closure to this thing, and the police never followed up on those sightings of him shortly after he disappeared. I need to know if there actually was something to them. Maybe the bastard really did just go off somewhere for some reason, and people really did recognize him."

At that point Jim chimed in, "Remember, Ike, it was curiosity that killed the cat."

Then Bill added, "For Christ's sake, Ike, you've got a great career ahead of you. Don't screw it up now. If you keep this up, they may well reopen the case, just for you, and not in a good way."

Despite this unequivocal advice, I did go to see Roberts again. It was clear from the start that he didn't want to waste any more time on the case, but reluctantly agreed to see me.

"Better make this short," he demanded the moment I entered his office. "I've got a lot of things on my plate right now, and this sure isn't one of them."

"I promise not to take more than a few minutes of your time," I responded. "For starters, can you at least confirm that the Randolph case is closed?"

"Yes, I can. What's next?"

"You have said there were several sightings of him after he disappeared. What happened with those?"

"Only presumed sightings, not confirmed ones. They were never corroborated. We certainly weren't going to waste time chasing after them."

"OK, but can you tell me how many there were and where they were located?"

"Why the hell do you want to know? What would you do with that information if you got it anyway? What are you going to do, start a private detective agency now? Haven't you got better things to do?"

"All I am asking is that you humor me and let me have the information about those sightings. They're not confidential or anything, are they?"

"No, they're not. Just go by the front desk on your way out and I'll have them waiting for you. And let this be the last time I hear from you."

CHAPTER 23

Armed with this new information, I went back to Tom's place hoping it would turn into something significant. Convinced by now that Randolph had staged his own disappearance, I started to plot the sightings. One was in New Mexico and one in Arkansas, two were in Arizona and two more in Texas. At first the distribution seemed random, except that they were all in the south and southwest. There were none east of the Mississippi. That seemed odd until I lined them up sequentially according to their dates. Then I recognized a pattern, a trajectory of a trek westward that started just a couple of days after Randolph disappeared. It began chronologically just on the other side of the Mississippi in Arkansas, then Texas, New Mexico, and finally Arizona, in that order. As for the lack of sightings on this side of the Mississippi, the only thing I could think of was that Randolph may have kept himself pretty much out of sight those first couple of days, until he got far enough away and news of his disappearance began to fade. Then he might have let his guard down.

As I continued to obsess about Randolph, my mind shifted back and forth between the sightings and the Qanon material, the only two potentially useful pieces of evidence I had. Could they somehow be related? Why, in particular, was there so much material by this one Perveux person? Why this apparent fixation on one obscure conspiracy peddler, one who didn't seem quite as crazy as the others? Could it be the professor in him that made Randolph attracted to such a person?

Then it hit me, and I couldn't wait for Tom to get home from work to share my eureka moment. I decided to make a sort of celebration out of telling him, so I bought the fixings for a steak-frites for two with salad, and had some of Tom's own Scotch waiting for him when he got home. I told Tom I had a surprise for him, but kept him in suspense while I prepared the meal.

Once we sat down to eat, I announced, "You'll never guess what I just figured out."

"No, I'm sure I won't," Tom answered. "What is it?"

"Well, I got the list of those Randolph sightings from the detective today. You know, the ones they never bothered to look into. I plotted them on a graph of time and place, and guess what. They are evidence of a perfect trek westward, starting in Arkansas and ending up in Arizona."

"So?" is all Tom could think to say.

"Sooo…, I asked myself, could Randolph have gone somewhere far away, like Arizona, where he could assume a different identity, an alter ego? And could that have something to do with the Qanon conspirators he seemed to be so interested in, many of whom have turned Arizona into a hotbed of that sort of thing? Then it struck me. Maybe he was not just a fan of those folks, maybe he is actually one of them himself. And who might that be if not the one whose own theories are more seemingly rational than the others? The one with the name a professor of French studies might adopt. Tom, our dearly departed Professor Randolph is Jacques Perveux! Barren Aaron is Jack the Pervert, and he's alive and well, practicing his new profession somewhere in Arizona."

Tom's reaction was classic. The first thing he said was, "Why didn't I think of that?"

Then, on second thought, he added, "Nah, no way. This is just how conspiracy theories get started, Ike. Don't become one of them yourself. You've been fixating on this guy for far too long. It's time to let it go, not dig the hole deeper. Don't ruin the good thing you have going with your textbook, your summer program, and the gorgeous Claudia. For the last time, Ike, forget Randolph."

"I appreciate your concern, Tom, but think about it. Here is a guy who all along has had a secret Qanon agenda and an alter ego to go with it, one with exactly the kind of name someone like him might use. I even googled the name Perveux. Guess what I found?

"I can't imagine. What?"

"Well, there are several actual people named Perveux, but they're in relatively obscure businesses, at least ones I've never heard of. But one reference led me to a kind of pop psychoanalysis of the name, something like a horoscope of people named Perveux, which could explain why he chose it for himself. Admittedly lots of things in there didn't match Randolph very well, but some others did, and remarkably so."

"Things like what?" Tom asked, unconvinced.

"I wrote some of them down. Listen to these. New things feel exciting. If somebody tries to limit your freedom, it is not appreciated. When realizing your interests, you feel no doubts. Once your beliefs are set, motivating your environment is the most natural thing. Your social intelligence allows you to capture the attention of your audience. You are a communicator."

When Tom didn't respond, I added, "I'll bet you Randolph is on some kind of a mission to spread his conspiracy ideas, which he couldn't do as a professor at Macallan. He needed a place where no one knew him to make it happen."

"So what are you going to do about it, Ike? Don't tell me you're going to try and find the son-of-a-bitch. Please tell me you won't do that."

"Well, I do have plenty of time between now and the start of next summer's program to look for him, to prove he's alive, and solve this mystery once and for all. It would even be good for me to take some time off for a while and see a bit of the country. They say Arizona is quite a beautiful place."

"Yes," Tom said, "and full of lots of crazy people, too. Gives the concept of the Wild West new meaning these days."

"Probably not any more so than a lot of other places," I added, which kind of put an end to our conversation.

And so the die was cast. As I was getting in my car to leave two days later, Tom didn't say good luck, he just shook his head and told me to be careful.

CHAPTER 24

I enjoyed the first day of my journey, out the New York State Thruway into Ohio and Indiana. Then things started to get boring, so I looked for another way to do this than via the interstate system. When I got into Illinois, I knew I had to start turning south. That's when I spotted a sign pointing to the famous Route 66.

Checking the map on my iPhone, I saw it would take me part of the way Randolph might have gone, to Oklahoma, then across the Texas panhandle into New Mexico and Arizona, the last three being states where five of the most recent sightings of Randolph were supposed to have occurred. Of course I had no way of knowing if Randolph ever took that route, or even if he traveled by car, since his own car was left in the garage back in Oban. But it would be worth it just to see the bit of Americana that I had heard historic Route 66 is famous for, even if it would take me a good bit longer passing through all those little towns along the way.

That indeed turned out to be the best part of my trip. Because it is still a local road, it beckoned me to stop numerous times to experience how things used to be in the America of the previous century. What caught my eye right away were the gas stations and other buildings looking just like they did in the 1940s. I used my iPhone camera to start creating my own personal album of them.

Each time I stopped, I would also pull out the photo of Randolph I brought with me to see if anyone recognized him. For the longest time I got nothing but blank stares. But finally, days later near Oklahoma City, the kid pumping gas recognized his picture right away. Even though it would have been some time ago, he didn't hesitate.

"I'll never forget that asshole," he said.

Then, hoping to find out whether Randolph was using his real name or his alter ego's, I asked, "You didn't by any chance get his name, did you?"

"I would'ov if he'd used a credit card. That's how come I remember the guy. He insisted on payin' for an eight-dollar top-off with a hundred-dollar bill. I knew he had smaller bills 'cause I saw 'em when he opened his wallet. I don't get many customers on this here route, so I gotta keep as many smaller bills as possible on hand."

"Sorry to hear that. But thanks anyway," I said, handing him exact change for my own top-off.

"That's OK," he said. "I knew he heard what I hollered at him as he drove off. Made me feel better about the whole thing."

I didn't bother to ask what he yelled at him. I'd had a few choice words for Randolph myself over the years. I knew how cathartic such things can be.

Though I was disappointed not being able to find out which name Randolph was using, at least I now had one confirmed sighting to justify my trip, one that also confirmed the wisdom (or the sheer luck) of having taken this particular route. After all, what were the odds Randolph would have come this very way.

That evening I decided to celebrate and ordered the biggest rib eye steak they had at a diner next door to the motel I stopped at for the night. I would have ordered a Scotch to start with but all they had was some cheap blended whisky in a half-gallon bottle, definitely not the kind of single malt I was accustomed to. I was, after all, out on Route 66 in the middle of nowhere. Then, when I went to order some wine to eat with my steak, the only kind they had was a nameless red from some winery in Texas. I couldn't imagine what a wine from Texas must be like, so I asked for a taste first. The waiter hesitated for a moment before responding.

"Well, we don't get many orders for wine out here, so I'd hate to open a bottle and have you not order it."

"Fair enough," I said. "So what do you think, am I going to like it?"

"Probably not," he answered, without hesitating this time.

So I settled for a beer and proceeded to sip it with my steak, pretending it was one of New York's State's famous champagnes from the Finger Lakes region around Oban.

I didn't get another hit with Randolph's picture until I got to Arizona. Checking into a motel in the Flagstaff area, the clerk behind the counter said of course he recognized the person in the photo.

"How could I forget a guy who complained all the time about his room?"

He gave me a big grin and then added, "I told him if he wanted a Hilton, there was one right in the center of town."

I also got the answer I expected when I asked him if he knew what name the guy was using. "Nah, he paid in cash. Had a wad of bills on him."

Then, knowing I could well be at the end of my journey there in Arizona, I had one more question.

"He didn't by any chance say anything about where he was headed, did he?"

"Nah," came the answer again, "but I do remember him saying something about living where the real people are, and then ranting about restoring the country to its former glory."

That night I wondered what Randolph might have meant with that comment about former glory. My first thought was what I myself was feeling, a sense of nostalgia after my trip down memory lane on Route 66. Then I remembered what Randolph was known for back at Macallan when he taught his courses on French history. He used to rave about the glory of the monarchy, especially Louis XIV, and how the French revolution destroyed the country.

That night in my dreams, images of the Sun King were juxtaposed intermittently with those of Donald Trump, a flowing black mane alternating with a frightful yellow mop. When I woke up the next morning, it occurred to me that Jacques Perveux might actually represent the perfect symbiosis of the King and the Donald in Randolph's twisted mind.

CHAPTER 25

At breakfast the next morning, I knew I had a critical decision to make. Assuming the Randolph sightings did actually terminate somewhere there in Arizona, that still left a lot of territory in one of the largest states in the country, the sixth largest in fact, to look for him. How to narrow down the search? Then, over my second cup of coffee, it suddenly occurred to me that these conspiracy types often solicit money to promote their agendas. Maybe I could find him that way. I chided myself for not having thought of that before.

I looked through the Perveux materials I brought with me one more time and sure enough, there was an address in one of them to send money. It was a P.O. Box number in Phoenix. Sifting through the materials further to verify the address, I found another one. It was also a P.O. Box number, but a different one in a different city, Tempe. By the time I completed my search, I'd found a third, this time right where I was, there in Flagstaff.

I didn't need to look at a map, however, to know that those three cities span most of the state, from north to south. That wouldn't narrow things down much at all. There was no way I could stake out all three sites at the same time and wait for him to pick up his money. Staying where I was now, in one of the three, would give me only a thirty percent chance of getting lucky. For all I knew, Randolph could very well be living in yet another city he wasn't using as a drop box at all.

In fact, as I thought more about it, that might be the most logical assumption. Why would Randolph risk remaining in any one of those cities for any length of time? Better to drop by once every few months, say, collect his money and get lost again. That would be the smartest way to remain incognito.

Pulling up a map of Arizona on my iPhone, I tried to think of where I myself would stay if I had to make repeated trips to retrieve my money at those three locations. Wouldn't it be somewhere midway between the two most distant ones?

After a while I settled on a couple of likely possibilities. Both were in the mountains south of Flagstaff and north of Phoenix and Tempe. One was Payson and the other Prescott. Looking at their descriptions on the internet, Prescott appeared more difficult to access than Payson, but it was twice the size and seemed to be an interesting town, someplace where I might like to stay, judging from the blurb by the local Chamber of Commerce. Mindful that it was nothing but a hunch, I nevertheless decided to make Prescott the place I would stake out first. So far my hunches had done pretty well by me, so why not go with this one as well? I would still have plenty of time if my hunch turned out to be wrong.

With that much time left to complete my mission, I figured there was no need to go to Prescott right away. I could stick around the Flagstaff area and enjoy some of the gorgeous Arizona scenery. Besides, the Grand Canyon was just up the road from where I was, and I had always wanted to see it.

Being new to the area, I didn't know that the rim of the canyon lies at about 7000 feet above sea level. Searching the web for information about it, I learned that the distance from the rim down to the Colorado River below is more than a mile. I also read that the trek down was well worth the effort and could be done in one of three ways: by hiking, biking, or even on the back of a mule. I decided on the most interesting option and made the earliest possible reservation for a mule ride two days hence.

To pass the time during those two days I spent the daylight hours playing tourist around Flagstaff and the evenings surfing the net for the latest Qanon activities in the area. I was hoping to find things *about* Perveux as much as *by* him. But there wasn't much, hardly anything in fact. I wondered if anybody actually read Randolph's stuff, since he evidently wasn't what you'd call a celebrity in the Qanon world. Then, late on the night before my scheduled mule ride, just as I was about to quit and get some sleep, I came across an article with the title "Who is Jacques Perveux?" Too tired to read it carefully, I gave it a quick once over, enough to realize it was something I'd have to study more thoroughly as soon as I got back from the trip down the canyon.

The mule ride was a two-day affair with an overnight stay at the bottom of the canyon on the other side of the river at a place called Phantom Ranch. The trip down took a few hours, the mules walking sure-footed on a trail that was often no wider than the animals themselves, sometimes with as much as a thousand-foot drop-off at the edge. Needless to say, there were no guard-rails. I knew if I were doing this on foot, my vertigo would kick in and I'd be a nervous wreck. But my mule gave me the sense of confidence I needed to enjoy the trip. And it gave me plenty of time to think some more about what I was getting myself into.

I wondered if this experience might be a metaphor of some kind. Could I trust myself to manage the situation I was willfully putting myself in searching for Randolph alone, with no mule in sight to hold on to? Tom's admonitions before I left Oban were ringing in my ears. I could be on a fool's errand, or I could find myself in serious jeopardy once I found him. There was no way of knowing what kind of people he might be associating with. Images of the Bundy standoff in Oregon flashed across my mind just at the moment my mule stumbled a bit, sending pieces of the trail cascading down the canyon.

Thankfully, the wonderful barbeque dinner and the lively conversation at the ranch on the other side of the river that evening took my mind off things. It made me think of Tom's parties, except that my current situation stopped me from even considering hooking up with one of the several single women whose company I enjoyed around the campfire. I was on a mission now, and was not about to let myself be distracted.

In fact, I excused myself early, went to my cabin and fell asleep almost immediately. In my dreams this time Randolph was riding the mule behind me, his image alternating with that of a witch on a broomstick. Every time the witch cackled, my own mule stumbled. When she suddenly swooped away to the bottom of the canyon, she was Randolph tumbling with his mule over the side. I woke up with a start and, needless to say, didn't get back to sleep for the rest of the night. That was the second dream, or was it nightmare, I'd had since embarking on this ill-advised mission. Maybe it wasn't too late to turn back.

The trek up from the river the next day seemed much longer than the one on the way down. I couldn't wait to get to my motel and study that article about Perveux. It, I thought, would tell me whether or not I should keep on with this.

What I read did indeed help me make up my mind. It emphasized the fact that no one seemed to know who Perveux was, since he had never shown himself in public. He was somebody hiding behind a mask, it said, working in secret. At one point the article suggested that Perveux wasn't really one of them, not a real conspiracist. It didn't exactly say why, but it did note that he writes more like an academic trying to indoctrinate a class of students. That struck me as not only very perceptive, assuming Perveux was indeed the professor, but also rather ironic. Weren't conservatives supposed to be the ones who accuse teachers of indoctrinating their students with progressive ideas, not the other way around?

What really got my attention, though, was how the article ended, on a very chilling note that could only be considered a threat. It was a blatant warning that Perveux needed to be ostracized from the movement, done away with by force if necessary. What I couldn't figure out was why such vitriol against someone who wrote some of the least controversial Qanon literature. Or maybe that was the point.

All of this unnerved me even more. I might be walking into some kind of civil war I didn't understand. But I was not going to let this stop me. I just had to remember I wasn't in New York anymore. I was in the Wild West now.

CHAPTER 26

It was with this disturbing thought that I packed up my things and headed off the next morning on what I hoped would be the final leg of my journey. To get to Prescott, the map on my iPhone told me to take route 89A south, just outside Flagstaff. That would take me a short way down Oak Creek Canyon to the red rock country around the town of Sedona before turning more westerly up to the Prescott Valley.

Seeing how absolutely gorgeous the scenery was around Sedona, I decided to stop there and spend the rest of the day enjoying what I had only previously seen in pictures. I parked the car and strolled around town, looking in at several of the art galleries the town is known for. A particular piece of Indian jewelry caught my eye right away, with its intricate interplay of turquoise, coral and silver. I bought it, thinking ahead to next summer and Claudia.

I spent the rest of the afternoon driving around the red rock landscape, imagining this could also be a place to make home someday. I found a place to eat dinner just outside town as the sun was setting, turning the rock formations into more shades of red than I thought possible. At one moment it looked like the whole landscape was on fire. Still consumed with thoughts about the wisdom of my mission, the image made me think I may be burning bridges to the life I would never see again.

The next morning the rising sun turned the landscape into yet another blaze of color. This time it was more like those images of Christ at Easter, where the sun's rays shine down over His shoulder. Enough of witches on broomsticks and burning bridges, I thought. Maybe this is the positive sign I need.

Back in the car after breakfast, Route 89A took me out of the desert and into the mountains towards Prescott. The scenery changed as the road began to twist and turn through stands of pine trees, and the red sandstone rocks gave way to the granite Dells, as the road sign said they're called, of Prescott Valley.

Eventually 89A dead-ended into state route 89 into Prescott itself. Arriving in town, I couldn't escape the feeling I really was in the old Wild West. I saw signs pointing out locations where Doc Holliday and Wyatt Earp's brother Virgil once stayed. Eventually I spied a modest but nice-looking hotel near the town square. I checked in and asked for a monthly rate. I figured a month should be enough to prove my hunch right or wrong.

For the next several days I wandered around town, stopping in at a store every once in a while to see if there was anything I needed. My first impulse was to buy a hat at the western hat store on the main square. I'd never seen so many different styles of cowboy hats before, or colors either for that matter. I settled on a modest one so I could blend in as inconspicuously as possible with the locals. With that thought in mind, I also dropped in to a clothing store. The jeans I was wearing might be OK, I thought, but the shirts I had with me were definitely East Coast. The next thing that drew my attention was the shoe store next door. I thought about buying a pair of cowboy boots to complete the outfit, but looking around I saw that only about half the local people were wearing them. This wasn't after all a movie set.

With my new hat on my head and a bag full of shirts in my hand, I went back to my hotel to change. Once more suitably attired, I decided to use the large park on the square as a vantage point from which to people-watch without being obvious about it.

On that very first day I thought I saw Randolph, but after several more such false sightings, I knew I needed to be more discerning. I didn't think Randolph would have tried to change his appearance, like growing a beard or something, because he certainly hadn't on his way out here. The two people back on Route 66 recognized him right away from the old picture I showed them. I assumed he would probably have done what I just did and simply dressed more like everyone else out here.

After several days of getting nowhere, alternating sitting in the park and taking walks around the town, I began to rethink my strategy. Since the main square seemed to be more of a tourist spot than anything else, it was probably unlikely Randolph would spend much time there anyway. My next thought was to look in areas where there were banks Randolph might be using to deposit the checks and withdraw the money he retrieved from his different drop boxes around the state. Being a relatively small city of about thirty-five thousand people, as the guidebook I picked up at the hotel said, I assumed there couldn't be that many bank branches in town he might frequent. But when I went on line to look, I found there were no fewer than thirty listed with addresses in the city, and even more in the surrounding Prescott Valley.

Feeling even more foolish, I tried to think of other ways I might bump into him, assuming he was there at all. I was obviously not very good at this sort of thing, so I had to get smarter. After a few more days it occurred to me that Randolph might well be hanging around right-wing groups in town, circulating among like-minded people where he could feel comfortable without attracting attention to himself.

With this in mind, I went on line to find out what sort of right-wing meetings might be taking place in the vicinity. After only a half-hour or so of searching, I found there was one scheduled for the following week, right in town. I jotted down the address and looked it up on the map in my guidebook.

Arriving at the appointed time, I discovered that the meeting was in an old church of all things. How appropriate, I thought, that people who believe in unverifiable theories would be meeting in a house where people worship otherworldly things.

Instead of going right in, I waited until the meeting had already begun, so I could sit unnoticed at the back. A couple of bouncer-looking types stopped me at the door and asked my name and a few other questions. I made up a name and said I was visiting from another state and wanted to be among "my" people while I was in town. They welcomed me in and gave me some pieces of literature to peruse.

Except for those speaking on the platform, all I could make out were the backs of people's heads. It didn't take me long to get bored with the ranting coming from the front of the room, so I started leafing through the literature they'd given me at the door. I didn't get very far before I heard Perveux's name being mentioned from the stage. I immediately put down the literature I was reading and listened as a commotion started in the room. Some people were saying they liked his stuff while others claimed he must be an impostor since no one had ever met him or even seen him. Then someone suggested just what I thought was implied in the article I had read, that Perveux was trying to subvert the movement by turning it into just another acceptable alternative to current political thinking.

"We need a revolution here," another person bellowed, "not appeasement. We've got to get rid of them all and start again from scratch, the way the great autocrats of history have done. We are through talking with them on their own terms. They are going to have to learn to deal with us on ours."

What I didn't notice sitting at the back of the room was one individual who was not participating in the commotion. Being able to see only the backs of people's heads, I had no way of knowing that this person was smiling quietly to himself at all the fuss.

As the meeting came to a close and people started to file out, I used my position at the rear of the room to be the first one out the door. Then I found an inconspicuous spot under some trees where I could survey the crowd coming out. Unfortunately, with so many cowboy hats drawn down over people's faces, I didn't get that many good looks. There were a couple of people I thought may have noticed me standing in the shadows, but they just walked on by with the others.

Feeling rather dejected at not having gotten very far with this idea either, I went back to my room to consider what to do next. All I could think of was to keep trying and see when another of these meetings might take place.

CHAPTER 27

The next morning I got up late and went to have breakfast at a restaurant I'd come to like. As usual I ordered the hearty western breakfast, as they called it, and started perusing the newspaper I'd bought on the way over.

The coffee came first, and just as I started sipping it, a guy approached my table and asked if he could join me. Assuming it might be one of the regulars who'd seen me eating alone there before, I said sure without looking up from my paper. It wasn't until the guy sat down that I glanced across the table.

And nearly spilled my coffee.

Before I could utter a word, the man said, "So you finally found me. I always thought it would be you. None of the others were smart enough."

It took me a few minutes to recover from the shock. Seeing Randolph sitting there with a sly grin on his face reminded me immediately of the smiling shaft. When I finally recovered, all I could think of to say was, "So who am I talking to, Aaron Randolph or Jacques Perveux?"

"Neither one, actually," came the haughty reply. "It's Cecil Barnes now, in the flesh. Aaron Randolph has vanished and Jacques Perveux is his alter ego who survives for the purpose of creating a better world, because the ultra-crazies don't understand how to do it."

"Oh," is all I could say, still unnerved. I didn't know what to make of Randolph approaching me like this. Should I be worried for my safety or glad to have suddenly accomplished my goal?

Sensing my discomfort, as he had done at similarly difficult moments with me back in the chairman's office at Macallan, Randolph (aka Perveux, aka Barnes) filled the vacuum in a disarmingly friendly tone. "Tell me," he asked, "how did you find me, in this of all places?"

"It's a long story," I responded. "Are you sure you want to hear it? We've only just met, and I'm still not sure who I'm talking with."

At that moment the waitress brought my breakfast and asked Randolph if he wanted to order something.

"Well," he answered, "since my colleague here has a long story to tell, I might as well eat something too. I'll have what he's having."

Then, "Please, Ike, do proceed. I'm all ears."

"Well for starters, that little stunt you pulled back in Oban cost me endless grief with the police."

"How so? If you're talking about my disappearance, you had nothing to do with it."

"That's not what the police thought. They were treating the whole business as a potential murder investigation, with me as the prime suspect. The only way I could clear my name was to prove you were alive somewhere."

"Well, now you have your proof. But why did they point the finger at you?"

"Motive, dear professor, motive," I said in a sarcastic tone, determined not to sound like I was still under his thumb. "I'm the one whose tenure decision you overturned, or have you forgotten?"

"No, I haven't forgotten. Believe it or not, Ike, my decision wasn't personal. If it's any consolation, I always thought you were the smartest one of the bunch. If only you weren't pushing language teaching as an end in itself, I'd have supported you."

"Well, I still am pushing language teaching, as you say. And quite successfully too, I might add."

"Good for you. You'll have to tell me more about it. But I'm still curious. How'd you know where to find me?"

"I didn't. I just followed a hunch. There were a few reports from people who said they thought they'd seen you shortly after you disappeared. The cops wouldn't take the reports seriously and refused to follow up on them. So I decided to do it myself. I studied the sightings and saw they led straight to here. I got in my car and followed the path."

"Oh my. I didn't realize I'd left such a trail."

"Let's just say you made an impression on people along the way that was hard to forget."

"Whatever. But Arizona's a big state. What made you pick such an out-of-the-way place like Prescott?"

"For the same reason I figured you would. It's not one where people are likely to come looking for you, as either Randolph or Perveux."

"But there are lots of old western towns like this out here. Why this one?"

"Because it seems to be the most appealing place to live that is equidistant from each of the three drop-box locations you, I mean Perveux, use for people to send money."

"Very clever, very clever indeed. Now tell me, how'd you figure I was Perveux in the first place?"

"Well, the presence of those Qanon materials you left at your house stood out as something important no one knew about you. And the presence of the Perveux articles stood out rather conspicuously among them. I figured someone with a French name like that publishing material praising authoritarian forms of government would be a perfect fit for a professor who teaches the glory of the monarchy and denigrates the French revolution."

"Are you saying that's what I preached in my classes?"

"That's certainly what the students said. It's right there in your teacher evaluations. And it's even evident in what I've read in your academic publications, skillfully hidden between the lines, of course. My sense is that the real Randolph only surfaces in the guise of Perveux. I'd love to know more about what you're up to while I'm here."

"And I'd love to tell you, now that you've found me. But I've got things to attend to just now. How about dinner this evening?"

"If you promise not to disappear again."

"No, once is enough for now. If you like Italian, my favorite place is Papa's, southern Italian and Sicilian. I'd be happy to make the reservation, say for seven?"

"Sounds good. I'll find it."

Randolph insisted on paying for breakfast, and I went back to my hotel to process what had just happened.

Once back in my room, I immediately thought of called Tom to let him know I'd found Randolph. At first Tom acted surprised, but admitted that of all people, I would be the one to accomplish even something as ill-advised as this. He suggested I take some photos of Randolph and me together, holding up a newspaper or something that showed the date the picture was taken, to prove Randolph was alive.

"Send it to me," Tom said, "and I'll personally see that Detective Roberts gets it."

"Will do. And would you please get a letter from Roberts stating that I am now cleared of any and all suspicion and that the case is officially closed."

"No problem, Ike. So tell me, where the hell did you find him?"

"In a town called Prescott, up in the Arizona mountains."

"Sounds like the perfect hiding place. I can't wait to hear the whole story. So when are you coming home?"

After a long pause, I answered, "I'm not sure yet, Tom. I may stick around here for a while. This is a really nice town and I still have more to talk with Randolph about. Frankly, I'm not in a hurry to leave."

"I don't like the sound of that, Ike. Listen, don't ruin a good thing and get your ass back here, the sooner the better."

"Don't worry. I promise to let you know when I hit the road again."

CHAPTER 28

I spent the rest of the afternoon thinking about what I was going to say to Randolph that evening. I found the restaurant easily enough and was ushered to the table where he was already seated. He ordered a bottle of Chianti while we perused the menus. I selected one of the house specialties, the osso buco ravioli. He ordered "the usual", his favorite linguini in clam sauce.

Having rehearsed what I wanted to talk about, I initiated the conversation before Randolph had a chance to take control again.

"Now that I've told you my story," I began, "it's your turn to tell me yours. Why did you give up a tenured senior position in the university to launch a Qanon crusade, of all things?"

Then I got an earful.

"Simply put," he began, "because the university is just another institution dominated by radical liberal thinking. Makes it impossible to get anything done. Students even demand so-called safe places so they can promote their self-serving agenda without fear of being challenged. All in the guise of rights they claim were somehow guaranteed by the constitution. Abortion rights, gay rights, workers' rights, students' rights. The list goes on. But other peoples' rights like property rights, gun rights, religious freedom, rights that are actually in the constitution as it was written are considered fungible, subject to interpretation depending on the situation."

The more Randolph talked the more boisterous and agitated he became.

"This kind of thinking," he went on, "dominates not just the universities but our institutions generally, furthering an agenda that real Americans don't want. That's why it's called the deep state, buried so deep it'll take drastic action to root it out. Even as a senior administrator at the university, I was powerless to do anything about it. The system was too entrenched."

"How, if I may ask, do you define a real American?" I interrupted, looking for a way to puncture a hole somewhere in his diatribe.

"Those who are genuine citizens, who believe in our laws and the constitution the way it was written, of course. Not the immigrants who crash our borders and then demand rights they haven't earned. Not the blacks who violate our laws and think only their lives matter. Not the Asians who come here and take all the seats in critical classes at the university, keeping real American students from being able to enroll. At some point this lunacy has to stop."

Randolph paused to eat and down a second glass of wine. I used the moment to try a different tack.

"So your idea of stopping the lunacy, as you put it, is by concocting conspiracy theories that incite the very lawlessness you decry? I don't get it."

"Don't be a smart Aleck, Ike. You may be a smart guy, but there's a lot you don't understand. So let me try and explain it to you. We're in a fight to save the country, now that the laissez-faire attitude toward immigration has pitted the demographics against us. For the first time in history real Americans soon will be, if they aren't already, in the minority in their own country. Since our institutions won't help us," he continued, getting even more agitated, "the only recourse we have is to put enough fear in people to motivate them for the fight ahead. And if there ever was a situation where the end justifies the means, this is it."

"I still don't understand. Why these conspiracy theories?"

"Because, my dear friend, they work. We need to increase the number of concerned citizens, and the more fear we put in them, the more they tend to respond. Since the democrats are so inept at messaging their own policies, we don't need to have policies of our own. People don't understand wonkish talk anyway. They react to what concerns them viscerally. Face it, Ike, this country has the stupidest electorate of any advanced nation in the world. And that's not only my opinion. Just ask Bill Maher. All you need to do is push their buttons and you've got 'em. They'll believe anything if you feed it to them consistently enough."

"My god, Randolph, I never thought you'd agree with Bill Maher."

"Only when he attacks his own libs."

"Now that I think of it," I added somewhat pensively, "you are more like Maher than those crazies you associate with. The commotion at the meeting yesterday was all about you being not crazy enough, from what I could tell. So where are you in all this?"

"Let me put it to you this way, Ike. These die hards are not going to get very far challenging American democracy the way they're doing it. They'll cause a lot of chaos, even death and destruction, but in the end the institutions of the state will still prevail because the numbers just don't add up. The crazies will never amount to more than about a third of the population, never enough to overthrow the government. We have to get the independents and the frustrated democrats to come over to our side. And that can only be done by offering them believable narratives, making them see the evil that exists in the deep state by feeding them stories that sound credible and are harder to disprove. Some fool wrote an article recently that castigated me for not delivering enough red meat to suit his extreme agenda. What an idiot."

"That article is just what I wanted to talk with you about," I said, jumping at the chance.

"Well, hold the thought. When we're done eating we'll go down the street to my favorite bar and finish this over a proper cognac."

I insisted on paying for the meal this time, hoping Randolph would let the waiter take the picture Tom advised me to get. He didn't want to at first, but acquiesced when I told him I needed it to clear my name.

I was left wondering what Randolph meant by "finish this" as we found a couple of comfortable leather chairs towards the back of the bar. It had a rather sinister tone to it that only heightened my apprehension.

"So what about that article?" he began, the moment the drinks arrived.

"You know it ends with an undisguised threat against your life, right?" I responded.

"Sure, but I, meaning Perveux, get that sort of thing all the time. You must have witnessed those idiots at the meeting yesterday arguing about whether I was either a god or the devil! I saw you after the meeting broke up, trying to hide in the shadows. Just remember, I'm Cecil Barnes now, so they would have no way to make the connection."

"But what if someone is as determined as I was to find you? It obviously can be done."

"OK, Ike, enough of this," Randolph said, raising his voice so loud several people turned around to look. "I've been sitting right under their noses for several years now, and they don't have a clue. Look, you got what you came for, so if that's all you have to say, why don't you just go back home and be grateful I'm not going to do anything to you about this. But you damn well better not blow my cover, or losing your tenure will be nothing compared with what I could do. Maybe I shouldn't have denied you tenure. Then I wouldn't have had to deal with you anymore. Go on, get out of here."

Maybe that's what Randolph meant by "finish this", I thought, as he slapped some bills on the table and pushed me towards the door. Several people turned around again to watch us go.

That night and throughout the next day, I couldn't get Randolph out of my mind. I had been toying with the idea of staying in Prescott for a while to enjoy the place some more, but given the way the meeting ended, living in the same town as him seemed out of the question now. There still were some loose ends I wished I could have tied up, like finding out how exactly he engineered his disappearance in Oban. But I obviously wasn't going to get the chance now.

I decided to spend just one more day in Prescott, then I packed my car and gave Tom a ring, as promised, to let him know I was on my way home. The relief I sensed in Tom's voice was palpable.

CHAPTER 29

Although I regretted how badly our meeting ended, I was elated that I finally got what I came for as I drove out of town. Proceeding up route 89 to get to the junction with 89A back to Flagstaff took me past the famous granite Dells of Prescott. I hadn't paid much attention to them when I first drove into town, being preoccupied with my quest. This time the incredible stone formations beckoned, and I decided to spend my last hours enjoying one more landscape unique to the west. I pulled off the road at a place the sign said was Watson Lake Park.

Two hours later, still a bit sad I had to leave, I got back on the highway and headed home. Just as I was about to make the turn onto 89A, I noticed a cop car coming up behind me with its lights flashing. As I pulled to the side of the road to let it pass, the cop pulled up behind me. Bewildered, I rolled down my window just as a big burly Arizona State Trooper in full western gear strutted up to my car. Before I could ask what the problem was, he demanded to see my license and registration. Then he went back to his vehicle to verify the documents. As soon as he returned, he ordered me to get out of the car. I had barely gotten two feet on the ground when he spun me around and ordered me to put my hands on the roof, frisked me, took my hands down behind my back and cuffed me. Shaking like a leaf, I tried again to ask him what was going on, but all that came out of my mouth was gibberish.

The trooper answered my mumbling with one terse sentence, "You're under arrest for first degree murder."

Stunned and speechless, I endured the ride back into town in the trooper's car in silence. I was marched into the police station and immediately put into what seemed to be an interrogation room: four windowless walls, a large table, several chairs with a single one on one side facing a mirror on the wall opposite. I was uncuffed, plopped into the single one and left alone for what seemed like an eternity. My god, I thought, this is exactly like in the movies. This can't be happening. There has to be some mistake.

Finally a man entered, tossed a copy of the local morning paper in front of me, left and closed the door. Picking up the paper, I read in bold letters above the fold the headline, "Local Man Found Dead in His Apartment". The article described Cecil Barnes as an older man who had recently picked Prescott as a place to retire.

Then, below a picture accompanying the article, I read the words "Have you seen this man?" There in the picture was me leaving the bar Randolph and I were in two nights before. Randolph's figure was in the background.

I barely had time to gather my thoughts when the door opened again and a man dressed in a coat and tie entered the room. He introduced himself as Detective Roberts, of all things. Hearing the name gave me a fright like I'd seen the ghost of my nemesis at the police station in Oban. How can this possibly be? Twice accused of the same crime I didn't commit? By a clone of the same detective, no less? Is this a dream?

Apparently I must have muttered the last thought aloud because the detective, the new Roberts, said, "No, fella, this ain't no dream. You wanna tell us about that picture?"

Trying to calm down, I answered, "It looks like someone took a picture of me walking out of the bar I was in a couple of nights ago."

"Very good," the detective said, "and who do you suppose is the guy behind you?"

Not having had time to think clearly yet, I hesitated before responding. The guy in the picture was Randolph, of course, but I had to decide who to tell the detective it was: Randolph, Perveux, or Barnes. The wrong answer could get me in more trouble than I apparently already was. In order to buy some time to think, I feigned difficulty recognizing Randolph because he was out of focus behind me in the picture.

Finally, figuring the people there in Prescott knew him only as Barnes, I answered, "It looks like Cecil Barnes, the guy I was having a drink with that night."

"Excellent," the detective said in a haughty voice. "And how exactly do you know him?"

Now the hole I was in got even deeper. Which man again? I couldn't say I knew him as Perveux because no one knew who that was and it would open a can of worms I'd never be able to explain my way out of. That left either "my former colleague in New York" or "a guy I met in Prescott." Either of those would also be difficult to explain. So to buy some time, I said the only thing I could think of.

"I have no idea what's going on here, so I need to talk to a lawyer."

Having requested to consult a lawyer, I knew I couldn't be asked any more questions. But the detective was a step ahead of me. He pulled out his cell phone, handed it to me and said, "There you go, fella, call your lawyer."

"But," I answered, my voice cracking, "I don't know any lawyers here. I'm visiting from the east coast."

"Fine," the detective said. "We can get a public defender for you in less than an hour. How's that?"

My brain started working a bit faster now. What on earth, I thought, could I tell a public defender, someone who has never met me, to make him believe the complicated story I'd have to tell him to save my ass. No one would ever believe it. So I tried to stall some more.

"I don't need a public defender," I argued. "I just need to get in contact with someone back east, but it may take a while."

To my relief, that ended the interview, but it didn't stop them from booking me into the local county jail.

I didn't have a lawyer on the east coast either, never having had the need for one. So as soon as they let me, I got a hold of the person whose advice I now wished I'd taken before embarking on this mission in the first place.

When I started telling Tom what had happened, I could almost feel him stifling the impulse to say I told you so. Instead, he told me not to worry, he knew exactly who to get in touch with.

"Let me call Sarah," he said.

Taken aback by the suggestion, I replied, "How can we ask Sarah to defend the person she split up with not that long ago, someone who is all the way on the other side of the country, no less?"

"Don't worry," Tom said. "She and I stay in touch, so I know she's never lost her fondness for you. She feels badly about what happened and would do anything to make it up to you. I'll call her right away."

Even if she wanted to, I couldn't imagine Sarah being able to leave her law practice and come all the way out west to defend me. At best I figured she might be able to give me advice and help me find a good local lawyer. When I didn't hear back for another day, I feared she may even have refused to get involved.

What a poor judge of character that turned out to be. The next phone call I got was from Sarah herself. She immediately apologized for having taken so long to get in touch, and asked how I was managing in the jail. Then she explained the situation.

"When Tom called me, I didn't know how to answer at first. There were several issues that had to be taken care of before I could get involved. My law firm had no problem with me defending you, Ike, but I'm not licensed to practice law in Arizona. Law licenses are issued state by state, and a lawyer in one cannot practice in another unless there is a reciprocity agreement between the two. New York does allow reciprocity, but Arizona does not."

"But you can still give me legal advice, no?" I asked, impatient to find a way out of my dilemma.

"Hold on, Ike, I'm getting there. It has taken some time, but we've come up with a solution. We've found a law firm in Prescott that has agreed to take your case and let me act as associate counsel. I won't be allowed to address the court myself or examine witnesses, but I will be able to sit with you at the defense table and advise as the case proceeds. I'll be meeting with them in Prescott the day after tomorrow to plan a strategy. So hang in there, Ike, and I'll see you soon."

I don't remember how I expressed my gratitude for what Sarah was willing to do for me, but I know it was profuse. Still, as I sat in jail contemplating my fate, I couldn't help wondering if the denial of tenure in the grassy hills of upstate New York was to be duplicated by a denial of justice among the granite hills of Prescott, Arizona.

CHAPTER 30

To my surprise and utter delight, Sarah greeted me in the visitors' room at the jail with open arms. It felt for a moment like we'd never left each other. She didn't waste any time putting on her lawyer's hat, though. She wanted to know how I got into such a mess. She did several eyerolls as I told her there was not one Randolph but three. She had to ask me to repeat myself a couple times just to get it straight.

Her immediate thought was that no jury would buy such a story.

"It's not only too complicated, Ike, it defies credibility. We need to keep things simple and eliminate any mention of this guy Pervoo, or whatever his name is, and the whole Qanon business. Just make it about your needing to clear your name regarding Randolph's disappearance. We can defend that by proving you needed him alive, not dead."

While that made perfect sense, I was convinced the Perveux business had to be the key, the reason Randolph was killed in the first place.

"That Internet article 'Who is Jacques Perveux' provides clear evidence of a threat against Randolph's life," I insisted. "Mentioning it would be a way to establish reasonable doubt by implicating someone else with an obvious motive."

"That might work, Ike," Sarah replied, "but then we'd have to prove that Randolph was indeed Perveux, and the only person other than yourself who could possibly verify that is dead. It seems to have been Randolph's own carefully guarded secret."

Our conversation ended without coming to any conclusion for the time being. Then Sarah, all business now, went off to introduce herself to the law firm she'd be working with.

I remained locked in my new home, clad in my unbecoming orange attire, but not feeling nearly as alone as before, thanks to Sarah. She came to see me the very next day with news about how things had gone with the local law firm.

"Right off the bat," she told me, "they wanted to make sure I understood that they had agreed to take your case only because of the assurances I had given them about your character. The character issue, they said, would have to be the centerpiece of your case. They did have a number of concerns, however."

"What concerns?" I replied. "Please tell me."

"In the first place, they needed verification that the dead man was in fact Randolph and not Cecil Barnes. So far all anyone has is your word for that. The local authorities haven't made a positive identification yet, awaiting various lab reports and further discussions with officials in Oban. Until that is completed, the body in the morgue is still Cecil Barnes."

"OK, I get that. What else?."

"More disturbing, though, is what they said they learned about you when they checked with the Oban police regarding Randolph's disappearance, information the prosecution is bound to discover as well."

"I think I know what you're going to say," I interrupted, my hopes dwindling fast, "but go ahead."

"As you can imagine, the report they got wasn't flattering. Obviously, the information they used back then to make you a person of interest and potential suspect could be used again here by the prosecution. Only this time the fact that there has actually been a murder might be all that would be needed, they thought, to get a conviction. So, they suggested, maybe we should be thinking about a possible plea deal, to at least reduce the severity of a potential sentence."

Needless to say, when Sarah told me this, I went ballistic.

"No way am I going to plead guilty to something I didn't do," I screamed. "They must be crazy to suggest that."

"I figured you'd feel that way, Ike, and told them so. But you have to understand that the way you reacted just now is precisely the sort of thing the prosecution will bring up. That little spat you had with your study abroad director in France is sure to be used by the prosecution in this case. You really have to keep it together from here on out, Ike, since there is an actual body to contend with now."

Sensing we might be at an impasse, Sarah said, "So tell me again, Ike, what do you propose we do?"

"Like I said before, I think the Perveux angle is the one to follow. Why don't we engage a private investigator to find out who wrote that threatening article. That would lead us to the real killer and the prosecution would no longer have a case."

Sarah reported back to the law firm that afternoon with my suggestion. They did agree to hire a PI, and the next time she came to see me at the jail she started fleshing out the defense strategy they had decided to employ.

"Once the prosecution finds out Barnes is indeed Randolph," she began, "they will have to base their case on what they know about your involvement with Randolph. Even if they bring up the Oban police report, we can argue that your previous behavior with that director in France was nothing but a youthful indiscretion. You were, after all, barely out of high school at the time. Then we can argue that the only plausible reason for you coming to Arizona was to prove Randolph was alive, since the authorities in New York declined to do so. The character issue should help us convince a jury you'd have to have been crazy to actually do what you were accused of doing when Randolph disappeared.”

“That sounds pretty good to me,” I responded.

“Except,” Sarah continued, “the lead attorney on your case here, Deke Connerly, thought that will only work if we succeed in building a strong enough case about your character.”

Seeing how nervous I still was, Sarah continued, with a bit of a smile, “Don’t worry, Ike. I assured them I have intimate knowledge of who you really are and can testify to that in court. I told Deke I thought we should wait to hear the prosecution’s case and if it’s stronger than we anticipate, we can then introduce the Qanon angle and the threats Randolph brought upon himself by pretending to be Perveux. We wouldn’t necessarily need the PI to have found who wrote that article, we would only need to plant the seed in the minds of the jury that there was someone a lot more interested in seeing Randolph dead than you.”

“OK,” I responded, somewhat relieved, “but I’m still worried.”

“I completely understand, Ike. But there is something else that we only just learned that could help a lot. It seems Randolph was shot with a bullet to the head while he was asleep in bed around two o’clock that morning, the very morning after the altercation between the two of you that was overheard at the bar. The crime scene apparently had all the signs of a professional hit: no struggle, a single shot to the head, no shell casings found, and no stray fingerprints either. Definitely seemed more like a mob hit than a crime of passion.”

Hearing this, my ears perked up again, and my spirits, too.

“What about the fact,” I asked, “that I have never owned a gun or even shot one in my entire life? I told the authorities that during my initial interrogation. How could I have possibly pulled off that kind of a hit? I'm finally beginning to see the picture here. Someone must have witnessed that altercation in the bar, overheard us talking about Randolph being Perveux, then followed him home and killed him that very night."

"Excellent theory. But we don't have a shred of evidence to prove it yet, so it's only conjecture at this point."

"Well, let's hope the PI comes through."

With this strategy still percolating, I had my preliminary hearing before the judge. I pleaded not guilty of course, but was denied bail due to the charge being first degree murder and the possibility, the likelihood the prosecution contended, that I would flee back to the east coast, or even to Europe, if I were released. There being little my legal team could do to refute that without giving away their character defense before the trial had even begun, so I was remanded back to jail. Everyone agreed to play it by ear from here on out, to see how the prosecution's case unfolded once the trial began before deciding whether or not to introduce the Perveux angle.

During this time, Sarah and I spent several hours a week together in the visitors' room at the jail, talking about what had transpired in our lives since our separation. Despite the fact that the room was about as inviting a place to have an intimate conversation as the main hall at Grand Central Station, I was able for the first time in weeks to take my mind off my situation.

We talked about the success of my summer language program and the publication of my textbook, about the work Sarah was doing with her law firm and how close she was now to being named a partner. We discussed how she and Jeremy were doing and whether I had a new woman in my life. I told her about Claudia and the possibility I may actually decide to live in Italy for a while, assuming my situation gets resolved.

The moments I got to spend with Sarah reminded me of the wonderful times we had together and how much I missed being with her. The fact that she had traveled this far to be with me in my hour of need made the feeling that much more poignant.

CHAPTER 31

At long last the date of the trial arrived and I got to exchange the orange jumpsuit for a decent coat and tie. Having settled on the wait-and-see strategy for presenting our defense, we were anxious to find out how the prosecution would proceed.

The very first thing the prosecutor addressed in his opening statement was the issue of the deceased's name. He made it clear that the murder victim had been conclusively identified as Professor Aaron Randolph, despite being known locally as Cecil Barnes.

"The fact that Randolph was using the name Cecil Barnes," he insisted, "should have no bearing on this case. The defense may try to use the name issue as a red herring, to divert attention from what is actually a very simple story. We will show that the accused had a long adversarial history with this professor, one he was hell bent on putting an end to. And the end," he intoned in the most dramatic fashion he could muster, "was indeed final."

Right away, making such a thing about the names made me suspicious, and Sarah too. Could they know more about the names Randolph was using than they were letting on? Could this be a trap, to lull us into thinking they're not aware of the whole Perveux business? They never mentioned anything about it in the discovery material they were required to provide us before the trial began, but that wouldn't be the first time, Sarah informed me, that a D.A.'s office "accidentally" omitted some crucial bit of evidence.

The rest of the prosecutor's opening statement proceeded along the lines Sarah had thought it would.

"Our case," he stated, "will be based on the fact that Mister Bell had long held a grudge against Professor

Randolph, ever since the professor denied him tenure at a certain university in the east. His obsession with the man was so intense," he dramatically proclaimed, "he even followed him to the other side of the continent to exact his revenge."

Of particular note in these remarks, to me especially, was the prosecutor's reference to Randolph as Professor Randolph, while insisting on calling me Mister Bell. I was sure that was intentional, trying to plant the impression in the minds of the jurors that I was less worthy of respect within my own academic community, and therefore more likely to act outside its norms.

Also, conspicuously absent from the prosecutor's opening remarks, Sarah and I both noticed, was any reference to Randolph's unexplained disappearance. That had to be intentional as well.

When it was our turn to present our opening statement, my lead attorney, Deke Connerly, focused on these very issues. He made an even more forceful point of referring to me as Professor Bell, even when no title was necessary. He used this as an opportunity to present what he said was the real me to the jury.

"Here is a young professor," he began, "who has created a highly successful academic career for himself, undaunted by having been denied tenure."

Then he stated what the case ought to be about.

"What we have here is not an act of revenge but quite the opposite, the defendant's need to prove that Randolph was alive. What the prosecutor neglected to tell you was that Randolph simply vanished one day from his university in the east and came out here to live under an assumed name as Cecil Barnes. At a loss to explain his disappearance, the local police treated it as more than just a missing person case. They considered it a potential murder investigation, and they named my client as the likely suspect for no other reason than his having been denied tenure by Randolph the previous year.

Living under this cloud, Professor Bell felt obliged to clear his name, to prove that Randolph was indeed alive. He made use of evidence that the local police refused to investigate, a series of reported sightings of Randolph shortly after his disappearance. Once he found Randolph, the last thing on his mind was to commit the very crime he was trying to prove himself innocent of."

After a short pause to let the jury digest this information, Deke concluded, "Beyond that, we will show that Professor Bell has never bought or used a firearm in his life, let alone one in a gangland style murder he could never have managed to pull off in the first place."

Deke purposely did not mention anything about the possibility of there being another party eager to see Randolph dead. He left that for the jury to imagine, reserving it for later, if needed.

With the opening statements having taken so long, the judge adjourned the proceedings for the day, announcing that the prosecution's case would commence first thing in the morning.

The next day, the prosecution began by calling to the stand the detective who had first inspected the crime scene. He noted that the room showed no evidence of violence, suggesting the victim was asleep in his bed when he was murdered. Then he described the single gunshot wound to the head as the obvious cause of death. He finished by saying that access to the house was apparently gained by jimmying the lock on a back door.

When it was our turn to cross examine, Deke began by asking the detective if my fingerprints had been found in the room or anywhere else in the house.

"No," he answered, "but he could have been wearing gloves."

"OK," Deke continued. "Did you find the bullet casing from the gun that was fired."

Again, the answer was, "No."

Then he asked, "What in your experience, detective, would you normally conclude if a killer knew how to jimmy a lock, left no prints, picked up his spent shell, and left no evidence at all of having been at the crime scene?"

At first the detective feigned not understanding the question. So Deke continued, in the most sarcastic tone he could muster, "Honestly, detective, did it not cross your mind that this had all the earmarks of a professional killing?"

This got the detective angry, which I could see from the way his face turned red as he answered, "Of course I thought of that. But it doesn't prove a thing. Anyone who's watched a lot of movies would know how to stage something like that."

"Even a professor of linguistics who has never even operated a firearm?"

"Objection," the prosecutor intervened. "Argumentative and introduces a fact not in evidence."

"Sustained," the judge intoned.

"Sorry," Deke said, "I got a little ahead of myself there. But there is still one obvious thing the detective hasn't told us yet. How, detective, in the face of all this evidence, or lack thereof, did you settle upon my client, of all people, as the perpetrator? It obviously didn't just come out of the blue."

"No, not at all," he responded. "But I'm not the person you need to ask. That was handled by the investigative team."

"Fine then, we'll wait to hear from them. I have no more questions."

The next person to take the stand was in fact the prosecution's chief investigator. As he did so, Sarah leaned over to me and whispered, "Here goes, hold your breath." We knew that what the jury was about to hear would either hurt our case or give us the answers we had been looking for to prove who actually did the killing.

Once the investigator was sworn in and seated, the prosecutor began right away, "So, tell us, Chief Investigator Wilcox, how did you determine that the defendant here was the killer?"

"We were informed of an altercation someone had with Professor Randolph the night before he was killed. They were overheard raising their voices at one another in a bar in town. Several patrons turned to see who they were, and watched them as they got up right afterwards and walked out. One of the patrons recognized Cecil Barnes, or Randolph as we now know him, and made a mental note of the person he was with. Then when he heard that the person he knew as Barnes had been killed, he came to us to report what he had witnessed."

"And what did you do with that information?" the prosecutor asked.

"We had the owner of the bar show us any tapes they had from their surveillance cameras, to see who Barnes, I mean Randolph, was with that evening. That's where the picture came from that we had printed in the paper the next day, asking if anyone had seen this man."

"And is this man in the courtroom here today?"

"Yes, he is."

"Would you point him out to us, please?"

"It's Mister Bell, the defendant there."

"Thank you. Please continue."

"When that picture was published in the paper, the first person to call us was the manager at the hotel where Mister Bell was staying. Once we found out who he was from the hotel manager, we started a full-scale investigation of his background. His own internet postings and web page took us to jurisdictions in upstate New York, to among other things a town called Oban. The police in Oban were very helpful. When we mentioned the defendant's name, the detective there told us they had just closed a missing person case involving a certain Professor Randolph, one in which Mister Bell had been implicated. Naturally we then asked what the missing person case was all about. Do you want me to go on?"

"By all means, please do."

"The detective told me that their investigation of Professor Randolph's disappearance centered at first on it being considered a simple missing person case. Then, after interviewing a number of people, one of whom had had a bad experience with Randolph, they started treating his disappearance as a potential murder investigation instead."

"And who was this person who had the bad experience with Randolph?"

"It was Mister Bell there."

"And did they describe the nature of that experience?"

"Yes. The said that Randolph had just denied him tenure, and he was about to lose his job in just a few more months. So the authorities made him their primary suspect. Technically he remained only a person of interest, though, because there was as yet no evidence a crime had been committed."

"Tell me, detective, was there any other information about Mister Bell the police in Oban told you that made him a suspect?"

At this point Sarah sensed what was coming and whispered something to Deke. He was ready to pounce the minute he heard the detective say, "Oh yes. They mentioned an incident between Mister Bell and the director of a program he attended overseas."

"Objection, your honor," Deke yelled, jumping up from his seat. "This so-called incident is based entirely on hearsay. Moreover, it is irrelevant to this case and would be highly prejudicial."

"Gentlemen," the judge said to both attorneys, "approach the bench."

After several minutes of discussion, which no one in the courtroom was allowed to hear, of course, the judge sent the attorneys back to their tables and spoke directly to the jury.

"The report you are about to hear," he intoned, "is not to be taken as evidence that the defendant ever did or would do what he is accused of in this trial. Furthermore, since the incident occurred some time ago, when the defendant was a junior in college, it does not even indicate his current state of mind. Please proceed."

Then Wilcox told the story of my quarrel with my study abroad director in France, and the threatening tone, as he put it, I had taken during that incident. When he finished, the prosecutor said, "Very helpful. Thank you."

Then, turning to Deke, "Your witness, counselor."

Deke asked permission to approach the witness, presumably to make the conversation he was about to have as personal as possible. Addressing the story the jury had just heard, he began, "Didn't the detective in Oban also tell you, Mister Wilcox, that Professor Bell denied the specifics of what that study director had told him, that the whole incident had been blown out of proportion in the director's mind over the years?"

"Not in those specific terms, but generally, yes."

"What else did the detective in Oban tell you about his interaction with Professor Bell?"

"He said Bell was convinced Randolph had disappeared on his own and kept insisting on them trying to find him."

"And did they say on what grounds Professor Bell had to keep insisting in this manner?"

"I'm not sure what you're getting at."

"Well, let me spell it out for you. He kept asking the authorities, did he not, why they had not taken seriously the several sightings of Randolph that had been reported in the meantime."

"Oh, that, yes. And they said he got rather heated about it."

"Gee, I wonder why. Could it be that my client's life was on the line and the police were doing nothing to investigate the most likely exonerating evidence?"

"Careful, counselor," the judge intervened. "Let's keep this to the facts."

"I am, Your Honor," Deke responded. "With all due respect, this is exactly what this case is all about. My client was doing nothing but trying to establish his innocence, and the authorities refused to follow up on the most crucial evidence they had that would prove Randolph was alive. It's no wonder Professor Bell was forced to take matters into his own hands and follow up with those sightings on his own."

"That's enough, counselor," the judge interrupted again. "You can save your argument for when your turn comes to present your case."

"Alright, Your Honor. If I may, I have just one more question for this witness."

"Proceed."

"You haven't told us yet, Mister Wilcox, who it was who told you about the discussion Professor Randolph and my client had in the bar that evening. Would you enlighten us now, please?"

"He said his name was Ken Jackson, not that it matters, I suppose."

"Well, it most certainly does matter, Mister Wilcox. The defense would like to know, and the jury too, I am sure, if you had ever had dealings with this man before, or even knew him at all before he just happened to appear at your office. And if not, did you think to check him out?"

"No, we didn't know him and no, we saw no need to check him out, as you put it. We are always grateful when a citizen comes forward with information that may help solve a case."

"I'm sure you are, but did it ever cross your mind that this Ken Jackson person may have had an ulterior motive in bringing this information to you?"

"No, not then and not now either for that matter."

"Well, we shall see about that," Deke countered, planting another seed in the minds of the jury. "I have no further questions of this witness, your Honor."

Since it was about lunchtime, the judge called a recess until two o'clock that afternoon. On the way out of the courtroom, the prosecutor caught up with Deke and asked to speak with him privately. I soon found out what they discussed.

CHAPTER 32

As soon as Deke finished his private chat with the prosecutor, we went to a restaurant down the street and huddled over lunch. Deke then relayed what the prosecutor wanted to talk about.

"Believe it or not, he just proposed a plea deal, provided we agree now and don't proceed with our defense. He must not be convinced he can win the case if he's doing so this early. Questioning the motive of that Ken Jackson person must have spooked him. He probably thought we weren't going to have any witnesses other than you, Ike, until I brought that up. Don't worry, I'm not going to accept the deal, but it does mean we may have something here."

"We need to get hold of our PI guy," Sarah said, "and have him track down this Ken Jackson person right away, now that we know his name. This could change the whole complexion of our case."

"I am now convinced more than ever," I added, "that everything hinges on the Perveux business. Jackson must have overheard us use Perveux's name in the conversation we had in the bar and figured I'd make the perfect patsy to blame his murder on. After all, it happened right after that conversation took place."

"In the meantime, though, we have to proceed with our case the way we planned," Deke said, "until we find Jackson."

As soon as court reconvened, the prosecution rested its case. The judge then invited Deke to begin presenting our case. The plan was, since we had no other witnesses to the events involved but me, Sarah would take the stand first as a character witness. This caused the prosecutor to object, on the grounds that a member of the defendant's legal team could not also testify in the case. The two lawyers started arguing the point, but the judge quickly intervened. He ruled that she could testify because she was a civilian acting only in an advisory capacity with my legal team, and as such had no legal standing with the court.

Sarah then went to the witness chair and proceeded to paint a portrait of the Ike I knew she knew so well.

"I think I know Professor Bell better than anyone at this point," she began. "He and I lived together during the most trying times of his life, first the denial of tenure and then his treatment by the police with regard to Randolph's disappearance. What I witnessed on a daily basis was a person of incredible integrity and force of will. In the first instance, rather than complain about the loss of tenure, he established a highly successful academic career on his own, published a popular textbook and turned someone else's failing study abroad program into a model of foreign language training. Then, with the threat of a murder charge hanging over his head, he succeeded in solving a missing person case, also on his own, with no help from the police."

At this point Deke interrupted.

"You used the words 'force of will' to describe his character, Sarah. What exactly did you mean by that? I ask because some may misconstrue that as some kind of assertive or aggressive behavior."

"What I intended by that was rather perseverance and determination in the face of incredible odds, forces over which Ike had no control. Sure, at times he got angry. Who wouldn't in a situation like that? But he always channeled his frustration into something positive and productive. The court here has already heard evidence of that."

When Sarah finished and it was the prosecutor's turn to cross examine, he had only one question for her. "If Mister Bell is such a wonderful person," he asked, still insisting on using Mister instead of Professor, "why did you and he break up?"

How the prosecution knew about their separation came as a bit of a surprise, but not apparently to Sarah, who as the accomplished lawyer she was, had anticipated something like that. She didn't hesitate for a second.

"That," she said, "has a very simple if bittersweet answer. Ike and I loved each other very much, and I think I can speak for both of us that the feeling has never gone away. The fact that I came all the way across the country to help him prove his innocence is testament to that. But I was previously married, and eventually my former husband and I realized we owed it to each other to give our marriage another chance. It says a lot about Professor Bell's character that he has always respected that and has wished us nothing but the best ever since."

Hearing this, a subdued applause broke out in the courtroom. That brought an equally subdued admonishment from the judge, who proceeded to thank Sarah and tell her she could now stand down. Then, just as I was about to take the stand myself, Deke leaned over to me and said, "Don't let that applause go to your head. Stay focused and on message the whole time."

Deke started by asking me why I followed Randolph to Arizona in the first place. He intentionally started calling me Ike instead of Professor Bell now to humanize the questioning as much as possible.

"Can you explain, Ike, why you went on a crusade to find Professor Randolph, when all there was back home was a simple missing person case that would have resolved itself eventually anyway. It sounds like you were obsessed with this man."

"If I was obsessed with anything," I responded, "it was never Randolph himself. I was already well beyond thinking about the tenure thing, having successfully established a second career on my own in less than two years. It was the situation the police were putting me in that wouldn't go away, making me the prime suspect in a murder I not only knew I didn't commit but was certain didn't even exist. With apologies to the D.A. here, I had been told many times how often zealous prosecutors, wanting to make a name for themselves, have successfully convicted someone of murder even though no actual body was ever found. Under the circumstances, I felt I was a sitting duck for just such a prosecution, for the only reason that a missing person had once denied me tenure. Since the authorities in Oban refused to follow up on the evidence they already had that suggested Randolph was still alive, I felt I had no choice but to try and get to the truth myself."

"And what evidence was that? I know we've been over this before, but in your own words, how did you deal with it?"

"I simply looked at the time line for the sightings of Randolph that the police in Oban refused to take seriously. What I found was a distinct pattern, of a person who had traveled in a direct line from the east coast through Arkansas, Texas, and New Mexico, ending up in Arizona. That time line coincided quite well with the amount of time it would have taken Randolph to get where he was headed before interest in the case died away and no one would be looking for him anymore."

"And what did you do with this discovery?"

"Well, I had some time before my next summer program in Italy was due to start, more than six months, so I decided to see if I could trace his steps westward and prove he was still alive, to clear my name once and for all."

"And what did you find, before meeting up with Randolph that is?"

"Frankly, it was rather serendipitous. By the time I got to Illinois, I was tired of traveling the interstates and decided to take Route 66 from then on. I had no reason to suspect Randolph would have taken that route, but just in case, whenever I stopped for gas, to eat, or to spend the night, I would show people the picture of Randolph I had brought with me. And more than once people recognized his picture right away. That's when I knew he was alive."

"But how did you know their identifications were accurate?"

"They recognized the man in the picture because of the way he always drew attention to himself. Overbearing and demanding, complaining about everything that didn't please him, just as he used to do as a professor at the university, and did again at the bar that night."

"OK, so when you finally arrived in Arizona, how on earth did you happen to find him here in Prescott, of all places? This is a pretty big state, so you must have had some idea of where he might be, no?"

"Yes and no," I responded, reminding myself that I must not divulge anything to do with the Perveux business at this point. "I figured since the sightings ceased in Arizona, he must have found a place somewhere out here where he planned to stay. He used to say he hated big cities and also hated hot weather, so that already took a lot of places out of the running. He also used to comment all the time about how he really liked the climate in upstate New York, so I started looking for places around here that might fit that description. I knew it was only one chance in a million, but Prescott seemed to me to fit the bill pretty well. A nice town in a similarly hilly and forested landscape with a distinct change of seasons."

"And what did you do once you got here?"

"I just hung around, mostly in the park in the middle of the town square, where I could watch the goings on without being conspicuous."

"And then what? You just happened to see him one day?"

"No, actually, it was he who saw me. I was close to losing confidence in my decision and was about to try another town when I was having breakfast in a café on the square one morning. He just came up to my table and sat down. I remember his exact words: 'So you finally found me. I knew it would be you.'"

So far this recitation had been carefully rehearsed so as not to make mention of the main reason I picked Prescott, or how Randolph knew I was in town. I wasn't lying, just sinning by omission. Deke then continued with his questioning, both of us hoping I would stay on message and not get careless.

"Please tell us exactly what happened after that."

"Apparently now that the game was up, Randolph didn't mind talking about himself, relished doing so in fact. He told me what I already suspected, that he had changed his name, so no one knew him as anything but this somewhat gruff fellow called Barnes who had settled down in Prescott. He wanted to know how I found him and I wanted to know how he managed his disappearance. I told him my story over breakfast and we agreed to meet later for dinner to finish the discussion. We had dinner at one of his favorite restaurants and afterwards adjourned to this bar, where I started pressing him on why he left a perfectly good tenured position on the faculty at Macallan University. That got him in one of his belligerent moods again as he started ranting about the evil left-wing ideas the current academic system foists on the youth of this country. Then I think I said something like how that very system had done some pretty evil things to me as well, assuming he would take it the way it was meant, as a joke, and calm down. But he didn't. He abruptly ended the conversation and we headed out of the bar."

That last bit about the joke wasn't quite true, of course. It wasn't something I actually said to Randolph, but it was certainly something I was thinking at the time. Nor was it something I had rehearsed with my legal team ahead of time. I was getting nervous on the stand, trying so hard not to mention the real reason Randolph and I were meeting that I just tried to ad-lib my way out.

Evidently upset at my not having stayed on message, my attorney quickly changed the subject.

"Did you ever find out how Randolph managed to effect his disappearance?"

"Unfortunately, no."

"So you never got in touch with him after that?"

"No, he didn't give me his phone number and I never even learned where he lived."

"And you had no idea he had been killed in the meantime either?"

"None. I only found out after I had packed my bags and left, when I was about to turn onto the highway heading back to Flagstaff and a state trooper pulled me over. The cop refused to tell me anything even then. I only found out when they took me to the police station and tossed a copy of the local paper in front of me. There was my picture walking out of the bar with Cecil Barnes, as it said, right on the front page."

"One final question, Ike. Have you ever owned a gun or fired one?"

"No, never."

"So now you find yourself here, accused of a murder you didn't commit, in fact couldn't have committed, all because you tried to clear you name of a murder that hadn't happened. I can't even imagine how you must feel."

Then, looking away from me towards the prosecutor's table, Deke said, "The witness is yours now, counselor. Please treat him with the respect he deserves."

That last comment almost brought another admonition from the judge, but he limited himself to a withering look at my attorney instead.

Since it was getting late in the afternoon, the judge adjourned the proceedings until the following morning. It was a good thing he did because that evening our private investigator, whom I had not actually met before, came back with some crucial information.

I tried not to smile as he introduced himself as Rick Rambeau. He was a big burly guy, with a bushy mustache. He looked every bit the part of a wild west character, replete with hat and boots. He told us he'd located the Jackson person. And being the tough guy he looked like, with the name to match, he had pressured Jackson into admitting he worked for the people who had put out the internet post threatening Perveux's life. He had even succeeded in persuading Jackson to testify. He didn't elaborate on what form the persuasion took, only something along the lines of ruing the day if he skipped town.

Obviously pleased with this turn of events, Sarah and I were nevertheless taken aback a bit by the type of persuasion we sensed Rambeau had used on our behalf. When we mentioned this later to Deke, he just shrugged his shoulders and said, "You have to remember you're in the Wild West now, folks. Out here we have a different view of how to get things done. We treat our clients with kid gloves, but when it comes to the opposition, the gloves come off. But don't worry, our methods are scrupulously legal."

We spent the rest of the evening discussing when and if to let this revelation enter into my answers to the prosecutor's inevitable questioning on cross. If I did, it was sure to open a pandora's box and undoubtedly complicate the case. But it would also provide solid evidence of another motive behind

Randolph's death that had nothing to do with me.

"Remember," Sarah told me, "only answer the questions asked. Don't volunteer any additional information. And don't assume the jury is on your side once the prosecutor starts in."

CHAPTER 33

The trial resumed at ten o'clock the next morning with the prosecutor's cross examination. Unlike my lawyer, the prosecutor did not approach me on the witness stand. Instead, he headed over to the jury box and stood there, obliging me to look directly at the jury with my answers. He began in a sarcastic tone, showing his disdain for the final remarks Deke made on my behalf the day before.

"With all due respect, Professor Bell, there are certain aspects of your story that don't make sense to me, and I'm sure to the jury as well. For example, it seems inconceivable that you just happened to pick our community here in Prescott, out of all the other similar communities in this state, to establish your stake-out of Professor Randolph. Because it was a prearranged stake-out, was it not?"

"Yes, I suppose you could call it that," I responded, not knowing quite what he meant.

"And you want us to believe that of all the myriad other possibilities, this would be the one place you decided Randolph would want to spend the rest of his life? Come on now, professor, what are you not telling us?"

"Well, like I said, I did eliminate a lot of other places, places Randolph would probably not want to live in, big cities like Phoenix, Tucson, and Flagstaff, for example. But he might well want to visit them, I reasoned, so I picked one somewhere in the middle from which he wouldn't have to travel so far. Seemed logical to me at the time."

"I see. But I still don't understand. Tell me again why you thought he wouldn't want to live in Phoenix, Tucson, or Flagstaff? Was there any other reason except you thought he didn't like big cities?"

"Yes, actually, there was. I figured he wouldn't want to be seen in a place with lots of people who might recognize him. He was after all on the run. No one would necessarily come looking for him up here."

"Except you, of course."

"Objection, your Honor," Deke jumped up. "May we keep to the facts here, please?"

"Sustained," is all the judge said, somewhat reluctantly, seeming to sympathize with the prosecutor.

Frustrated by not having gotten anywhere with that line of questioning, the prosecutor decided to change his approach. "Let's just assume, then, that you are some sort of clairvoyant individual and move on."

"Ob-jec-tion," Deke repeated in an exasperated tone.

"Well," the judge responded this time, "the prosecution is offering to move on. But I'll sustain the objection as to the tone. The jury will disregard any personal commentary, by either side. This may be the Wild West, gentlemen, but my courtroom is not a rodeo."

Still standing right next to the jury box, the prosecutor resumed his interrogation. "Would you tell us again, please, what it was you and the professor were discussing that night in the bar when things got so heated, heated enough that other patrons in the bar took notice."

"Heated for him, but not for me. I simply asked him why he would give up a perfectly good job at the university and disappear like that. Then he started ranting about how universities are ruining the minds of young people with leftist propaganda and so forth, and he didn't want to be implicated in it anymore."

"Go on, professor, what else was said during that conversation? You're leaving something out, aren't you?"

Hearing this, I started to sweat and shifted my position in the witness chair. Could this be the moment, I thought, when he drops the Perveux bomb on me? Again, I tried to stall for time. "I'm not sure what you mean."

"Well, in your previous recounting of the conversation, you mentioned that you made what you claimed was some kind of a joke. Isn't that right?"

Thinking I'd dodged a bullet, I said, "Well yes, I did try to lighten the mood, since Randolph was getting loud and people were looking at us."

"And this joke, as you call it, as you recounted it in your earlier testimony. It was about the academic system having ruined you as well, isn't that right?"

"Yes, but only as a joke."

"Do you really mean to tell this jury, professor, that raising the issue of your tenure decision right in front of the person who made that decision, the person you had gone to such great lengths to find, was nothing but a joke? That seems very hard to believe. Sounds more like airing a grudge that you have never gotten over."

"Objection," my lawyer yelled again. "The prosecutor is putting his own thoughts in the mind of the defendant."

"Objection sustained," said the judge. "Do you want to rephrase that in the form of a question, counselor?"

"Yes, thank you Your Honor. Tell me, professor, why on earth would you make a joke about something like that, right in the face of the man who did it to you? Seems completely counterintuitive."

"Not if the person making the joke really has gotten over it, as I have more than demonstrated I have."

"Well, I guess we'll have to let the jury decide that now, won't we? I have no more questions, your honor."

Then the judge asked Deke if he had anything to add on redirect. He hesitated for a moment and then requested a recess "to consult with my client." The judge agreed to break early for lunch and reconvene at two o'clock.

"I was afraid this might happen," Deke said the moment we huddled again in that café down the street. "If only you hadn't mentioned that so-called joke, Ike, we might be in the clear by now. But the prosecution has reinforced the presumption that it wasn't a joke, that you really were there to exact revenge on Randolph. And he just put a big fat exclamation point on it. I'm not sure how we can counter that now, on redirect. Or even if we should try. Maybe we should just take our chances with the jury."

"But that's exactly how I was thinking at the time. I was just trying to avoid mention of the Perveux business, as we agreed. Isn't there anything else we can do now," I pleaded.

"There is, of course," he answered, "but it would involve opening up the whole can of worms. That might be worth a try now, since we have that Jackson fellow who can testify about the threat against Perveux. But we still haven't met with him, so we don't know yet if he will cooperate once he's on the stand. I could ask the judge for a stay so we can get our ducks in order. But that in itself might indicate that our case is weak."

At this point Sarah, who had so far remained quiet, offered a suggestion.

"We could," she proposed, "ask for a stay on the grounds we have uncovered some new evidence. Then we could get Jackson in here and plan a new course of action."

"Good thought," Deke responded, "except we'd have to ask for the stay the moment we got back in that courtroom. By then we'd already be committed to a course of action we haven't yet worked out. We need to get hold of Rambeau right away and make sure we've at least got Jackson locked in first."

When we did get in touch with Rambeau, he said he had some bad news. Even though Jackson had been under round-the-clock surveillance, he somehow managed to slip away. And Rambeau hadn't been able to find him since.

So now we had no choice. We had to rest our case and hope for the best. Which Deke did as soon as we were back in the courtroom. The judge then recessed the proceedings until the following morning, telling both lawyers to be ready to make their closing arguments.

CHAPTER 34

The next day, following the normal practice, the plaintiff's side went first with its summation. The prosecutor did a masterful job of using the heart of my case, the character issue, against me, just as Deke feared he might. In the best scornful tone he could muster, he referred to my having "magically" picked Prescott as the place to look for Randolph, asking the jury to wonder what I had not been telling them. Then he mocked the very idea that raising the tenure issue in front of Randolph could have been a joke, ending his presentation melodramatically with the words, "Murder is no joke, ladies and gentlemen. You need to find this man guilty."

Upon hearing this presentation, Deke knew he could no longer use the character issue in his summation. So he tossed aside the notes he had prepared and approached the jury. He first asked them to consider how preposterous it would have to have been for me to go all the way to Arizona to prove my innocence, only to commit the very crime I was trying to clear my name of. Then he made a bold gamble.

"Actually, the prosecutor is correct," he told the jury. "There are things the defense has not mentioned in the course of this trial. Things that would not only exonerate my client but show that someone else had every reason to murder Randolph. But since we do not yet have sufficient proof, we could not present that evidence in court."

Needless to say, making a claim like that after the fact drew an immediate reaction from the prosecutor, who jumped to his feet to object. Even before he could do so, the judge banged his gavel and addressed the jury himself.

"I could let the prosecution use its prerogative to respond to this extraordinary revelation," the judge intoned, "but I'm going to do it myself. I could order a mistrial, but I trust the good sense of you the jurors. So I'm going to tell you that since this court has no idea what the defense was just referring to, I'm hereby instructing you to ignore the entire matter and base your decision solely on the evidence that has been presented in this courtroom. As for you, counselor, I could cite you for contempt, but I'll let you finish your summation and deal with you later."

All that Deke could do at that point was summarize what evidence had already been submitted. He tried to salvage the damaged character issue as best he could, asking the jury once again to consider how preposterous it would be to think anyone, least of all someone like me, could commit the crime from which I had gone to such lengths to exonerate myself. He concluded by concentrating on the nature of the murder itself, how implausible it was that I could possibly have committed a picture-perfect gangland style murder, never having owned or even used a gun before.

The judge then proceeded to read the jury the standard set of instructions before sending them off to begin their deliberations.

Two days later, the jury still had not come to a decision. Two times they asked the judge to explain a particular point of law. The third time they told him they were deadlocked. The judge instructed them to keep trying, and reminded them this was not a case involving the death penalty, only life in prison with or without parole. If there were only one or two holdouts, he added, they should reconsider all the evidence together and keep going until everyone was on board. He ended by telling them he would not accept a hung jury in this case.

With the rest of my life hanging in the balance, I spent what seemed like an eternity in a special cell adjacent to the courtroom waiting for the verdict. At least I was not required to change back into the orange jumpsuit. Sarah came to see me several times a day, trying to keep my spirits up. She told me that if I were convicted, she would move heaven and earth to get the evidence we knew existed and secure a retrial.

Towards the end of the third day, the word went out that the jury was returning to the courtroom, and I was ushered back in. The judge asked me to stand while the jury foreman read the verdict.

"Guilty of murder in the first degree, with the possibility of parole."

Sarah turned to me and we hugged like we'd never hugged before. Neither of us wanted to let the other go. Even the bailiff waited patiently for us to relinquish our embrace before leading me away.

On the way back to the holding cell, I couldn't help thinking how ironic it was that I couldn't get tenure in the academic system but I managed to get it now in the legal system, tenured to a life behind bars. It seemed my whole life had been on one big tenure track, one I'd had no control over, no matter what I did. It made me sick to realize that after all this, the trial had produced exactly what the plea bargain would have given me in the first place.

CHAPTER 35

The legal system eventually did do something positive for me, however. As soon as the judge dismissed the jury and thanked them for their service, he ordered my legal team to come to his chambers right away, and invited the prosecutor as well. In what apparently was an unusual move, he also ordered me to join them, since I was still in the holding cell next to the courtroom. What I witnessed at that meeting was as eye-opening for me as it was for the judge and prosecutor, for entirely different reasons.

Visibly angry at first, the judge demanded to know what was behind the stunt, as he called it, that Deke pulled at the start of his summation.

"Unless there is some very convincing explanation," he declared, "I will have no choice but to cite you for contempt, sir. So what do you have to say for yourself?"

It would be an understatement to say that both the judge and the prosecutor were stunned to hear what Deke told them, that Randolph had not two but three names. He revealed the Perveux alias for the first time and produced the internet article threatening Perveux's life. Then he recounted how our PI had succeeded in getting the Jackson fellow to admit what had actually happened, and how he'd gone to the police in order to finger me.

With disbelief written all over his face, the prosecutor said, "That's quite a story, counselor. If it's true, why didn't you put your star witness, Jackson, on the stand? Then the jury could have decided for themselves whether or not to believe all this."

"Because," Deke admitted, a bit meekly, "Jackson got away despite our having him under round-the-clock surveillance. I could have called our PI as a witness, but his testimony would have only been hearsay, and neither you nor the judge would have allowed it."

"That's right," the judge said, "I would have had to suppress all of this evidence without a first-hand witness to verify it. So what do you think we should do in light of all this now, Mister Prosecutor?"

"I have to admit," he answered, "I was rather surprised that we were able to obtain a conviction with so little concrete evidence on our side, only a presumption of guilt based on the defendant's supposed frame of mind. As I'm sure Mister Connerly here realized, I offered that plea deal because I thought we might have the weaker case. But the defendant's case was also weak, what with his bizarre fixation on the deceased and a strange story to justify his innocence, even without this new Perveux business. But," he said after some reflection, "if that Jackson fellow did come to us just to finger Professor Bell, I do think we have an obligation to pursue the matter further."

"What exactly do you mean by further?" Deke asked.

"Well, unless Your Honor is willing to vacate the defendant's conviction now, which I don't suppose you are, sir, then I will at least not insist Bell be sent to a maximum-security prison out here in the West, as we were prepared to do given his first-degree murder conviction. I propose we let him serve his time in a minimum-security facility back East, near his home, while we sort this whole thing out."

As Sarah listened to this unusual turn of events, the prosecutor finally became a human being in her eyes. He became Daryl Hanson, the man who just promised to find the truth, the person she would now stay in touch with for as long as it took to find justice for me.

By the end of that meeting, everyone was on a first name basis. Sarah told me she even considered asking if, under the circumstances, I could be put under house arrest rather than in prison, but then thought better of it. This was probably not the time, she said, to look such an unusual gift horse in the mouth. But Daryl did arrange to let her accompany me on the plane taking me back to New York with the police escort.

Daryl's willingness to do the right thing had quite an effect on her, Sarah told me some time later. As a trial lawyer herself, she had seen all too often how the system fails the innocent and rewards the guilty. She had even harbored thoughts of quitting and finding some more honorable profession, she said.

What I witnessed at that meeting also had quite an effect on me. I had just heard with my own ears someone describe how the supposed search for truth and justice the legal system is meant to stand for is little more than a kind of chess game. The lawyer who tells the better story, the narrative that wins over the minds of the jury, is the one that prevails. The defendant in all of this remains a pawn who has no choice but to allow them to play the game and hope for the best. Obviously, we had the weaker narrative this time. What really upset me as I thought about it was that even if we had gotten Jackson on the stand, the outcome still would have depended on whether the jury believed the story he told. It depressed me deeply as I sat in the plane on my way to prison in New York, thinking this is the way matters of life and death are decided.

CHAPTER 36

The Otisville Prison Camp is located in southeastern New York, only about 200 miles, or a three-hour drive, from Syracuse. It is not exactly a country club, but it is as comfortable and safe a place as one could wish for if one had to be deprived of one's freedom. It is a minimum-security facility adjacent to the medium-security Otisville Prison itself, considered one of the ten cushiest federal prisons in the country.

The Camp has an open, campus-like layout with plenty of recreational activities available including facilities for playing flag football or soccer, baseball, tennis, bocce ball, handball, and more. Inmates can play cards or pool, watch movies, use the exercise room and either the leisure or the law library. There is also a commissary where they can buy everything from medications to shoes and sweat suits.

When I arrived at the prison, I was given only a few minutes to say good-bye to Sarah. She promised to keep me informed of the progress on my case, and to come see me on weekends whenever she could get away. I was then escorted inside and given a modest strip-search, not the invasive kind you see in the movies, and a fresh set of clothes. I and the other newcomer I came in with were then given a tour of the facility and read the rules we would have to live by for the duration of our time. We were to share a two-person cubicle-like room in one of the dormitories on the campus.

Since so much time had now gone by since I started on my ill-fated journey west, I knew there was little chance my case could be resolved before the next summer program in Siena was set to begin. So I needed to let the consortium know I wouldn't be available. I set up a conference call from the prison and gave them a carefully worded explanation of what had transpired since the previous summer. I then asked if I could have a leave of absence from the program for a year, and hopefully be available again the following summer. I couldn't imagine I would be spending the rest of my life in this place.

The consortium was more than happy to oblige and even asked what they could do to help. The best thing, I suggested, would be to have whoever takes my place consult with me and become as knowledgeable about the unique nature of the program as possible before it was scheduled to begin.

In the meantime, back in Arizona, both the prosecution and my defense team continued trying to find Ken Jackson. But, I was told, they were having a hell of a time. Every time they thought they'd got a lead, the guy disappeared again. After a while they decided to change tactics and had our PI Rambeau go undercover and infiltrate the Qanon movement in town to see what he could find out.

He felt so bad about having failed to produce Jackson at my trial, he called me personally to let me know how that went.

"It didn't take long before I was considered one of them," he said, adding with a hearty laugh, "I'm used to working undercover, so I had no trouble playing as much of an asshole as the rest of them."

His tone changed to more of a swagger as he continued to tell the story.

"Once I felt pretty secure, I began to casually drop Perveux's name, to see what kind of reaction I would get. At first, not much happened. I figured maybe it was something they didn't want to talk about in front of a newcomer, I couldn't tell. Then one evening, after one of their gatherings, I got invited to join a small group of them at a local bar. It turned out to be the very bar you and Randolph were seen together on that night, of all things. From what I could tell, it was a favorite watering hole for this particular group. After speaking in hushed tones through the first two rounds of drinks, they finally started to loosen up. They began bragging about their latest activities, more than one of which, they said, involved the demise of certain individuals with whom, as they delicately put it, they had had disagreements.

"You can imagine how my ears perked up when I heard Perveux's name among their conquests. They mentioned something having taken place right there in that bar. I pretended not to know what they were talking about, so they told me that was where they overheard a guy going on about leaving some university or other and using the name Perveux. Then they had a good laugh explaining that he was a guy they'd been looking for, how they'd killed him and framed 'the schmuck he was with'—their words, Ike, not mine—for the murder.

"That alone would have been enough for me to hear, but they went even further. Turned out his real name was Randolph, they said, not Barnes as he called himself, and the schmuck who was with him actually got convicted.

"To ensure my cover was still secure, I joined the cackles of laughter and even ordered another round of drinks to celebrate the news. Since I'd got what I came for, I wanted to get out of there as fast as I could, but I needed to stay a while longer just to make it look real. Then I made a point of looking at my watch, told them I had to go, threw a bunch of bills on the table and took off. Once I got in my car, I looked at my watch to see if I got the picture I needed when I checked the time back there, then I took out the recording device I had in my pocket to make sure I got the entire conversation on tape as well.

"So that's the story so far, my friend. Hang in there and we'll see where all this goes."

Needless to say, hearing this lifted my spirits enormously. I could just picture those guys sitting across the room from where Randolph and I were that night, watching us. I got so excited, Sarah had to remind me the next time she came to see me that the game had only just begun. A photograph and a recording would not be enough to exonerate me, she said. The authorities still had to find the guys, who Rambeau only knew by their first names, indict them, try them and get a conviction. That could take months if not years. My tenure in the justice system had apparently only just begun.

But my meetings with Sarah still helped a lot. I needed someone to talk to about how things were going at the Camp. Although I was depressed a lot of the time, conditions were such that I could work quite comfortably on my research and keep in reasonable shape physically. My roommate was a quite a piece of work, and our nightly chats after lights out took my mind off things. He even offered to teach me once how easy it is to embezzle money, should I ever want to. Since that was what he was in prison for, I wasn't sure how good of a teacher he could be.

I was curious to know how Sarah and Jeremy were doing, and she had to admit her being away in Arizona for so long hadn't done their relationship any good. He was jealous of her spending so much time out there with me, and he wasn't happy with her weekend visits to the Camp now either. She suspected he may even have reverted to his old habits in her absence. I wasn't sure how to react to this, since I had never lost my fondness for her, nor she for me, it seemed.

Tom also came down to see me whenever he could get away from Macallan. Bill came with him from time to time too. When he did, the two of them would stay over in the nearby town of Mount Hope so they could spend an extra day with me. That's when we got to talk at length about things. They were both concerned that the trial and prison seemed to have taken more of a toll on me than I knew myself.

"We're worried about you, Ike," Tom said at one point. "You need to take care of yourself in here."

"Oh," I answered, "I'm doing OK. This is not such a bad place. It certainly could have been a lot worse if they'd sent me to San Quentin or something."

"Still," Bill chimed in, "you don't look quite as fit as you used to. Are you sure you're OK physically?"

"Well," I answered, "you know I've had this heart condition since I was a kid. Nothing serious, they say, but it does get me down once in a while. I try to exercise as much as possible here, but as you know, I've never been much for sports, so I don't participate in the games they play here. Their so-called flag football seems more like professional football to me. I stick with bocce ball. It's safer."

"But have you been checked out by a doctor since you came here?" Tom asked.

"No, not yet. I suppose I should, no?"

"Absolutely," they both said almost simultaneously.

At other times the conversation turned to how I was keeping myself busy. I had to admit that I was already getting bored with the daily routine, even if I was allowed to work on my research when I wanted to.

"That's the other thing we need to talk with you about," Tom said. "According to what we hear from Sarah, you could be in here for quite some time, years rather than months."

"We've been considering," Bill said, completing the thought, "what you could do in here beyond your normal routine. Some project or other, perhaps."

Hearing the word project got me thinking. "Of course," I exclaimed, "why didn't I think of that. My whole life has been creating projects, for myself in France and for the student program in Italy. Why not try to do something like that here as well? Problem is, of course, how. This is a prison, after all."

"That may be," Tom declared, "but it seems more like a country club to me. Got to be a way to work things out in a place like this."

CHAPTER 37

And so we put our heads together and came up with a plan to keep me sane. My third bite of the apple, we called it. The way we figured it, the inmates at this Camp were not lifers or hardened criminals. Most of them were guilty of nothing more than so-called victim-less or white-collar crimes, and were only here for a time before being able to return to their former lives. There was a good chance some of them might appreciate learning something new they could use when they got out, maybe even something to turn their lives around.

"You mean something like another language, perhaps?" I said with a grin, as if I'd just pulled the idea at random out of a hat. "Hell, I might even be able to make that work. Maybe not French or Italian, but a program in Spanish might work in here," I added, getting serious. "I speak a little Spanish and there are a number of Spanish speakers here I could use as informal instructors. They wouldn't have to know how to teach. They'd just need to engage people in conversations and let the learning take care of itself. Who knows, it might even become another game for them to pass the time of day."

Designing such a program kept me so preoccupied after Tom and Bill left, I lost track of the weeks and months that passed. When the day came to unveil it, I went to the prison authorities to get their approval first. I didn't want to commit myself to something that could well backfire on me. The Camp might be more like a country club as Tom suggested, but some of the staff were just as harsh here as in any prison, meaner than any of the prisoners themselves for sure. I couldn't afford to get on their bad side. I knew what that could be like because one of the inmates I'd befriended since I arrived was gay, and they made that poor guy's life hell. I almost intervened once, but my roommate warned me off.

Surprisingly, the warden was sympathetic to my plan, almost enthusiastic because, he told me, it could take some of the pressure off keeping the inmates out of trouble. He suggested taking things one step at a time, however, to see how both the inmates and the guards would react. He told me to make up a questionnaire to find out the level of interest within the prison population.

When I did this, I of course got a few snide and racially motivated responses, but was surprised how many said they'd like to take me up on the idea. Some of them mentioned the very boredom I was experiencing myself as the reason. They specifically cited the lack of programming or educational opportunities at the Camp. Several said they would look forward to having something useful to do indoors during "these damn cold New York winters". I was also surprised to see how many acknowledged the value of knowing Spanish in the U.S. And I was especially delighted to hear the Spanish speakers themselves say they wanted to be involved. I didn't even have to ask them.

As for the staff, they indicated they would welcome anything to keep the inmates occupied and out of trouble, just as the warden had predicted.

Within days of the warden's office announcing official approval of the program, no fewer than five "Spanish tables" spontaneously materialized in the cafeteria at meal time. No longer were the Spanish speakers all sitting apart from the rest of the inmates as they used to. At least one of them was now seated at each of the new language tables. And everyone seemed to be enjoying themselves, with waves of laughter coming from time to time throughout the meals.

This occurred most often, it seemed, when someone used a word that they didn't know had a certain off-color meaning. That would prompt the native speakers to provide all sorts of similar words their "students" eagerly jotted down on napkins or whatever scraps of paper they had at hand. This type of learning might not be very professional, I knew, but it was just what the doctor ordered to get my third iteration of intensive language training off the ground.

I also knew, though, that I had to put more structure into my program. This wasn't, after all, just a free-for-all. There needed to be some sort of formal instruction. So I ordered several copies of a basic Spanish grammar for the Camp library. That would have to suffice as teaching materials in the absence of a proper corps of instructors. Several of the inmates told me how much they appreciated having a grammar to consult. They couldn't learn the language just by hearing it, they said. They needed to visualize the structure of a sentence in order for it to make sense. I was more than happy to spend time in the library with them myself to provide the kind of instruction the rest of the cohort wasn't interested in.

I also ordered several sets of interactive software so those who wished could engage in conversations with Spanish speakers enacting real life cultural experiences. This was an American prison, after all, and I didn't want them learning nothing but local street language. At the same time, though, I cringed at the thought of having them sit with earphones talking to an unseen stranger the way I was forced to on my junior year abroad. But the situation here made all the difference.

Providing a program like this within the confines of prison walls was a challenge the likes of which I had never faced before. It made me think how much being deprived of a normal life outside was weighing on me. One night, to cheer myself up as I was trying to get to sleep, I recalled my favorite line from West Side Story. A member of either the Jets or the Sharks, I couldn't remember which of the two gangs, blames his behavior on his bad upbringing and exclaims, "Hey, I'm depraved on account of I'm deprived." It made me chuckle to realize how that line works the other way around for the white-collar types in a place like this. My amusement quickly dissipated, however, once I contemplated why I was in here.

In a remarkably short time, though, the fervor to learn Spanish spread like a fever throughout the camp. Where they were at first learning all the words and expressions involved with eating at meal time, they began quickly picking up enough vocabulary to understand the commentary during televised sports events on the Spanish language channels. Where there used to be only one TV in the Camp tuned to a Spanish language channel, the ratio quickly became about fifty-fifty. I even heard Spanish being used in the pick-up games they played out in the yard. The ones who took the experience most seriously also watched Spanish language movies to see how much they could understand without looking at the subtitles.

As with everything else in life, however, there came a downside just as things were looking up. It took a while for me to realize how the guards really felt about the phenomenon that was overtaking "their" Camp. I heard that the ones who didn't understand Spanish, a few of whom were veritable rednecks, didn't like it one bit. They had gone to the warden to complain that they couldn't control a situation if they couldn't understand what was being said. Apparently, they even claimed that Spanish had now become a secret language the inmates were using to thwart them throughout the Camp. And they pointed the finger at, who else, "that Ike guy".

That had to have put the warden between a rock and a hard place. He thought he had the staff's buy-in before he approved my project. But he hadn't anticipated how successful it would become, or how quickly. And it was too late now to abort my bilingual baby. He had to do something to appease the guards.

What the warden didn't know was that the guards had already been taking their anger out on me. They twice searched my cell, looking, they claimed, for contraband. They harassed me every opportunity they got, with hot water that mysteriously stopped working when I was alone in the shower room, with no more meat loaf left when my turn came at the line in the cafeteria. Stupid little things which I understood were meant specifically for me. But rather than go whining to the warden, I took it as a compliment that what I was doing was actually working. I may ultimately have to pay a price, but just the satisfaction of seeing my program working in a place I never expected it would, made it all seem worthwhile. So I kept my head down and hoped for the best.

After a while, however, things did not get better. In fact, they went from bad to worse. The harassment increased to the point where my cellmate offered to come to my rescue. I had had numerous late-night chats with Art alone in our dorm room and had gotten to know him pretty well. He was a skinny little runt, but he acted like he owned the world, even if the world had not returned the favor. His persevering spirit was almost admirable, even if neither of us would ever want to walk in the other's shoes. How could we? A university professor and a corporate embezzler! As if to prove the point, Art was not one of the inmates who opted to join my language program. He had better things to do, he claimed.

All the more reason, perhaps, why he could see how bad things were getting for me from the outside.

It turned out Art had a thing going with one of the guards. That's why, when our dorm room was searched, nothing belonging to him was ever touched. As things got worse, he actually suggested it was his turn to make it up to me.

That was only the catalyst, I would soon learn, for what Art really had in mind. And it was definitely not on the up and up. Since he had only a five-year sentence, he was due to be released soon. So he had made a deal with his guard friend. If he could get the other guards to withdraw their objections to my program and stop harassing me, that would solve the warden's problem and put his guard friend in the warden's good graces. Then, instead of boring, routine guard duty, he could ask for a promotion to work in the warden's office. Once on the inside, he could do Art's bidding with the Camp's accounts.

For the next six months or so, the plan worked remarkably well. My program prospered, the harassment stopped, and the guard was rewarded with a position in the warden's office. But the real test came only once Art was on the outside again and could direct the embezzlement scheme from there. Then the money started flowing. There wasn't much at first, since the Camp was only a derivative of the main prison facility next door. But a short time later, when the guard friend learned how to access the prison system itself, the real payoff began.

It did so for some time until, that is, there was a hitch. Whereas I was known as a good, some said even great, teacher, Art, on the other hand, was anything but. Where they used to say I could train anyone short of a monkey to learn a language, Art didn't do so well training his guard friend how to manipulate the Camp's accounts without getting caught. And that's how all hell broke loose a year or so after Art was released to carry on his scheme from the outside.

CHAPTER 38

While all this was going on, it turned out, Rambeau and the Prescott D.A.'s office had been busy trying to locate Ken Jackson. The reason they were having difficulty, I heard, was because none of the suspects stuck around in the Prescott area once the word got out that the D.A. was still looking for people to question about my case.

After almost a year of searching, Sarah told me that the D.A. had decided not to spend any more of the taxpayer's money trying to find the guys. But he didn't close the case. He left it open so my legal team could continue the search if they wanted to. True to his name, Rambeau wouldn't give up. He still couldn't bear the thought of me remaining in prison because of his failure. And like before, he delighted in relating the story of how he finally got Jackson.

"I stayed on that asshole's trail for months before I finally caught up with him," he told me over the phone. "He was miles away in Texas just about to cross the border into Mexico. He seemed rather exhausted from trying to stay one step ahead of me all this time, so I didn't need to use too much persuasion to get him in the car back to Prescott. I kept him well lubricated the whole trip with little airline bottles of whiskey from the 7-eleven store I stopped at on the way. And by the time we finally arrived, he had spilled more about the murder than I could possibly have hoped for."

I'll never forget how he ended the story. It took me a moment or two to get the joke. With his hearty laugh booming in my ears over the phone, he said, "You wouldn't believe it, Ike, the guy spilled more than he drank."

With Jackson finally in custody, my legal team pleaded with the D.A. to prosecute him immediately and not wait to find the guy who actually pulled the trigger. We needed his story on the record so I could be freed. Doing so, however, posed a unique problem: how to get him to testify against himself

Once again, it was Sarah who came up with the solution, and what she told me afterwards in one of her too-infrequent visits was brilliant.

"We were pretty sure," she said, "that Jackson was not personally involved in the plot to kill Randolph. He was only the messenger who brought your presence in the bar that night to the attention of the police. But he obviously knew everything, so my idea was to get the prosecution, the judge, and Jackson himself to all agree in advance that he only receive probation, provided he waive his right to a jury trial and tell us everything he knew in front of the judge in a bench trial. Then, two weeks later, Jackson did appear before the judge and answered all the prosecutor's questions. Satisfied with his testimony, the judge then sentenced him to the agreed-upon five years' probation. Now it's up to the judge to either nullify your conviction, Ike, or at least reduce your sentence to time served. We'll have to wait to see what he will do. So don't count your chickens just yet."

It turned out that Sarah was also right about counting chickens too soon. Sure enough, before I could breathe a sigh of relief, fate intervened yet again to complicate my life.

Imagine, if you will, how the warden back at the Otisville Camp felt about having been duped not only by one of the prisoners but by one of his very own guards. He was so pissed off, his desire for retribution did not stop with having them both tried for embezzlement. He figured I must also have been a party to the scheme, since my program benefited from it. So he was hell-bent on punishing me as well. Since my project had already taken on a life of its own, he couldn't do much about that. But he did ask the local authorities to add five more years to my sentence as an accomplice.

Once again I found myself the innocent victim of a miscarriage of justice. Naturally I turned to Sarah, and what she had to tell me was not good news. She said that my situation would be affected by whichever way the judge in Arizona ultimately ruled on my case. And either way it did not look good.

"If the judge resentences you to time already served," she told me, "the authorities here in New York could just tack on the extra five years the warden demanded. If on the other hand, the judge vacates your sentence entirely, they could decide to try you all over again as an accomplice to the embezzlement scheme."

Two weeks later, the judge did make his ruling. He gave me a full pardon and vacated my sentence. And with that, my next experience with the legal system began, just as Sarah had foreseen. The Orange County D.A. immediately charged me with conspiracy to commit fraud by being a partner to the embezzlement scheme, and kept me incarcerated at the Camp until my new trial.

Unlike the last time, however, when Sarah could only be an associate working with the law firm in Arizona, her own firm agreed to undertake my defense this time and appointed her as lead counsel.

Her first act was to object when the D.A. insisted on trying me together with the other two men as an equal partner in the embezzlement scheme.

Meeting with the prosecutor in the judge's chambers, she insisted, "That would put my client at an unfair disadvantage, Your Honor. He has his own legal team here, and we will be mounting an entirely different defense from the other two."

The prosecutor ultimately relented, and I had a preliminary hearing before a separate judge and prosecuting attorney. As soon as that hearing was called to order, Sarah spoke up again.

"We are asking for a change of venue, Your Honor, so the case can be tried in Onondaga County, in Syracuse where my law firm is located."

Immediately the new prosecutor interrupted, "We object to such a move, Your Honor."

"On what grounds?" the judge asked.

"In the first place, there has been no pretrial publicity here to affect this man's case. Moreover, there is no judicial interest in this case outside this courtroom and this jurisdiction. The defense has no grounds to ask for a change of venue."

Hearing this, Sarah gave the prosecutor one of her most practiced courtroom looks and said to the judge, "All we're asking for is a little professional courtesy, Your Honor."

Before the judge could respond, the prosecutor returned Sarah's look and said, "Alright, I will withdraw my objection, but I do insist that the defendant remain in custody and not be granted bail."

"That, Your Honor," Sarah insisted yet again, "would amount to adding insult to injury. My client has been in prison now for several years for a crime he has just been exonerated of. To compound the previous miscarriage of justice by keeping him incarcerated now for another crime, one we will prove he had absolutely no knowledge of, would be unconscionable."

"Well," the judge admitted, "since we are not dealing with a capital offense here, I am inclined to agree. Bail is set at $50,000."

And with that, Sarah and I began the next chapter of our life together.

What I didn't know, because Sarah hadn't told me yet, was that she and Jeremy were no longer living together. Just as she had feared, trying to rekindle their previous marriage ran into a major snag when she had to spend so much time in Arizona on my behalf. This time Jeremy didn't just get lonely, his longing for female companionship resulted in him falling in love with another woman. Though he tried to hide it for a while, he eventually came clean and they parted amicably once more. Jeremy's two-year leave of absence from Macallan was about to expire anyway, so he would have had to relinquish his position at the university entirely if he stayed away any longer.

The timing of all this was especially fortunate for me. After hearing about the separation, I didn't have to ask, Sarah suggested I live with her while out on bail, at least until I was free of the legal system. Then we could decide what kind of future we might want together. We had more important things to deal with now, like making sure I would *have* a future.

The trial itself turned out to be rather more straightforward than either of us anticipated. In a very smart move, Sarah advised me to waive my rights to a jury trial, just as she had done with Jackson back in Arizona, so she could try my case directly before the judge. Having gotten the change of venue to her home turf put her in a position to personally know the judge who was eventually assigned to it. He was an elegant older gentleman, who looked every bit a judge with his full head of silver-colored hair. Judge Augustus Thomas had been on the bench for years and had a reputation for fairness. Moreover, Sarah felt confident the prosecution would not have much of a case, unless they could find witnesses willing to lie and testify to my knowing something I obviously didn't know.

When the trial began, the prosecutor put my former cellmate Art on the stand. But he was forced to treat him as a hostile witness because no matter how hard he tried, he couldn't get Art to say I was actually part of his scheme. On cross examination, on the other hand, he readily answered Sarah's questions.

"So did you ever," she demanded, "engage my client in your scheme?"

After a short pause he responded, "Well no, I don't recall ever telling him what we were up to. We didn't know how he might react if we did."

"So may we infer then," Sarah proceeded, "that you used him as a patsy to get your own scheme off the ground?"

"Well, I guess you could say that, yes."

"OK, if not you, then did your guard friend ever tell my client about your scheme?"

That brought the prosecutor out of his chair. "Objection, Your Honor. How," he demanded, "would this man know what the guard said or didn't say to Mister Bell? And even if he did know, it would only be hearsay."

The judge sustained the objection but did not restrain his own curiosity.

"There is a simple way to resolve this question, counselor. Call the guard to the witness stand and let us hear from him directly, since he seems to be the only other individual with personal knowledge of this scheme."

When the prosecutor didn't answer right away, the judge got visibly annoyed. "Is there something you are not telling this court, sir, that we should have been made aware of? So far your sole witness is testifying for the defense."

"Well, your Honor," he answered, "we did interview the guard and all he would say was that he didn't trust Mister Bell here to keep his mouth shut. He wouldn't say whether or not he told him, so we decided not to subpoena him."

Hearing this, the judge, this elegant silver-haired gentleman, became irate. "Do you or do you not, counselor, have any other witnesses to bring before this court?"

When the prosecutor meekly said no, the judge slammed his gavel down on the bench so hard it glanced off the little block of wood it was supposed to land on, which went flying across the room.

"I am declaring a mistrial right here and now," the judge almost yelled, "and I want to see you, Mister Prosecutor, in my chambers immediately. As for the defendant, you, sir, are free to go, with apologies for what the court has done to you. You should never have been brought to trial here in the first place. Go with God and my blessing too."

CHAPTER 39

With the trial over and the judge's blessing still ringing in my ears, I felt I was finally free of the system that had plagued me for so long. Sarah said she didn't know who was happier, me or her. The fact that we had endured so much of this together only strengthened the bond between us. I was no longer just staying with her until my ordeal with the legal system was over. We became a true couple again, more in love with each other than we had ever been.

Once I regained my equilibrium, I was anxious to contact the consortium to find out what had transpired in the meantime with my program in Siena. What I learned was not good news. I knew from having watched newscasts in prison that the economy had been in recession, but I wasn't aware of how bad it had gotten. Families couldn't afford to send their kids abroad when they could barely afford to keep them in college to begin with. As a result, the consortium had been forced to close a number of its programs, including the one in Siena. They couldn't say when or if the program would ever be able to reopen.

While this news was obviously disappointing, I couldn't blame any system this time. I just needed to think about a new path for my future. And who better to think about it with than Sarah. Fortunately, there was no real urgency for me to find another job. As it happened, that idea was all but taken off the table by two events that occurred soon afterwards.

Within months of having successfully defended me, Sarah was finally awarded the partnership she'd been hoping for. The firm's masthead now read Smith, Jessup and Blake; and in that one stroke our financial future together was secured. At the same time, the stress I had been under for the past few years had taken more of a toll on me than I realized. I had sought medical attention at the prison, as Tom and Bill had insisted, but I never got a proper physical, only some medication to keep things under control. I knew I needed to see a real doctor now, and when I did, he insisted I put aside any thoughts of work and get the rest I needed to recuperate.

Resting for me, of course, meant keeping busy doing the sorts of things I found relaxing. Primary among them, as usual, was cooking, and Sarah's promotion to a partnership gave me all the excuse I needed to have a culinary celebration. I decided it would not be a one-off thing, like the coq-au-vin production the last time, but my own version of a movable feast. For the next several months I prepared a special gourmet meal every weekend. It was steak-au-poivre one week, followed by shrimp and grits the next, then linguine alla vongole, veal parmigiana, salmon almondine, and so on, never making the same meal more than once. Sarah was delighted, of course, but she knew I couldn't keep this up forever.

As usual, she was right, but not for the reason either of us could have foreseen.

Just as I was running out of ideas for a new concoction, I saw an advertisement for a job that intrigued me no end. It was the chairmanship of the foreign language department at a college there in Syracuse, the very one I used to go to for my study abroad consortium meetings.

In my current state of mind, I thought the nature of the job and the timing of it couldn't be better. Sarah, on the other hand, wasn't so sure.

"Don't you think it might be a bit too soon after escaping the fangs of the legal system to go jumping back into the jaws of academe?"

"Well, maybe," I answered, smiling at the clever phrasing, "but this position could be perfect for me. It's a small, well-regarded private college which specializes in undergraduate education. Unlike Macallan, knowledge of a foreign language is considered an integral part of a well-rounded education there. The college's literature makes that quite clear. And I'd be chair of their language department, practically a dream job for me."

"Well," Sarah conceded, "I can't object. I know how much this would mean to you."

"Look at it this way," I added. "Since the college is right here in Syracuse, we can continue to live together, go to work and come home each day to some delicious left-overs from my weekend culinary exploits."

After several successful interviews with the college administration and faculty, I was offered the position with tenure and a generous salary. And so I found myself, as I told Sarah afterwards, trying to one-up her with my own metaphors, "getting back on the horse that threw me years before. Only this time," I couldn't resist adding, "I think I've found a mild-mannered mare rather than a bucking bronco."

One of the reasons I was so sure about that was the warm reception I had received from everyone at the college, even from the one professor I figured would vote against me. That was none other than the person I had replaced as director of the Siena program. He was one of the distinguished older professors in the department, whose opinion seemed to hold a lot of weight. Not only was he very gracious towards me during the interview process, he was one of the strongest voices recommending me for the position and commending me for the fine job I did turning the Siena program around.

I had never been in a position of power and responsibility like this before, however, and I had to admit it did give me pause. I thought of how supportive my modest little team of teachers and staff had been in Siena, and how readily the consortium had given me what I needed to make that program work. Running a department, even in a small liberal arts college like this, I knew, was going to be something else again. I would have to negotiate with the administration to ensure my department got its fair share of resources. Even within the department, I would have to determine how to share those resources among the various language factions and still keep everyone happy. I could only hope that the warm feeling I got during the interviews promised fewer personal grievances among my colleagues than at Macallan.

Pondering all this, I almost started to feel sorry for Randolph having to deal with the likes of Professor Doyle. But that feeling didn't last very long. I had my own situation to think of now.

As soon as my contract was finalized, I got in touch with my good friend Tom to share the news. He had been on sabbatical when I got out of prison, so we had a lot to catch up on. Tom came up to Syracuse this time to spend the weekend with us.

Tom had never been to Sarah's place before and was impressed by how cozy and inviting it seemed. An old apartment with large high-ceilinged rooms and lots of wood paneling, located right in the city center. As someone whose own home was large enough for entertaining and still intimate at the same time, Tom thought Sarah's place ran a close second.

"You know, Ike," he said, "this place will be perfect for faculty get-togethers, now that you'll be chair of the department. Unless," he added with a sly grin, "you intend to become another Randolph and keep everybody away."

"Not on your life, Tom," I responded. "You know how I love to cook, so we'll be doing a fair amount of entertaining."

As I said that, I looked at Sarah to be sure she was OK with it.

"That's fine with me," she said. "I'll play hostess while Ike plays chef."

"I noticed you have quite a modern kitchen for an old building like this, Sarah," Tom said. "Ike must really be in his element in there."

"I had the kitchen remodeled when I bought the place, Tom, and it has the kind of appliances Ike likes, especially the combination gas range and electric oven. There's also a beautiful patio out back. It's got a barbeque grill with the gas piped in from the house, so Ike won't have to worry about a propane tank going dry on him in the middle of a party. But my favorite thing about this apartment is its location, close enough to my law office, so I can walk to work whenever the weather permits."

"Speaking of which," Tom interjected, "I never pictured you as a city boy, Ike. How do you like living here in the city center?"

"I'm OK with that. And anyway, I'll now have the best of both worlds, since the college is located in an idyllic site just outside the city limits. It even has a name that evokes its bucolic setting, Grosvenor Grove."

"That's an interesting name for a college. What do you know about it?" Tom asked.

"I was curious about the name, too, so I did some research beyond what the college's own brochures say. Would you believe the Grosvenor and Macallan names are historically joined at the hip, Tom?"

"Really? How so? I don't know that much about the history of the Macallan name, except that it has to do with some really fine Scotch."

"Speaking of which," Sarah interrupted, "it's not too early to break out the Scotch. How about we have some while you guys do your language thing."

I didn't sense any irritation in Sarah's voice, knowing how secure she was in her own profession. So I made a big deal of bringing out a suitable scotch for the occasion, a Macallan 18. Then we settled in a comfortable corner of the living room.

"Well," I began, "it seems that both names date back to the French conquest of Britain by William the Conqueror in that pivotal year in English history, 1066. William was a Norman but the Bretons fought on his side, since both were originally French speaking Celtic tribes from just across the channel, in what is now Normandy and Brittany. Turns out the name Macallan, which originally meant son of Alan, first appeared in England as a surname among William's Breton followers shortly after he assumed the throne as King of England. And one of the Normans who helped William conquer Britain was someone called Hugh le Gran Veneur, or Hugh the Great Huntsman. Now this guy was apparently a man of some girth because he gained the nickname Hugh le Gros Veneur, or Hugh the Fat Huntsman, a moniker he is said to have worn with pride. And this is the surname that got passed down to this day in its anglicized form as Grosvenor. So there you have it, two peas in the same pod."

"You do love that historical stuff, don't you, Ike?" Tom remarked. "You should teach a course on what that French conquest of Britain did to the English language."

"Oh, what was that?" Sarah inquired.

"Are you sure you're up for another of my stories? We may need another Scotch."

"I'm all ears," Sarah replied, getting up to refill our glasses.

"Well, since you asked, here it is in a nutshell. Even after Guillaume le Conquereur became William the King of England, he refused to learn English. After all, why should he? It was his country now and he was the king. So the court and the upper classes more or less had to learn French as well, in order to maintain their social status. Consequently, proper English became infused with a lot of French vocabulary. The lower classes, on the other hand, got left behind in all this, left to continue speaking their local dialects. Ever hear a cockney Englishman speak? You'll hardly understand a word of it. The English we use today derives from the upper-class use of the language back then, which explains why more than half of our words are of French origin. I think the number is supposed to be 58%, if I'm not mistaken."

"You know," Tom suggested, "if you taught a course on the French origins of English words, the kids would love it. You could show them how relatively easy it would be to learn French as a second language."

"I might just do that, Tom. Come to think of it, isn't it ironic how the tables have been turned. Nowadays the French complain about how their language is being overtaken by English. I guess what was good for the goose is good for the gander. By the way, do you know where the term Great Britain comes from?"

"Let me guess," Sarah answered. "It's from French."

"Yup. Since Brittany, or Bretagne in French, was only a small province, the Bretons called the country they conquered La Grande Bretagne. Vive la France!"

CHAPTER 40

If a cat has nine lives, I was now on my fourth, eager to pursue my passion in yet another incarnation. First there was Macallan, then Siena, after that the Otisville Camp, and now Grosvenor Grove. Reminiscing about all this while settling in to my new office in the lovely rural countryside made going to work a pleasure, equal to the honeymoon the faculty gave me during my first year at the college. As I pondered my good fortune, it made me think about the honeymoon I hoped to have one day with Sarah.

But work was work, and I had a challenging job to do. Rather than impose my own vision on a department as diverse as the one I had now inherited, where more than half a dozen languages were offered, I used this initial period to listen and learn about my colleagues and their various approaches to foreign language teaching. I could see from the start that their methodologies were varied enough that no single approach or vision would be possible. The need for exceptional language instruction itself would have to be the guiding principle.

One colleague who turned out to be most helpful in my inaugural year was once again the professor I had replaced as director in Siena, John Darling. His very name bespoke his kindly temperament, and his genuine humility struck me as rather unique for a professor, especially a senior tenured one. Darling readily admitted he had no head for administration and had been pleased when I took over the Siena program. But he was an excellent judge of character, happy to help me get to know my new colleagues and eager to see me succeed. He had the look of a judge, with the same kindly face and head of flowing silver hair as the one who had finally freed me from the legal system. He offered to be my eyes and ears whenever I needed him.

I decided to adopt a three-pronged strategy to smooth my entrée into the department. I first invited the faculty, spouses included, to our apartment for an informal get-together with lots of food and drink and only one rule: no talking shop. Sarah relished her role as hostess that evening, using her considerable courtroom skills to keep conversations informal whenever they started to veer off into work-related subjects.

"I guess it's hard to keep academics from being academics," she would joke, and receive knowing smiles from the spouses, both male and female.

Later that evening after everyone had left, Sarah and I sized up the evening with a nightcap of Scotch on the rocks. "That was a very successful ice-breaker, don't you think?" She quipped.

Back at the department the next day, I held my first faculty meeting. I used the occasion to describe how I viewed my role as chairperson, being careful not to say chairman. Then I asked each member to state what he or she thought was the most important issue facing the department at the present time. That gave me a good idea how to prioritize things during that inaugural year.

Finally, as the third leg of my strategy, I invited each of my new colleagues to meet with me individually over the course of the next two weeks for a personal chat.

My idea for the confidential chats was not to encourage talking behind peoples' backs, though I expected I'd learn a lot they would rather not say in front of their colleagues. Rather, I wanted to have a better idea why someone felt the way they did should an important issue arise.

This strategy worked remarkably well in getting things off to a good start. It helped me deal with one particularly sensitive issue that occurred towards the end of that very year.

The student evaluations of the most recently hired assistant professor, Nicole Watson, had not been good, and I needed to find out what the problem was. So I asked her to come to my office to discuss the situation.

As soon as I mentioned her evaluations, she said adamantly, "It is only the male students who don't like my classes."

Hearing that triggered my recollection of the confidential talk we'd had when I first arrived. I had sensed then that she had issues with her male colleagues. Now it appeared the same sentiment held for the students as well. My suspicion was more than confirmed when I asked her what she had been doing to address the situation.

"It's not up to me to do anything," she insisted. "It's they who need to change their attitude. I've been thinking of going to the college grievance committee before this issue becomes one that affects my chances for tenure."

That comment, and the vehemence with which it was made put me in an awkward position. Here I was, the dominant male in the department with the responsibility to evaluate her performance, not to mention determine her salary. I couldn't appear to be using my position against her with a subject as potentially explosive as this. I had to figure out how to convince a female junior colleague with strong gender issues to see things in a different light.

I was not a psychologist, far from it, but I was a linguist, and I had read her student evaluations carefully before meeting with her. I did not detect any hostility there towards her as a person, only dissatisfaction with her teaching methods. In fact, one of the students, evidently a male, even said so in so many words. I had to find a way to get her off the gender thing and become a better teacher.

That initial private meeting I'd had with her at the beginning of the year bore fruit in yet another way. I remembered her telling me she was bilingual, having been brought up by an American father and a French mother who insisted on speaking French at home. That background, coupled with her superior graduate work, not only got her the job at Grosvenor, but got her assigned to teach the most advanced French course in the department as well.

A careful reading of her personnel file also told me something else. She never had teaching assistantships that would have provided her with that experience in graduate school, like the rest of her fellow grad students. Because of her exceptional intellect and superior French skills, the faculty at the university where she got her degree wanted her for themselves, and gave her research assistantships instead. While that garnered her excellent recommendations when the time came to look for a job, it also put her at a decided disadvantage now that she'd got one. And it could mean everything when her tenure decision was due to come up.

Knowing all this gave me the opportunity to help solve her problem without addressing the gender issue. I offered myself as a mentor, explaining that I would be happy to provide the teacher training she was deprived of in grad school. Framing the issue this way gained her respect, and she graciously accepted my offer. It pleased me no end to think I now had the opportunity to help a well-qualified person like Nicole realize her potential in a system that was as fraught with injustice as this one. It made me think of the time Randolph told me I was "the smartest one of the bunch." I thought much the same about Nicole now; but unlike Randolph, I was determined to do whatever I could to help her. I could only hope that her feelings about women's rights, as much as I respected them, would not get in the way.

CHAPTER 41

Having two successful careers in the same household made life at home idyllic. Sarah and I were in the prime of our lives, enjoying each other's company more than ever. The subject of getting married was getting to the point of having to find a good reason not to.

Even though I now had a full-time job, I still made time to prepare gourmet meals just for the two of us. Not every weekend as before, just whenever the occasion called for something special. One such weekend, well into the second year of living together again, I decided to make one of my favorites, Julia Child's original recipe for butterflied leg of lamb.

To be sure I hadn't forgotten any of the details, I found my old copy of *Julia Child and Company*, buried among the dozens of cookbooks that made our kitchen look more like a library. I had learned over the years not to try butterflying the meat myself. I'd tried it a couple of times before and always ended up with chopped lamb. This time I watched the local butcher do it for me with just a few deft strokes of his knife. Once I got home, I marinated the meat with olive oil, light soy sauce, pressed garlic, chopped rosemary leaves, and fresh squeezed lemon juice, just like Julia said. Then I put it in the fridge to let it get used to itself until Sarah came home from another Saturday at work preparing briefs.

While it was normal for us to eat dinner most weekends with a bottle of wine and candles on the dining table, I could tell Sarah sensed something different when she came in the door this time. I told her I was just trying to see if I remembered how to make a butterflied leg of lamb, and asked her to join me in the kitchen.

I had bought a bunch of English shelling peas at the farmers' market that morning, and had already put two baking potatoes in the oven at 450 degrees to get them going. Then I poured two Scotches—neither of them Oban or Macallan this time, so as not to dwell on the past—and challenged her to a contest to see who could shell the most peas in the shortest time.

Unbeknownst to me, Sarah had shelled a lot of peas before, so she knew the trick. By the time she had shelled twice as many as me, I gave up.

"OK, smart ass," I said, comparing my meager pile with hers. "What's the secret?"

"Easy," she answered, "just don't do what they tell you to. Don't waste time pulling down the string on the back of the pod and trying to crack it open from there, like you were doing. Just turn it over to the other side and pop it open with your thumbs. Works like a charm every time."

I then started working feverishly to catch up, only to realize I was dropping so many peas on the floor, I was losing even more ground.

Laughing hysterically, Sarah said, "Watch where you step, Ike. We're not here to make mushy peas."

Finally, with the peas shelled and the Scotches downed, I checked the oven and saw that the potatoes were already done. I left them there, put the lamb in next to them, turned down the heat to 375 and reset the timer for another 35 minutes, just like Julia said for medium rare.

Watching all this, Sarah asked, "Weren't the potatoes done?"

"Maybe, yes. But don't worry, you can never overcook a baked potato. It just gets nice and fluffy on the inside and crispy on the outside."

When the meat was done and resting, I put the peas on low heat in a pan with butter and a pinch of lavender salt, making sure to warm them up just enough but not cook them through.

"They should," I joked, "still taste like fresh garden peas, not mushy peas."

The dinner itself was, of course, scrumptious, but I could tell Sarah was still wondering what I was up to.

"Something's going on here, Ike. This isn't about the dinner, is it?"

"It is and it isn't," I answered. "Let's clear the dishes first. Then I'll explain."

Once we finished cleaning up, I grabbed our bottle of cognac and led her over to the couch in the living room. She looked really puzzled when I made like I was reaching for the TV remote and instead pulled a package out from under the coffee table where I'd hidden it. It was nicely wrapped, about the size of a thick book.

"Ok, I give up, Ike. What's the occasion?"

"Open it and you'll find out."

When she opened it, she found another smaller package inside. She didn't ask what the second one was. She gave me a look that said it all. As she opened it, she covered her mouth with her hand the way women always seem to do at times like this, and let out a sound somewhere between a gasp and a scream.

We set the date in June, as soon as school was out for the summer, with a honeymoon to follow in July. I had planned the timing carefully, knowing this would be the last summer I would have free for a while. I had successfully negotiated with my dean to create the summer program I always wanted, starting the following year. That would keep me busy year-round.

Not only did I get my summer program, the dean also offered to reserve the college chapel for our wedding. The chapel, built in the style of a classic wooden country church, served as a non-denominational meeting place for ceremonial events, where the president of the college usually presided. Our wedding was to be just such an event, and the college president, an ordained minister himself, offered to perform the ceremony.

CHAPTER 42

When the day came, Tom and Bill were the first ones besides family we invited. Tom was more than happy to serve as my best man. Jim Taylor had finally left Macallan for greener pastures and greater fame. He sent congratulations and best wishes from somewhere deep in the heart of Africa. He was busy initiating a whole new genre of French literature. Sarah's law firm closed its office for the day so everyone could attend. The chapel was barely large enough to hold everyone from the college itself who wanted to attend.

There were audible oohs and aahs when Sarah came down the aisle. She was not wearing white, having been married before, but a gorgeous multi-colored dress. In place of a veil, she wore a tiara made of flowers that accentuated her golden locks and complemented the colors of her dress. For my part, I shunned the traditional tuxedo and even the three-piece suit. It being late June, I wore off-white slacks and a fancy tailored light-blue jacket. I even managed to find a tie whose colors matched those of Sarah's dress.

Surprisingly, or maybe not so surprisingly, the most memorable moments of the day occurred not at the ceremony itself but at the reception afterwards, when both the ties and the tongues got loosened. The college president delivered a lovely speech about how much the college appreciated me and my lovely bride. Then the fun began.

My dad mentioned how proud he was of me, especially the way I had dealt with my time at "the camp".

"But," he added jokingly, "I never understood why I couldn't see him without showing proof I was actually his father. That never happened at the other camp we used to send him to every summer as a boy."

Actually, my dad did come to see me several times when I was there, more times in fact than those years I was at Macallan. It meant a lot to me.

Then it was Sarah's father's turn. He congratulated her on becoming a partner in the firm, and me on becoming chairperson of my department. Then, assuming the likely discrepancy in our salaries, he asked, "Is it true, Sarah, that you made Ike sign a prenup?"

When it was Bill's turn, he wanted to know what I had learned from my nemesis Randolph about handling the job of department chair.

"Any useful ideas there?" he asked.

I paused for a moment and answered, "I just think about what he would do and do exactly the opposite. Works every time."

The best moments came, naturally, when Tom got up and did his thing as best man. He began by recalling how I thought I had reached intellectual nirvana as an untenured assistant professor at Macallan.

"A university named after a bottle of Scotch, by the way," he added.

"However," he went on, "fate proved how ephemeral nirvana can be. So when that system let him down, what did Ike do? Why, challenge another system, of course. And this time he did get his tenure, only it was a sentence of life in the federal prison system."

Getting only a muted reaction, as if people weren't sure how to react, Tom quickly finished the thought.

"The fact that Ike sits here today suggests we can all learn from his experience. Just look at what he's made of it. He has proven you can beat the system so long as you realize it's not about the system. It's all about yourself, how you deal with things you can't control. That's when you find out who you really are. Here is a man, my best friend Ike, who not only turned the denial of tenure into a successful program abroad, but also managed to turn his time in a federal prison into an opportunity to give other inmates a skill they can use to turn their own lives around."

When people started to applaud, Tom interrupted and said, "But wait, the system wasn't finished with him yet. He managed to get screwed yet again by a warden out for revenge." Then, pausing for effect, he went on. "So where did Ike finally find justice? In a judge who saw through the failures of his own legal system and gave Ike back his life."

Tom then turned to a gentleman at the back of the room who had remained quiet throughout the whole proceeding, and asked him to please come forward. Somewhat reluctantly, a silver-haired gentleman came to the podium and Tom introduced him.

"This is Judge Augustus Thomas, the person who finally put an end to Ike's trials with the legal system. And he did it in a remarkably energetic way, one that gave a unique quality to the pronouncement of a mistrial. He slammed his gavel down on the bench so hard, the little block of wood it was supposed to land on landed instead right at the prosecutor's feet."

After the laughter and the applause died down, the judge spoke with noticeable humility.

"I didn't do anything back then but my job. The man getting married here today has made himself the life he has always deserved, and has obviously had the good fortune to also find the perfect woman to share it with. Let me just use the words I enjoy saying when an innocent person is found not guilty: You are free to go, sir, and in this case may God bless you both."

Hearing that, everyone raised their glasses one more time with a chorus of "here, here". Tom waited until they'd finished, then said, "I'm not done yet, folks. I want you to know who this perfect woman is the judge just referred to, and who it is who found whom. One thing for sure, she wasn't one of Ike's famous one-night stands back then in Oban, mind you."

That brought muffled laughter as people looked at Sarah to gauge her reaction. She gave Tom that knowing smile of hers and raised her glass as if to toast the remark. Then Tom continued, "Well, maybe Ike initially thought she would be, but he soon found out differently. I have known Sarah longer than I've known Ike, and I always felt she was someone very special. That was proven, if proof be needed, when I told her later about Ike's first problem with the law in Arizona. They were no longer seeing each other at the time, but she never hesitated a moment, got right on a plane to the other side of the continent, and stayed by his side throughout his entire ordeal. Ike, my friend, all I can say is you are one lucky bastard."

The look on Sarah's face at that moment was different from any I had seen before. It wasn't the one I'd seen her use with opposing counsel in courtrooms for sure, nor was it like that "what are you up to now" one when I tried to surprise her with a new culinary concoction. It was different even from one she gave me when I presented her the engagement ring. But it said all I needed to know.

CHAPTER 43

A week later, we were on an Air France flight from JFK to CDG, about to start the honeymoon I had been looking forward to for so long. I was finally getting to show Sarah my beloved Paris.

Once the plane landed at Charles de Gaulle airport and we cleared customs, we got a cab into the city. I gave the driver the address, a charming boutique hotel on the rue Bonaparte, right in the center of the Latin Quarter, a block from the Place St. Germain des Prés. It was already late afternoon when we checked in, so I proposed we have dinner around the corner at the famous Café de Flore. We got a seat right at the sidewalk so Sarah could enjoy people-watching at one of the most bustling spots in the city.

We used the time at dinner to finalize plans for our stay. We agreed to spend the first day visiting some of the major tourist spots like everyone else does: the Eiffel Tower, the Champs-Elysées, and the Louvre. The rest of the time I wanted to show her my favorite haunts from my year as a student.

The next morning, Sarah got to experience the traditional French breakfast of café-au-lait and a tartine (thin baguette or ficelle fresh from the bakery, sliced lengthwise and slathered with French country butter and home-made jam). Then we set out for the Eiffel Tower.

"If you can ignore the mob of tourists," I told her as we bought our tickets and queued up to get on the elevator, "the view will be well worth it."

As indeed it was, on a bright summer day.

Afterwards we went over to the Champs-Elysées and stopped for lunch at a busy bistro. When Sarah gasped at the prices, I said, "That's what we get for doing the tourist thing. I hardly ever came to this area of the city when I lived here, but you have to walk down the Champs-Elysées at least once. Nothing like it anywhere else in the world."

When we got to the Place de la Concorde and entered the Louvre, we had to make a decision. It would take several days to see all the exhibits, so we had to choose. Sarah opted for concentrating on modern European art, which she'd enjoyed studying in college. We went to see the Mona Lisa, of course, and I insisted on showing her my favorite room, the vast hall where some of the most famous nineteenth century French paintings are displayed. There was Gericault's huge, awe-inspiring romantic masterpiece, the Raft of the Medusa, and a few steps away on the same enormous wall, Delacroix's Liberty Leading the People. It depicted, I told her, the second French revolution.

"You mean France had two of them?" she asked, looking a bit sheepish that she didn't know.

Recalling Randolph's obsession with the monarchy, I joked, "Yes it did. It took two revolutions for France to rid itself of kings and emperors."

At which point Sarah couldn't help adding, "If we don't watch out, we may need a second revolution ourselves should the white supremacists take over."

Several hours and many exhibits later, Sarah indicated she was ready to leave. "Enough museum for one day," she admitted. "But I'm curious. They seem to have everything under the sun here, but hardly any impressionist paintings, my favorites. What's up with that?"

"That's because there are several other museums that have nothing but the impressionists," I told her. "There's the Quay d'Orsay, the Orangerie, and the Monet Museum. Don't worry, we'll go to at least one of them while we're here."

As we sat down to breakfast the next morning and Sarah was

expertly slicing her *ficelle* down the middle and slathering it with butter, it started to rain. She looked at me with an air of disappointment, while I, on the other hand, was almost ecstatic.

"Ah," I exclaimed. "You haven't lived until you've had a romantic stroll through the streets of Paris in the warm summer rain, with a *parapluie* in one hand and your lover on the other arm."

Then we set off to the area where I had spent so much of my time as a student, the streets around the Sorbonne. We grabbed a large umbrella for two thoughtfully provided by the hotel at the door, and stepped outside. Since our hotel was already in the Latin Quarter, our stroll in the rain didn't take that long. Once there, I pointed out one of the old buildings where I had attended classes.

"You know, this is one of the oldest universities in the world. It was founded in the thirteenth century. It's changed a lot since then, of course, but back when I was here, it still felt pretty old. I'll never forget trying to find a seat in one of those ancient auditoriums, where you could hardly hear the professor from the back rows and you could barely see him through the haze of cigarette smoke. At least we didn't have to speak Latin to understand the lectures, as they did back then."

"Wait a minute," Sarah interrupted. "You mean they really taught courses here in Latin?"

"Oh yes. Latin was still the language of the university centuries after the Romans left. Latin is, of course, the language French comes from, so it was just a matter of the universities being the last bastions of proper discourse. Why do you think the university district here is called the Latin Quarter?"

"I was going to ask you that. I never would have guessed. By the way, what is that big domed building over there. It looks just like the Pantheon in Rome."

"That's exactly what it was intended to look like. That's the French Panthéon. It imitates the Roman one in both form and spirit."

"I get the form part, but what about the spirit?"

"Well, the one in Rome is said to celebrate the various Greco-Roman gods, so the one here honors famous men and women in French history. A number of them are entombed there."

"Oh, I get it. Since the gods were already immortal, the French had to make their heroes immortal by burying them in the same type of building here in Paris, is that it?"

"Something like that. Want to pay them a visit?"

"Sure. Who am I going to visit with?"

"Well, off the top of my head, there's Voltaire, Rousseau, Victor Hugo, Emile Zola, Antoine de Saint-Exupéry, Alexandre Dumas, and the famous atomic physicists Pierre and Marie Curie, for starters."

Sarah seemed quite engrossed as we toured the building. Then, as we were leaving, she remarked, "There weren't that many tombs in there. They must have left a lot of famous people out. I wonder how they decided who would get the honors."

"Don't worry," I said, "the French have made up for it in spades. There is a huge cemetery here in Paris, the Père-Lachaise, where you can commune with hundreds more if you like."

"Like who, for example?"

"Well, let's see. The ones I remember are Balzac, Molière, Chopin, Edith Piaf, Oscar Wilde, Gertrude Stein, Simone Signoret, and quite notoriously Jim Morrison of the Doors. You know, don't you," I added with a grin, "that the doors closed and the lights went out forever on Jim right here in Paris, when he pushed the envelope one too many times."

Enjoying her groaning, I got on a roll. "Then there's another cemetery, at Montparnasse, where the philosopher-lovers Jean-Paul Sartre and Simone de Beauvoir share the same grave. You can just imagine them thinking great thoughts together in death just as they did in life. Isn't that sweet?"

Before she could groan again, I continued, "Then there's the big military complex, called Les Invalides, that houses Napoleon's tomb. I could go on, but you've probably had enough by now."

"Actually, no," she answered, "because you still haven't said a word about the kings of France, only Napoleon. Where are they buried? Being such a catholic country, they must be In Notre Dame or something, no?"

"Good guess, and a close one because they're all in another church, in the northern suburbs of Paris, called Saint Denis. But that's a long story. So let's go get a take-out lunch and sit in the Jardin de Luxembourg while I tell you. It's practically around the corner from here and the rain has stopped, so it should be a perfect time for a picnic in the park."

We ordered two classic *jambon-buerre* sandwiches (nothing but delicious French-style ham and butter on a fresh baguette) and a *demi-bouteille* (half-bottle) of wine from a café nearby. Then we found a bench under some trees in the park to enjoy everyone's favorite lunch spot in Paris. As we watched the little kids floating their toy boats on the pond, I opened the bottle of wine and sat back with what must have been a wistful look on my face.

"Are you OK," she asked.

"Couldn't feel better. I'm just thinking of all the times I ate this very lunch in this very place between classes. And now to do it again with you. I guess Tom was right, I am a lucky bastard."

When we finally broke the embrace that must have made everyone nearby think they were witnessing two star-crossed Parisian lovers, she said, "Now about those kings."

"Sorry, got distracted there for a moment. Well, almost all of them, from the first one onward, were entombed in the Eglise de Saint-Denis. At the height of the French revolution, however, the mobs raided the church, destroyed the tombs and removed all the remains to a mass grave on the grounds outside. Then, after the revolution, an effort was made to recover them, but by that time it was impossible to tell which bones belonged to whom. So all you see down in the crypt of the church today is an ossuary, a large wall engraved with the names of all the kings whose bones are stashed behind it."

When I finished, Sarah seemed speechless, so we emptied the rest of the wine and toasted the glory of France.

Once we finished eating I asked Sarah if she was up for another walk. We went over to the Ile de la Cité, the island in the middle of the Seine where the original Roman city used to be, the city they called Lutetia. I wanted to show her Notre Dame, but it was still inaccessible after the fire. So we settled on the magnificent Sainte Chapelle with its famous stained glass windows, and the enormous flower market nearby. Then we found a little bistro for dinner.

At breakfast the next morning, Sarah began to muse about what she had experienced so far.

"Our time on the island yesterday made me think about how much of this city is oriented around the river. The Eiffel Tower was right at the river, so was the Louvre on the other side, and now Notre Dame and that fantastic chapel on the island in the middle. Lots of other cities are built on rivers, I know, but none of them seem to make so much of it as this one."

"Ah, now you're beginning to see why Paris is so special. Paris wouldn't be Paris without the Seine."

"And all those bridges," she added. "It makes the place so romantic."

"And I haven't even taken you on a walk in the evening along one of the banks yet."

"That reminds me of something else I wanted to ask you. Everyone talks about the left bank and the right bank. How do you know which is which?"

"That's easy. The left bank, or Rive Gauche, is the bank on your left as you face downstream. The Rive Droite is on the right."

"OK, I think somewhere I knew that. But how can you tell which way the river is flowing here? It goes so slowly it looks more like a big green pond. Besides, it also makes that wide turn I saw over there near the Eiffel Tower."

"Confuses everybody, including me when I first came here," I admitted. "But there is a trick."

I pulled out the little red pocket book of city maps I'd kept all these years, my little bouquin rouge, as it used to be called, and showed her.

"Look here. The map is of course oriented with north at the top like most maps, and the river, as you can see, goes from one side to the other, more or less horizontally if you ignore that turn over there by the Eiffel Tower. All you have to know is that the Seine flows from east to west through the city, from right to left on the map. Hence the left bank is on the south side of the river and the right on the north. But they don't say north or south here. They say right bank or left bank."

"OK, now I see. But that raises another question. I thought the Seine flowed north from here to the English Channel, not east to west?"

"You're right, but the river actually starts way over on the east side of the country and meanders its way ever so slowly northward. That's why it's so hard to see the flow. Paris is blessed with one of its greatest meanders along the way."

"Got it. So, my love, where are we going to meander today?"

"Well, since we spent most of yesterday in the Latin Quarter, on the Rive Gauche, how about a day on the other side, the Rive Droite?"

"Fine by me."

"I'm thinking of spending the day in the Marais. The word means marsh or swamp because that's what most of that area used to be before it was drained and developed. Today it is one of the trendiest sections in the city, with lots of historic mansions and fancy boutiques. It's also the site of the famous Jewish quarter. You're going to love its village feel."

We finished our breakfast and hopped on the metro to the Marais. As if to prove my point about it feeling like a village, the first thing we saw once we started wandering through the streets was a line of local Parisians on the opposite sidewalk escorting their children to grade school. There were mothers with little ones hanging onto their arms and fathers with sons perched on their shoulders. As we stopped to watch, I recognized the gate where a woman was ushering the children into the school. As the line thinned, she beckoned to us, encouraging us to come inside and enjoy the adjacent garden.

"This," I told Sarah as we followed the last of the families through the gate, "is one of the many private gardens I used to visit. Most people know about the parks Paris is famous for, but few are aware of how many charming little enclaves like this there are, hidden away behind stone walls. They're actually private gardens, but anyone is welcome to enjoy them."

This one had an enormous aviary in the center, surrounded by all sorts of trees, shrubs, and flowering plants. Benches were placed strategically throughout the space, which was enclosed on three sides by a stone wall that hid the garden from the street. The fourth side was occupied by an elegant eighteenth-century mansion that had evidently been converted into the school. Once inside the gate, it was impossible to tell you were still in the middle of one of the busiest cities in Europe. The only sounds we could hear were those of the birds and the occasional happy voices of the children.

Relaxing together on one of the benches, I started reminiscing about the times I used to spend in gardens like this.

"On weekends, when I wasn't in the Jardin de Luxembourg having my jambon-beurre sandwich, I'd find one of these gardens and sit with my study books. I found a little paperback once that described more than a dozen of these hidden gems. It told you where they were and how to find the entrances. I think I had visited every one of them before my year ended."

As we sat there enjoying the moment, Sarah acknowledged how much it meant to her that fate had brought us back together again, able to enjoy a moment like this.

"Isn't it strange," she mused, "how it took the worst of fortunes to create the fortunate life we have now."

"Yeah, each of us had to strike out twice before we hit the home run, didn't we?" I quipped. "But it wasn't so much fate that brought us back together. I think we earned it."

"Amen to that," was all Sarah said before we became two Parisian lovers again taking advantage of our private little hideaway.

Though we were reluctant to leave such an idyllic place, the streets of the Marais beckoned. For the rest of the morning,

Sarah made me stop every block or two so she could nose around the unique boutiques. Naturally she found things we just had to have. When I protested about having to schlep more luggage, she just smiled and asked the merchants to ship them for us.

By lunch time we found a café where we could linger for a while over a nice selection of wines, cheeses and charcuterie. We were discussing what to do for the afternoon when Sarah asked, "Didn't I see a building back there that said Picasso Museum?"

"Yes," I answered, "it's one of the treasures of the Marais. You want to go? It's got hundreds of his works, many of them from his own personal collection. The best part is they're presented chronologically, so you can appreciate his evolution as an artist."

We spent the rest of the afternoon learning more about Picasso than either of us thought possible.

For the next two days, I filled our itinerary with the things I most wanted Sarah to see before we had to return home. We did go to the Père la Chaise cemetery. She liked cemeteries, she said, because she found them comforting.

"Comforting in what way?" I asked.

"Because you get to commune with the spirits of other people."

"You mean you talk to them," I asked again, trying not to sound flippant or dismissive.

"Not in so many words," she responded, smiling at her own clever retort. "It's more of a spiritual thing. Takes you out of your own narrow world for a while. Makes you think. This place is better than indoors at the Pantheon, where everything is encased in stone. Here the stones are part of the natural landscape, the way they should be."

I had to admit I had not seen this side of her before, but it helped me appreciate how much Sarah's lawyerly persona did not describe who she really is. It also made me think about myself, how having been denied tenure had probably made me more of a human being than the one I might well have become if I had gotten it. That was something I needed to keep in mind when dealing with my new colleagues at the college, once this honeymoon and the one I enjoyed there were over. Funny how walking among the departed makes you think about things like that.

Sarah also got to visit her impressionist museum. I took her to the Quay d'Orsay. She was overwhelmed seeing so many impressionist works in one place, and equally awed at how they had transformed a nineteenth-century train station into a masterpiece of museum architecture.

"I don't know what is more impressive," she said, hinting at another pun, "the building or the art work."

Sarah also enjoyed the times we spent together strolling through some of the city's famous parks. I would make a point of finding a nice restaurant nearby, so we could enjoy a proper Parisian *dejeuner* followed by a walking siesta in the park afterwards. It was during one of those lunches when she asked me why there were so many different names for restaurants.

"Why is the one we're in called a restaurant, but others are called a café, a bistro, or even one that sounds like it must sell women's underwear."

"You mean a *brasserie*," I answered, laughing because I had had the same reaction when I first came to Paris.

"*Brasserie* is not to be confused with brassiere. The word *brasserie* originally meant brewery, and those establishments usually have a wide range of beers and other drinks. They also normally have tablecloths and a fixed menu of standard French fare, like my favorite steak frites. I think of them as more like a tavern or an inn, without the lodging of course. A *bistro*, on the other hand, serves drinks, naturally, and usually cheaper fare like stews and things on bare tables, more like a pub I'd say. They say the name comes from the Russian word for 'quickly', or 'hurry up', when Russian soldiers were in Paris after the Napoleonic wars. That's probably not true, but there is a sign claiming just that on a bistro at the Place du Tertre in Montmartre. At least they don't claim they were the first fast food restaurant!"

"This is fascinating. But what about the word *café*? The place we ate at our first night here was called Café de Flore. It seemed just like another casual restaurant to me."

"Well, cafés were originally coffee houses where people would meet over coffee or a drink. The early ones in Paris, like the Café de Flore, were famous as hangouts for artists, philosophers, and the like. They are perhaps the most casual of all the eateries, but they can get fancy at times, too. To tell the truth, I'm not sure these distinctions mean all that much these days. I don't know if you noticed, but I even saw signs saying things like *brasserie restaurant, bistro café*, and even one that said *café restaurant*. That last one sounded more like an oxymoron to me, since a café is the most casual and a restaurant the most formal, like the one we're in now. A restaurant normally has specific hours for lunch and again for dinner, like this one, and the menu depends on what the chef has in mind that day. Most of the other types serve throughout the day. You can tell they do if there's a sign outside saying *service continu*. But that's probably more than you ever wanted to know!"

"Not at all. I am beginning to see why those who don't speak French often say they don't like Paris, while those that do, like you, love the place. I'm just lucky I'm experiencing the city through your eyes now. It's been great."

When our last night together in Paris came, I told Sarah I had a special surprise in store. I told her to dress for dinner, ordered an Uber and asked the driver to take us to the quay by the Pont de l'Alma. As soon as we arrived, Sarah noticed the two *bateaux mouches* docked below, with one of them elegantly set for dinner on deck.

We were offered champagne as soon as we were seated on board. Once our first course was served, the boat got underway. Seeing the city from the Eiffel Tower like we did that first night was one thing, but it was nothing like cruising down the Seine gazing at the buildings and monuments of Paris being lit up by floodlights from the boat as we cruised by. Sarah especially loved having the opportunity to experience all the bridges the boat passed under, up close and personal. Each time we emerged on the other side of one, another impressive view of the city became illuminated. Our only disappointment was not being able to see the full beauty of Notre Dame, still encased in scaffolding. We vowed right then and there to come back again once the restoration was finished.

That night, our making love was somehow different and very special, as only a last night in Paris can be.

CHAPTER 44

The taxi ride back to Charles de Gaulle airport the next morning was quite an emotional moment for me. Watching my beloved Paris fading away behind me gave way to thoughts of what I was returning to in the States. Not only had I finally found nirvana in my chosen career, I had found the perfect partner to share it with. Paris could wait for another visit now.

With all the curve balls life had thrown at me, however, I had finally learned that nirvana is only a state of mind. I knew I would have my work cut out for me if I wanted it to last. At least as a tenured professor and chair of the department I was more in control now, not so much at the mercy of the system as before. But that put the burden on me now to make the system work.

Things did go relatively smoothly with the higher-ups in the administration. The rough spots occurred within my own department, when I had to decide how to divvy up the funds I got among the different language factions. In my first year on the job the Asian languages thought they were getting short-changed. Then in my second year the Italians thought the French and Spanish got better treatment. I knew I couldn't let this situation persist. I remembered all too well how Randolph would make enemies every year by his decision-making in this regard.

So I decided to try something new. I proposed an advisory board to consult with me on issues like this. To make things as democratic as possible, I suggested it be composed of three members, two tenured and one untenured, two from the larger European bloc of languages, one from the smaller non-European one. Furthermore, I proposed that membership on the board change every year, so everyone would get a chance to participate. The faculty had never heard of an idea like this from a chairperson before, but they endorsed it enthusiastically.

The worst times came when I had to make judgments about my colleagues' individual performances and set their salaries accordingly. Faculty always complain if they get less than they think they're worth, but I had gotten lucky so far. The administration had provided an extra pot of money each of my first years as chair, earmarked specifically for salaries. But I couldn't count on that in the future. Since personnel issues are confidential, I couldn't use my advisory board for that purpose. It was entirely up to me.

The only person who had so far made an issue of it was none other than Nicole Watson. If she didn't get the maximum amount of increase, she would insist it was because she was a woman. Although her publication record continued to be excellent, and her teaching had definitely improved, I still had to limit her committee assignments and other administrative responsibilities because of the way she kept antagonizing her male colleagues. Even her presence at faculty meetings caused a lot of unnecessary friction. I was sure this attitude would make it unlikely her male colleagues would vote for her when she came up for tenure. So I had to do something if I didn't want that to happen.

I decided to call her into my office for another heart-to-heart talk.

The moment she entered the office, I came out from behind my desk, motioned to one of the two chairs in front of it and sat in the other one myself. I began the conversation by praising her work and telling her how valuable a member of the department she had become.

"Your research," I told her, "has begun to bring a lot of credit to the department, both within the college and nationally. And we are very pleased with that."

"Thank you for saying so," she responded. Then, true to form, she added, "But will my male colleagues feel the same way when it comes to my getting tenure?"

If I was looking for a way to segue into the discussion I needed to have with her, she just handed it to me. A bit off balance because the opportunity came so quickly, I put the ball back in her court by asking, "What makes you say that?"

"Well," she replied, "it's pretty obvious that they don't respect me nearly as much as you seem to. At least you gave me the raise I deserved this past year."

That provided a good place for me to start.

"Your raises, Nicole, have been based solely on performance during the current year, with special consideration given to improvements over preceding years. I have scrupulously followed that pattern with everyone in the department since I have been chair. It is only your accomplishments that earned you the larger increase last year. And, I might add, the respect of the faculty as well."

That stymied her for a moment. Somewhat confused, she asked, "If that is true, then why in faculty meetings is my opinion not given the same respect as theirs?"

"But Nicole," I responded, "you're not the only female in the department, and I know for a fact that none of the other women feel that way. So if you do, you need to look inward."

"So you're saying it's all my fault?"

"Meaning only that it is entirely within your power to do something about it. What I'm saying is, it's a matter of collegiality. I know your male colleagues respect you as a scholar because they have told me so on a number of occasions. But they also tell me they don't understand why you harbor such resentment towards them, something they insist they don't deserve. And I must say I have to agree with them."

"So what am I supposed to do?"

"Well, I have an idea, something I've thought a lot about as you get closer to your tenure decision. If this were a European university, you'd be judged entirely on your academic credentials by a board of independent scholars. But here in the U.S. things are different and, I have to admit, more subjective. You will be judged not only on your scholarship but also on whether or not your fellow faculty members think you'd make a good colleague, someone they would want to work with for the rest of their academic lives. I don't say that's a good thing, but it is the reality of the system we deal with here."

I stopped a moment to see how Nicole would respond, but she seemed to be waiting to hear what the "idea" I mentioned was.

"So here's what I propose," I continued. "You know that the college is going to celebrate its fifty-year jubilee soon, and the dean wants our department to play a significant role. We'll need a committee of faculty to plan for that, and I'm going to ask for volunteers. I want you to be one of them and to play a major role. I don't think I have to tell you what that would mean for you and the department both if you did well. So what do you say?"

Instead of looking away, as she tended to do when being talked to like that, Nicole looked at me with what seemed like a tear in her eye and said, "Thank you for giving me this opportunity. I won't let you down. Or I guess I should I say, let myself down."

"I know you won't, Nicole. I'm counting on that."

CHAPTER 45

Even though things were going reasonably well, problems like this were apparently adding more stress on me than I realized. At least that's what my doctor told me when I went for my next annual physical.

"You cannot continue taking everything so much to heart, Ike, or you really will end up with heart problems," he said. "You've already been diagnosed with an irregular heartbeat, and you've had a couple of AFib incidents as well. You really need to take better care of yourself."

My response to my doctor's admonition was, as Sarah put it later, classic. Relieving stress usually meant starting something new that gave me pleasure. And I had the perfect antidote. I plunged head-long into preparing for the summer program I'd finally been able to produce. Using the same logic I used at the prison, I picked Spanish as the language to launch the program. The department faculty agreed with my decision provided, they said, I let other languages have a bite of the apple in future summers.

Usually pretty empty during the summer recess, the campus that summer was full of students required to speak Spanish wherever they were on campus, converting the college into what looked more like some Latin American university. The student cafeteria was made into a kind of *comedor*, and even the menu was modified to provide a range of Spanish and Latin American dishes. That was easy to do since so many of the kitchen staff were Latino, delighted with the chance to show off their native dishes, or as they put it, their mother's cooking. TVs in the common rooms were tuned to Spanish language stations. Friday nights became movie nights with

Spanish language films. I even found a Spanish language version of a play about Don Quixote which the advanced language students rehearsed all summer in preparation for a command performance at the end of the term.

The campus sports facilities were abuzz with activities where everyone was speaking Spanish. Not surprisingly, the soccer field became a focal point. The atmosphere at the games was quite bizarre, even hilarious at times because the teachers had to act as the referees. Needless to say, the refereeing they did was more language training on the run, so to speak, than anything to do with the rules of the game.

By the time the program was over, everyone including the president of the college was singing its praises.

The very next summer, the faculty voted to add French to the schedule. The focal point that year, not surprisingly, was once again the soccer field, but now the French were playing the Spanish to win the college cup, which quickly became known as the Grosvenor Goblet.

With these two summers behind me, I entered my fifth year as chair of the department. It had been a great ride. I didn't know who was more pleased, me or Sarah. Our relationship was thriving, each of us supporting the other's careers. Our friends considered ours the ideal marriage, and often told us so. The only thing lacking, they would inevitably add, was children.

Naturally, the subject had come up between us already several times, but we typically ended up deciding that our two careers would not provide a way to raise children properly. But time wasn't standing still, and we had to admit we weren't getting any younger. Sarah was at a critical stage in her life where this would soon become a now-or-never proposition. We knew we had a decision to make and the sooner the better.

My biggest challenge that fifth year was overseeing the department's participation in the college's fiftieth anniversary jubilee. The committee I had appointed did an excellent job making the department's reputation for first-rate foreign language instruction a focal point of the events. It was especially gratifying for me to hear the committee members praising Nicole for her leadership in producing the end result. They had not seen this side of her before, and it pleased me no end to think she might now get the tenure she deserved.

As part of the celebrations, the department committee insisted on including recognition of my having completed five years as chair. It was to take the form of a gala dinner in my honor at my favorite restaurant in town. Both Tom and Bill drove up for the occasion and spent an extra day at our place, reminiscing with Sarah and me about the past and toasting the future.

It wasn't long before the subject of having children came up there as well, and we had to admit we were seriously contemplating it. We had even discussed possible names for our child.

That prompted Sarah to raise a toast to "a future with little Isaac, Jr. running around the house."

"And if it's a girl?" Tom immediately asked.

"We've settled on Anna," I said, "so she can be called Anna Bell. We love the sound of it."

That brought a somewhat perplexed look from Bill. "Sounds a lot like Poe's Annabel Lee. You know, don't you, that his poem was about the death of a woman?"

"We thought about that," Sarah answered, "but it was also about a love so strong even death could not extinguish it. Our Anna Bell would symbolize that."

"Did I just hear a lawyer talking about symbols?" Tom joked. "I thought you lawyers were all about evidence and such."

"Ah," I intervened, "That's only Sarah's day job. You should have seen how transported she was when we toured the Père Lachaise cemetery in Paris, communing with the spirits."

"You guys can kid all you want," Sarah interrupted with a sly grin on her face, "but actually the jokes on you. I missed my period for the first time in my life this month, guys."

Once I regained my composure, all I could say was, "What? Why didn't you tell me?"

"I'm telling you now," she answered, assuming her best mock lawyerly manner. "But who knows, it might be a false alarm. I bought a pregnancy test kit yesterday to be sure, but haven't used it yet. I wanted you to be there when I do, Ike."

As soon as the festivities were over and Tom and Bill had left, Sarah and I went to the bathroom together for the revelation. That first test was inconclusive, but the next day we knew for sure that either Isaac Jr. or Anna Bell was on the way. Now it was time to make plans.

There was no way Sarah could take time off from her partnership in the firm, but I had a sabbatical coming after five years in the chairmanship. I could stay home for the next year and take care of the baby. I could essentially be on paternity leave and become, as I liked to put it, a diaper daddy. Needless to say, my doctor whole-heartedly approved of that solution.

There was just one further issue to resolve at the college, however. Who would assume the chairmanship for that year? That was where my relationship with the kindly John Darling once again came into play. Darling had been true to his word and had given me lots of good advice during those five years. And we had become close friends. Needless to say, he was well liked by just about everyone in the department, so when the time came, it seemed natural that he would be asked to become interim chairperson. Insisting as he had done many times before, that he didn't have a head for administration, he agreed to accept the job only on the condition I would be available to consult with at any time. I was more than happy to do so.

As my last duty before relinquishing the chairmanship, I presided over another successful summer program, with the Italians faced off against the Japanese this time for the coveted Grosvenor Goblet.

When the time was right, towards the end of Sarah's first trimester, we made an appointment with the ultrasound nurse. On the way back home after the session, we couldn't decide who was happier that the third person in the car with us was tiny Anna Bell.

Punctual as always, Sarah delivered Anna right on schedule. Then we began our new daily routine. Sarah prepared Anna's meals, as we jokingly referred to pumping extra milk before leaving for work. I did the feeding during the day. My favorite moments were when serving Anna her "brunch in a bottle", after which she would inevitably take a siesta and I would get back to my research and writing.

That year seemed to go by so fast, we hardly realized where the time went. For the most part, Sarah was able to maintain a nine-to-five schedule during the week and be home on weekends. She envied the time I got to spend with Anna, but said she was proud of how easily I adapted to fatherhood. I wondered at first why she said that, but on reflection I understood.

I guess it's true that you never know who you really are until you are faced with the need to find out.

In the meantime, Darling was doing a fine job as interim chair. He only had to consult with me a couple of times. The one time he did was when the annual performance evaluations were due and next year's salaries had to be determined.

There was no way he was going to step into the breach, he insisted, and leave me with his decisions on matters as delicate as that.

There was, however, one decision I could only make on my own: what to do about next summer's program. I would have been on leave for only nine months by then, rather than the full year my doctor had prescribed. If he had his way, I would relinquish the chairmanship as well, and go back to teaching classes like a normal professor.

In the end, I agreed to have another colleague run the summer program and promised Sarah and my doctor I would remain in the chairmanship only one more year.

CHAPTER 46

Towards the end of our first year with Anna, and my sabbatical over, we had to figure out how to resume two full-time jobs and still raise a one-year-old baby. That problem was solved by Sarah's mother complaining about not having been able to spend enough time with her granddaughter. Olivia arrived with enough luggage to stay a whole year. As soon as she got settled in, she began to run the house as if it were her own. I could have resented having my mother-in-law take over like that, but events quickly made me glad she was there.

Things began smoothly enough in my last year as chair, until the day my world once again turned upside down. Two months into the second semester, shortly before the Easter recess, the college's long-term and highly-esteemed president, the man who had presided over our wedding, suffered a stroke. It was so debilitating, it wasn't certain he would survive. Immediately, therefore, the administration sprang into action. The provost could have served as interim president for the rest of that year and the next while they searched for a new one, but he wanted to have a new president in place by the time the next academic year began.

That turned out to be a fateful decision. In their rush to appoint a new leader, the administration assembled a search committee right away. I was asked to be on it, but I declined, not wanting to add another responsibility so near the end of my last year as chair. And so the committee went forth without my voice, one they might well have wanted to hear.

The provost assumed the chairmanship of the committee, but refused to be considered for the job himself. Rather, he used his position to convince the members that what the college needed now, after two decades of the current administration, his administration, was an influx of new blood and new ideas. If I had been there, I might have tempered this push for change at all costs with a more balanced approach. I would have stressed the small-college values Grosvenor Grove had stood for during all those years, values I thought Macallan had lost when it became a full-fledged university.

In the end, change was indeed what we got, and just the kind I feared. The individual they selected, Jared Redding, was an entrepreneurial type in his mid-forties, with a degree in finance and a decidedly corporate frame of mind. He was the spitting image of the sort of administrators people call "the suits", only his was not just a coat and tie but a three-piece outfit every day and a pocket square to match. Right from the start he let it be known he intended to do what I feared most, take Grosvenor Grove to "greater heights", from a college to a university.

As soon as he took office, first thing in the next academic year when I was no longer chair, Redding appointed a team of "experts" to review every department in the college. They were instructed to identify programs that could be eliminated to make room for what he called "state-of-the-art investments in education."

What those state-of-the-art programs would be was not very well articulated, but which programs were to be eliminated definitely were. At the top of the list were so-called ancillary ones, like my summer language program. Our department itself came under particular scrutiny when the team of so-called experts declared, in uncompromising terms, that "anyone who wants to get somewhere in today's world either already speaks English or damn well better learn it."

No longer chair and powerless to stop it, my cherished summer program was replaced with, of all things, an intensive program for foreign students to learn English. Then, to add insult to injury, our departmental budget was cut almost in half, and my successor as chair, Kevin Smart, proved unable to do anything about that either.

Already regretting having relinquished the chairmanship at such a critical moment, I was now inclined to resign from the college entirely. I knew I could survive just fine without an institutional affiliation, having already proven that. In fact, that would probably have been the best thing I could have done as far as my doctor was concerned. But there were a few things that kept me from running away, made me feel I could still make a contribution. Or as Sarah put it, recalling the literature class she enjoyed so much in college, play Candide one more time. My doctor used a different literary analogy, asking "how many times are you going to tilt at windmills, dear Isaac, before your heart gives out?" I could just picture Tom nodding in agreement.

One of the things I had appreciated most about the faculty in my adopted college, that made it such a welcome place to work as opposed to the one at Macallan, was how well everyone seemed to get along. Even the hard decisions I had to make as chair were accepted with uncharacteristic grace by nearly all my colleagues. Now, however, the pressure being put on the department by the new administration changed all that. Everyone was at each other's throats, not knowing who among them would become the next victim of the draconian budget cuts being imposed. The frustration at our next faculty meeting was palpable.

"They can't do this," one of them exclaimed, displaying his ignorance of executive power. "It's not legal."

"I'm afraid it is," chairman Smart corrected him. "They can do pretty much what they want as long as they don't violate academic rules."

"So how are we going to meet their demands?" another asked.

"I'm not sure yet," Kevin answered, "At least the amount we have to come up with is less than the fifty percent we've been hearing about. By my calculation, it's more like thirty."

"That's still an impossible amount," yet another said. "What are we going to do? Cut positions or even eliminate whole languages?"

"Again, I'm not sure yet, but I've asked Ike to consult with me, to see what we can come up with. If any of you have specific suggestions, we'd very much like to hear them."

At that moment, John Darling spoke up. "Let me offer one right off the bat. Speaking only for myself, mind you, I think the decent thing someone like me could do, having served here for so long and being at retirement age anyway, is take that retirement now. I was planning on working another couple of years, but I'd be happy to bow out now if that would help."

"That is extremely gracious of you, John." Kevin responded. "Saving just two or three salaries through retirement would help a lot. But we'd miss you tremendously, John, you've been such a wonderful colleague."

Then, trying to lighten the mood a bit, he added, "You can be sure we'd hang a plaque honoring you in the most conspicuous place possible."

After some nervous laughter in the room, and having nothing more to add, Kevin adjourned the meeting, promising to schedule another one as soon as there was something more to report.

Kevin and I got together almost immediately afterwards, but not in his office. We agreed to meet at Kevin's home that very evening. His wife had an engagement elsewhere, so we had the place to ourselves. Kevin's home reminded me a lot of Tom's place. I'd been to his home before, most recently at the gathering he organized when he was first appointed chair. But not under circumstances like this. This time made me feel I was back in Oban, sitting with my friends in Tom's book-lined nook, figuring out how to deal with what life was throwing at me then. I was even inclined to ask Kevin if he had any Oban or Macallan Scotch to complete the picture.

It wasn't either Oban or Macallan that Kevin fetched, but it was Scotch, a Dalwhinnie fifteen-year-old, to be exact.

When we were seated, Kevin said, "I'm not sure there is anything to toast to just now, except Darling. That was really magnanimous of him today, wasn't it?"

"What an extraordinary man," I responded, almost getting emotional. "The best colleague anyone could hope for. This place will not be the same without him."

"Do you think the retirement idea will catch on?" Kevin asked. "No one else took him up on it at the meeting. Hopefully they're thinking about it, though. We have two colleagues older than John who might be willing."

"The way I figure it," I said, knowing the departmental budget inside out, "eliminating two senior positions this way and including only one or two more untenured ones would go a long way to solving the problem. What I wouldn't want to do, but am afraid we may have to, is stop offering some of the languages we're teaching now as well."

"That would be the most unpopular thing we could do, Ike, but it would certainly make Redding happy. He'd love to do away with as many foreign languages as he could. I'm sure that's why he targeted us so directly, to prove his point about English being the future of humanity, or whatever his cronies claim it is."

"You know, along those lines Kevin, I had an idea after I heard what he was going to do with my summer program. If he's turning it into an intensive English-for-foreign-students thing, that means he's planning on bringing in plenty of non-English-speaking students to the college. They'll need a way to support themselves during the academic year. We could offer them teaching assistantships, to keep our language classes going, and at a greatly reduced cost. Who knows, we might even be able to offer more languages than we do now that way. I remember my own graduate school training, when we had to learn some non-European language and used a foreign student when there was no one else to teach it. It was a lot of fun actually. We learned some of the most exotic languages that way."

"What a great idea, Ike, trading expensive professorships for assistantships."

"Don't you have a meeting with the president next week?" I asked. "You could present this to him then."

"I do, but you have to come along. You're a lot better than me at this sort of thing."

"I'd be happy to."

CHAPTER 47

The new president's office reminded me, rather chillingly, of Randolph's. Hardly a book in sight except some conspicuously displayed tomes about corporate success and the like. Plus several trophies and certificates on the walls. Even the furniture did not go with the style of the elegant older building it was in.

Redding noticeably did not come out from behind his desk to greet us. He stood as we entered and extended a hand across the desk. Then sat back down.

Great beginning, I thought. This can only go down-hill from here.

It didn't exactly go down-hill, but it did go sideways. In the most submissive tone he could muster, Kevin first described how we hoped to meet the budget reductions with retirements and untenured positions, trying to show the department's willingness to cooperate. Redding nodded his appreciation, but I could sense he was thinking we still didn't get the picture.

"If you think you can meet your new budget goals with that, then fine," Redding said. "But I doubt it. You'll need to do something different with the department."

"Well, we do have another proposal," I quickly chimed in, trying to keep the discussion going in our direction rather than Redding's.

"I'm all ears," Redding responded, somewhat haughtily.

Then I explained the assistantships-for-professorships idea. That got Redding's attention if not his enthusiasm.

"Interesting concept, gentlemen. Definitely something to think about. It would require my putting more money into a new program rather than eliminating older ones. But it's at least in line with the goals we've set forth for the college."

"I'm glad you see it that way," Kevin added somewhat meekly, which made me even more nervous. We've got to get on the offensive here, I thought, if we're going to turn this around.

Then I did something I hadn't told Kevin about yet, something that had been on my mind from the moment I heard about the new president's agenda.

"There is more we could do," I began, giving Kevin a look that said please don't kill me for this. "Something to promote the mission you've articulated in a more comprehensive manner. Since most business is global these days, we should develop a series of foreign-languages-for-business courses. Students would learn how to speak with business people in other countries, in their own languages. That would give Grosvenor graduates a leg up when applying for jobs with international firms, and almost everyone is international in one way or another now. Other universities offer such courses to complement their business school programs, as I'm sure you are aware. We could make our students competitive with theirs."

"I like the sound of that," Redding said. "I think I like it a lot. Look," he went on, "I don't want to be seen as some kind of corporate down-sizer. I just want this institution to realize its full potential, and what you propose now makes sense. Let me work on that with my staff, especially my English-only fanatics," he added with a smile, "and I'll get back with you."

"Talk about breaking the ice," Kevin said once we left Redding's office. "Nice master stroke, Ike."

"So, you're not upset at me for doing that?"

"Quite the contrary. I'm very grateful. You should never have given up the chairmanship. You know how to seize the moment in situations like that."

"I think I learned it from my lawyer wife!"

Back at the department the next week, Kevin held the faculty meeting he'd promised. He described what had taken place in the president's office and said he was waiting for a more formal response. In the meantime, he reported, one more senior colleague had come forth with his decision to retire at the end of the current academic year. That brought to two the number of full-time, tenured positions the department would not need to fill next year.

Then, concerned that the burden of any further cuts might have to be borne by the junior faculty, he turned to them.

"Let's all take a deep breath here, folks, and look at the bright side. There is something in this plan that can give our untenured colleagues some security. If Redding provides funds to offer a series of foreign languages-for-business courses, which he seemed to think was a good idea, I promise to protect the positions of any untenured member who takes on some of that responsibility."

There was an almost audible sigh of relief in the room after that, but I still felt obliged to advise caution.

"Although our meeting with the president ended on a positive note, there is still no telling what he will ultimately do. Remember, while the business language proposal promotes his larger agenda, it doesn't respond to the English-only partisans in his administration. Redding would have to convince his more radical supporters to see the larger picture. We're in for a rough ride for a while, but with good will, and if we keep our heads, we'll survive with the department intact."

The ride did indeed get rougher some weeks later, and in a surprisingly new way. The president announced he wanted Grosvenor Grove to become one of the nation's most advanced academic institutions by, of all things, doing away with tenure.

And with that one stroke, the senior faculty felt just as vulnerable as the junior ones.

Needless to say, the mood, not only in our department but in the college as a whole, took a nose dive. At first, most of the senior faculty brushed it off, declaring that tenure meant they had written contracts for life and couldn't be touched. Until, that is, the better-informed ones reminded them that tenured positions can be eliminated under certain circumstances, chief among them being budgetary necessity, precisely the tool the new president was already wielding quite effectively.

Those more informed colleagues also knew, however, that doing away with tenure entirely was not something that could simply be decreed. The president would have to gain the approval of the faculty to make such a radical change in the college's constitution and by-laws.

Which is just what Redding set out to do.

A few weeks later, Redding invited me to come back and see him in his office. This time, he came out from behind his desk not just to greet me but to sit with me on the big modern sofa he had made a centerpiece of his office decor.

"Can I get you a cup of coffee?" He began.

"No thank you, I'm fine," I responded, already thinking it might have been better to say yes.

"Well then, let me get right to it. I have asked you to come for two reasons, Ike. It is Ike, no?"

"Yes, of course."

"First off, I wanted to let you know what my secretary has just told your chairman that we are approving both your professorships-for-assistantships idea, as you call it, and your business language program. The money that I will put back in the department to fund these initiatives, together with the senior retirements, should solve your budgetary problem and enhance my own agenda as well. That's just the kind of spirit I've been looking for from the faculty."

"Well, I'm sure I can speak for the entire department in saying how much we appreciate that, sir."

"It's Jared, please."

Then, feeling emboldened by the sense of comradery I began to feel in the room, I ventured to add, "But now you are going to tell me the second reason you asked to see me, and I think I can guess what it is."

"I'm sure you can. It's the elephant that is going to be in every room around here for some time to come. As you know, I believe the concept of tenure is not only outdated, it is responsible for much of the stagnation, I would go so far as to say fossilization, in academic institutions in this country. In far too many instances, the granting of tenure removes much of the incentive to keep producing new ideas. Stop me, Ike, if you think I'm going too far."

"No, I'm with you so far."

"OK then. What disturbs me most is how many promising young scholars have their career ambitions destroyed by being denied tenure. And by whom, the tenured ones who cannot accept having their preferred views of the world challenged. From what I've been told, you have had personal experience in this regard."

"I have indeed. But it never stopped me."

"Exactly. That's the point I want to get to. Now I may not have a background in academia myself, but I have studied this issue carefully. Apparently, a primary motive for the institution of tenure in the first place was to protect academic freedom, to ensure that unpopular ideas would be allowed to flourish without fear of losing one's job. Ironically, however, the very process we use to grant tenure has had precisely the effect tenure was supposed to shield us from.

It nips unpopular ideas in the bud before they even get their feet on the ground."

Ignoring the horribly mixed metaphor, I responded somewhat hesitantly, "I would have to agree with you there too, of course, but I'm not sure doing away with the institution entirely is the answer either."

"Well as much as I would like to, I'm well aware I can't just decree it away. I need to find a way to achieve what I'm after without blowing the place up, as it were. That's why I have asked to see you. I want to appoint a committee to advise me on how to get past this. And I want you to chair it. I know what happened to you at Macallan and how you overcame that. I also know what you did for that young female colleague in your department, I think her name is Nicole something. You are the type of person who can appreciate both sides of the issue and help lead the committee to a solution that would be acceptable to both me and the faculty."

"That's an extremely tall order, Jared. But I'm not sure I can put myself through yet another struggle with the problems academia has inflicted upon itself. I am certain my doctor, and my wife too, would tell me not to, and I have finally begun to take them seriously. That's why I bowed out of the chairmanship when I did. That's also why I wasn't nearly as upset as I might otherwise have been when you took away my summer program," I added with a big grin.

We both had a good laugh at that. Then Redding got serious again.

"I wasn't aware of your health issues, Ike, but I really need someone like you with me here. I want this college to realize its full potential, and I can't do it alone. I certainly hope you will consider this."

In the end, all I could think to say was, "I'll need some time to think about this."

"That's all I can ask," he answered. "Let me know if there is anything I can do to make this easier for you, but please don't take too long to decide."

There was indeed a lot for me to think about over the next few days.

There was the advice I'd given Nicole Watson that saved her career on the one hand, and the advice I wished I'd given my good friend Phillip Cranston that might have saved his life on the other. There was loyalty to the institution that had adopted me versus the pleas of Sarah and my doctor to consider my health first. Now, with this new turn of events, I also felt conflicted about whether or not to accept a position that would give me the opportunity to do something about the one issue that has haunted me throughout my career. This was not going to be easy.

CHAPTER 48

I didn't go back to my office that afternoon. I left my once-idyllic Grove and went straight to our apartment in town. I was anxious for Sarah to get home too so I could talk things through with her. But I needed to do something else first.

As soon as I walked in the door, I asked Olivia if little Anna was awake. Getting a positive answer, I ran upstairs to her room. Sitting there cuddling her provided the comfort I needed to give me time to think.

I had no idea when I finally heard Sarah come home that the situation was about to get even more complicated than it already was. She seemed as anxious to talk with me as I was with her. When we sat down, we both started talking at the same time.

"Seems like we each have something to report," she said, "so why don't you go first."

"Well, you already know about Redding's latest bombshell with the tenure thing, but you'll never guess what he's up to now."

"I can't even imagine."

"He called me into his office again today, and told me he was approving both of our proposals for solving the budget crisis in the department."

"That's great news, Ike. So why do you seem upset?"

"That wasn't the only reason he asked to see me. He had something else in mind. He began by telling me how pleased he was with how we were responding to his agenda."

"He should be. The way you presented the department's case, you all but dared him to say no. Just don't tell me you two had a meeting of the minds and now you are all buddy-

buddy, Ike. He's a slick operator, and he knows how to co-opt people."

"Well, I'm not co-opted quite yet, but he did put me in a very difficult position."

"Let me guess. He tried to rope you into that tenure business. You know that's the last thing you need to get involved with now, Ike."

"Well, he said he's setting up a committee to work with him on that."

"And he wants you on it, I suppose."

"Worse, he wants me to *chair* it. Says I'm the perfect person because of my past experience having been on both sides of the issue, as he put it. Proves I've got an open mind, he said."

"Well, Ike, now we're about to see how open a mind you do have. Do you want to hear *my* news of the day?"

"Of course. But let's have a drink first. I have a feeling we both may need it."

"Good idea."

I poured two doubles without looking to see which Scotch I grabbed, and took a big swig of mine before sitting back down.

"Guess who visited our office today," Sarah began.

"Don't want to even try."

"None other than a delegation of senior professors from the college. They want our firm to represent them in the event Redding tries to abolish tenure."

"You've got to be kidding me. That would create an obvious conflict of interest if I were to chair the committee charged with resolving the issue. Just knowing your firm had been retained would completely compromise me and any decision the committee might take. How serious are they about this? How much does your firm need this case? Can't they pass it off to another one?"

"Sounds like you really want this responsibility, Ike. Do you? I thought you agreed to disengage from these sorts of things, not get more involved."

"As I see it, even if I said no to chairing the committee, I don't know how I could say no just to being on it. I succeeded in putting the department in Redding's good graces, and he responded in kind. How can I turn him down now."

"My God, Ike, stepping down from one chairmanship and walking right into another is like getting out of the frying pan into the fire. And this one's bound to be a lot hotter. You can bet on that."

"I know, Sarah, but what choice do I have?"

"I could advise my firm to accept the professors' retainer, and the conflict of interest would give you all the cover you needed to tell Redding no."

"But you wouldn't force my hand like that, would you?"

"To save you from damaging your health even further, I might well do that, yes. Anna and I need you far more than either Redding or the department."

"Am I therefore to sit on the sidelines while the institution I love makes one of the most momentous decisions in its history?" I declared in frustration.

"I think we need a time out for a few days to sort things through, Ike. How about this: I promise not to let my firm commit to anything in the meantime if you will not commit to Redding before we come to a decision on this together."

"Good idea."

Then, after a moment's pause, I said, "You know what we should do? Use the time to go to Oban. We could enjoy one of Tom's parties and see what he and Bill have to say about all this afterwards. They're the best counsel I've ever had. Can you get away for the weekend? I'm sure your mom can take care of Anna."

"Sounds like a plan."

"Then I'll get in touch with Tom."

The party at Tom's place was such a welcome relief, I didn't want it to end. Jeremy was there with his new wife, and everyone got along famously. But we had things to discuss the next day, so we didn't stay up until all hours of the morning the way we used to. I had warned Tom it had to be "pleasure before business" this time, not the other way around, so everyone was well rested and ready to get serious once the sun came up.

Tom prepared a hearty breakfast with lots of strong coffee to make sure everyone was functioning at a hundred percent. Then we adjourned to the same book-shelved alcove as we had so often before. It felt like old times again, except this time we had only more coffee to drink.

Tom suggested Sarah lay the groundwork for the day's discussion. "We need her lawyerly levelheadedness, not Ike's passionate portrayal," he joked.

I could only smile at my best friend's accurate depiction of the person whose future was once again on the line.

Sarah did indeed present things dispassionately, laying out all the pros and cons without prejudicing the issue with her personal concerns. When she finished, Tom succinctly summed up the situation.

"This Redding fellow is definitely a force to be reckoned with, but I have to say Ike is also the best person the college could have on an issue like this."

"As I understand it," Bill began in his customary shrewd manner, "this committee is being formed for one purpose and one purpose only, to get the president what he wants. The trick will be to give it to him in a way that will still be acceptable to the faculty, that won't upset their delicate sense of dignity."

"We know one thing for sure," Tom offered. "Anyone who already has tenure must be allowed to keep it. Unless Redding is willing to face a slew of lawsuits, which I doubt even he would want. He can use mechanisms like budgetary reductions to thin the ranks, but not much more."

"Keeping tenure for those who already have it would mollify a significant portion of the faculty," I noted with some relief. "Calm them down if not take them out of the picture entirely. Then we'd have to find some way to make the absence of tenure palatable to the rest of the college community."

"Don't forget all those who are in tenure-track positions now but don't already have it," Bill reminded us. "They, too, have contracts that promise them a decision. I can't imagine Redding telling them they'll all be denied tenure when their time comes."

"Adding them as well would account for nearly all the faculty positions in the college," I observed, feeling even better. "That would leave only the part-time ones and those on soft-money contracts, the ones who don't have access to tenure now anyway."

"I think that's just the point, guys," Bill said. "With all the tenured and tenurable ones out of the way, as it were, Redding will be able to establish a new system for all subsequent hires. I'll bet you anything he's looking at the long term, when one day down the road, long after he's gone probably, there won't be any tenured faculty left. He'll have left his legacy."

"So you think the committee's primary mission will be to create the new system, then?" I asked. "Not to alter the status quo for those who already have contracts?"

"Precisely."

"And your responsibility, Ike," Tom added, "would not be nearly as onerous. In fact, it might be quite rewarding to have the opportunity to put the Grove, as you call it, on the map as a pioneer in higher education."

"If I were you," Bill said, "I would bone up on what some of the younger, more progressive institutions in the country have already done in this regard, by not offering tenure in the first place. I've read about some of the issues they have had to deal with, especially faculty hiring and retention if you don't promise security of employment at some point in their careers."

"I've heard about that too, but I've never studied it," I responded. "So let me ask you, would you have opted for a career in academia if you had not been promised the possibility of tenure?"

"Hell yes," Tom answered for both himself and Bill. "We get performance reviews every year and salary raises accordingly, as long as there's money in the budget. Plus we've both been promoted to full professor based on our continued productivity since getting tenure. So the tenure system doesn't matter to people like us one way or the other. It only protects the unproductive ones and keeps the promising new ones from getting into the system in the first place. Do away with tenure and everyone's on an even playing field from the git-go."

Sarah had been quiet throughout all of this, but she had been listening carefully and taking it all in.

"Sounds to me like it's Redding three and Sarah zero, guys!" She said, only half-jokingly. "But I understand. When you describe it this way, the job doesn't seem quite as demanding for Ike as I thought. I'm sure you'd enjoy the creative part, Ike, and you'll be good at keeping everyone focused."

I was tempted to ask if that meant she would now tell her law firm to stay out of this, but decided to save that for when we were back home alone. I'd heard what I needed to, and was now more than ready to trade the coffee for some Scotch.

CHAPTER 49

Once back in Syracuse, I got the promise I needed from Sarah and made an appointment to see Redding. He did come out from behind his desk again, but we sat in separate chairs this time. I got right to the point. I described how I perceived the committee's mission, hoping my little Oban council had gauged the president's intentions correctly. He kept a poker face throughout, listening intently. There was a long moment of silence once I finished, which Redding finally broke.

"I thought you would see the situation this way, Ike. And I dare say you're probably right. I am well aware that I cannot eliminate tenure for those who already have contracts."

"Not unless you want to risk a torrent of lawsuits which, by the way, are already being talked about."

"So I've heard. But there should still be things we can do to speed up the process. The budget cuts I've already instituted have encouraged some of the oldest faculty to voluntarily retire, as you know. Still, I'd like the committee to consider ways to encourage more faculty to do the same. Things like additional monetary incentives beyond the standard retirement benefits the college already provides as a kind of severance package."

"We can certainly consider that, but to be fair, we'd have to extend the same benefits to those who have already been kind enough to volunteer."

"Yes, I suppose so."

"Just to be clear, then, you agree that the primary charge to the committee will be to propose a new system for hiring and retention of faculty in the future, on the understanding that all existing contracts will be honored."

"That would be the primary charge, yes. But I want the committee to consider other things as well. Not only additional incentives for tenured faculty to retire, but a new system for granting tenure to those on the tenure track who don't yet have it. As far as I'm concerned, the current system is unacceptable. It is far too subjective, especially in a small college like this. It borders on being incestuous, and I don't want that to be continued here while I'm president."

Having spent hours thinking about Nicole's situation as well as my own at Macallan, and remembering the discussion Claudia and I had about all this in Siena, I went a step farther.

"I not only agree, Jared," I said, "there is a specific proposal I can make to the committee to achieve just that. One similar to the system in European universities, which use independent boards of scholars to evaluate an individual's worthiness for tenure rather than one's immediate colleagues. It would need to be modified to work in an American context, of course, but that shouldn't be difficult to do."

"Splendid idea. I knew I picked the right person for this job, Ike. You're on board then, right?"

"Yes, I guess I am."

"Well then, welcome to my team!"

If I thought I had relieved much of the stress of my new assignment when the president agreed to my view of the committee's charge, there was still something I hadn't considered. Sarah of course had, and she brought it up almost as soon as I arrived back at the apartment that evening. I was hoping to have some sort of mini-celebration and had even bought some steaks on the way home, to make my favorite steak-frites, but she brought me up short.

"I'm happy for you, Ike," she said, "but I'm still worried about the situation you're putting yourself in. You may have found a way to avoid lawsuits by the faculty, but not their disapproval for your having sided with the president on something as vital to their interests as this. You may no longer be the colleague the faculty thought so much of. You could even become a pariah, a traitor to the establishment. And that's not something you need right now."

"Well," I said, getting angry, "if that's what happens, so be it. I'll be only too happy to challenge the establishment on this issue, at least at this one small academic institution. It'll be my swan song, one way or another."

"Please don't talk like that, Ike. You scare me. I want you around for a long time to come. And Lord knows, Anna needs you even more."

"Speaking of whom, let's ask your mom to bring her downstairs so we can start this nice dinner."

Once downstairs, Anna came running over to me, a bit too fast for her novice legs to handle. I caught her just in time to save another face-plant. Thank God they don't have far to fall, I thought as I smothered her with kisses.

Just as Sarah had predicted, things got difficult for me the moment Redding announced the formation of his new committee. Colleagues in my own department started avoiding me, lest they say something they might regret. To make matters worse, they began calling it the Bell committee. In a few weeks' time, it seemed like my only real friend left was my successor as chair, Kevin Smart.

"I don't know why you agreed to do this," Kevin said to me one day when things got really unpleasant, "but I respect you for it. You are just about the only person who could manage a situation like this and keep everything from blowing up in our faces."

"Thank you for saying that, Kevin. It means a lot to me," I responded,

"So how's the work going so far?" Kevin asked.

"Quite well, actually," I answered. "I have to admit that Redding is a very good judge of character. He chose a solid group of people to tackle this. Ironically, it is less stressful to deal with the committee than with my own colleagues now. It was very smart of him to announce the day he appointed the committee that existing contracts would be honored, to take that off the table right away. I think it calmed a lot of the anger that would otherwise be boiling over by now. I guess I should be thankful it's only at a simmer."

"Well, my friend, I wish you nothing but the best. I know you'll do the college proud. Let me know what I can do to help."

"Well," I answered with a smile, "you can start by telling my dear colleagues in the department that I love them all and hope they still love me too!"

The committee did indeed do good work. They divided up their responsibilities into the two remaining areas of concern, now that they didn't have to deal with the contract issue. Half of the committee researched those institutions that currently do not offer tenure, to learn about best practices. The other half concentrated on devising a new system for making tenure decisions for those who were still on the track.

In the end, what they came up with was this: The tenure decisions that were still on the books, so to speak, would henceforth be made by an all-college committee consisting of only one member from the candidate's own department, plus two members from other departments in the college, and one outside scholar from another, comparable institution. In the unlikely event of a tie, the college dean would make the final decision.

On the other front, all subsequent faculty hires would be given a six-year renewable contract, just as junior faculty ordinarily receive when they are initially hired. But it would no longer lead to the possibility of tenure. When the time came for renewal, they would either be offered another six-year renewable contract or let go. In due time, therefore, the entire college would be operating with six-year renewable contracts.

This new system, I started telling my colleagues, would be much like the U.S. Senate, with six-year renewable contracts rather than life-long tenure, as on the Supreme Court. And the effect, I liked to add, would be much the same. No longer would life-long members be able to use their personal prejudices to decide issues, like justices on the Supreme Court. Everyone would have to submit themselves to the judgment of their peers every six years, just like a U.S. Senator.

Then, as an addendum to the new hiring system, the committee also decided that anyone hired by the college who already had tenure elsewhere would have to accept the same six-year renewable contract, effectively relinquishing their tenure. That caused some members to worry that such a move might keep the college from attracting established scholars, but most thought that any truly productive scholar would have no problem with it. They might well prefer to work in such a refreshing and invigorating intellectual environment.

In an unexpected last-minute move, one committee member suggested that once a faculty member received three renewable contracts, he or she should be offered tenure rather than a fourth since, his theory went, they had already proven themselves. But that idea was laughed away by the others, insisting that anyone who still needed that kind of security ought to be put out to pasture anyway.

In the end, the college Senate voted favorably on the committee's work, and the constitution and by-laws of the college were amended accordingly. It was a good thing the decision was made by the Senate and not by a vote of the entire faculty. Given the atmosphere in the college at the time, the outcome might well have been different.

CHAPTER 50

For me, working with the committee proved to be one of the most enjoyable and rewarding experiences I'd had in academia. Living with my other colleagues, however, was quite a different story. It took a considerable toll on me in the ensuing year or so, both emotionally and physically. Sarah noticed how I seemed to get tired more easily during that time, and she insisted I see my doctor again for a checkup.

The doctor wanted me to get some more tests, to be sure my heart condition was only stress related and not something more serious.

Two weeks later when I got the results, they were not encouraging. They showed I had some sort of undiagnosed congenital condition which had been exacerbated by the stress I'd been under all these years. The doctor recommended I have an operation to get a better handle on the situation.

"You have to do what the doctor recommends," Sarah insisted.

"But the pressure is off me now," I countered, "so things should get better on their own, don't you think?"

"No, I don't think. You're being just like all the men I've known, forever putting off getting medical attention, even for the most obvious problems."

"Gee," I said facetiously, "how many men have you known, Sarah, to have formed such a firm opinion?"

"Very funny. Promise me you'll do as he says, Ike."

"Okay, okay. Just let me enjoy a few more weeks of peace and quiet here with you and Anna first."

"And mom."

"And mom."

Those few weeks passed too quickly as far as I was concerned. We scheduled the operation for the first available time, which I assumed would still give me several more weeks. Surprisingly, we got a slot the very next week. The operation itself was a success to the extent it confirmed the diagnosis, but worrisome because it showed my condition had deteriorated further. They could alter my medications to keep the problem at bay, the doctors said, but taking early retirement would be the best medicine if I wanted to prolong my life.

In any other situation, I would never have dreamed of taking retirement early. But the idea seemed almost appealing to me now, if only because I would not have to endure the reproachful stares of my colleagues at work. Few of them ever said anything to me directly, but conversations in the halls would cease when I walked by. Kevin tried to help me out by having departmental meetings focus strictly on departmental issues when I was in attendance, so the subject of my "betrayal" would not come up. Still, I was not the type of person who shied away from things like this.

"I appreciate the gesture," I told Kevin, "but you don't have to do that. I have challenged entrenched systems all my life, and this time is no exception. I'll manage."

Sarah did her best to get me to see things differently, of course.

"Look at all you've accomplished," she said, knowing how I hated to toot my own horn. "You've published an acclaimed textbook, created model intensive language programs both here and abroad, turned a prison system into a learning facility, and now successfully challenged the devil at the heart of academe. You should be very proud."

"I am, Sarah, believe me," I responded. "It's just that I hate to be perceived as slinking away in the face of disapproval from my colleagues. It seems so cowardly."

"Nonsense. They're not so much angry with you as they are upset at the very idea of change, especially change of this magnitude. They'll get over it, Ike. You need to think of yourself and not what other people think of you," she said.

In the end, Sarah prevailed. It was none other than Redding himself who hosted my retirement party once I recuperated from the operation. It was not a gala affair, given the mood around the college at the time. The best word to describe it, I thought, was respectful. There were expressions of gratitude for all I had done for the college, and sympathy for the health condition that was taking me away at such a critical juncture in the college's future.

The president praised me for helping guide the college toward that future. My departmental colleagues recalled the years they had enjoyed under my leadership. The former provost, speaking for the late president, told of the pride he had taken in marrying Sarah and me. Sarah recounted how happy Anna was at the thought of having her father to herself now. The party ended with toasts to my health.

The generous retirement package I received, replete with full health benefits, plus the royalties I was getting from my textbook, now in its third edition, dispelled any qualms I might have had about living off of Sarah's income. I had to admit how much I enjoyed being at home with little Anna, watching her grow. She was getting bigger every day, remaining upright most of the time now as she ran around the house. I spent my days alternating between playing with her, researching an article or two, and cooking gourmet meals.

For some reason, I couldn't explain why, I got on a pasta carbonara kick early on. I made a different version of the dish every week for more than a month. I alternated between using spaghetti at first, then fettuccini, and finally bucatini, trying to determine which one allowed the rich egg sauce to cling to it best. I finally settled on the bucatini with the hollow center that allowed the sauce to coat it inside as well as out. I would alternate between adding bacon one day, grilled chicken another, mushrooms the third, and so on until Sarah finally exclaimed, in her best courtroom tone of voice, "basta with the pasta, Ike!"

So then it was out to the back patio preparing barbeque recipes every evening. I loved cooking on the grill because of that gas line Sarah had installed so I never had to mess with charcoal or butane tanks. As long as it wasn't raining or snowing, Sarah would come home and find me out there, even wearing a winter coat if need be.

I would get on binges like this for some time until we both agreed it was once again time to try something different. After a while, her new phrase became "basta the lasta one, for God's sake. It's like watching reruns of Law and Order with you." I knew she was afraid I was bored. Never a good sign for a retiree.

She needn't have worried, though, because as time went by and little Anna became not-so-little Anna, I got myself a novice *sous-chef* that changed everything. Now, instead of playing the same games with her every day on the floor, I would prop her up on a stool in the kitchen and teach her all manner of new skills. Believe it or not, I eventually even got so far as training her on the proper use of knives. After all, I thought, what good is a *sous-chef* if she doesn't know the proper way to chop vegetables!

Surprisingly, she only nicked her finger once. It was not easy for her at first, when her fingers were still small, to curl them under the way you're supposed to, to keep them safe. I taught her the proper way to push the vegetable toward the knife and not the knife toward the fingers. She turned out to be an amazingly quick learner whose digital dexterity increased with the size of her fingers.

From that moment on, there were no more binges. There was something new to teach Anna every day. And it wasn't long before she was telling me when I made mistakes.

CHAPTER 51

In the meantime, Sarah's professional life was anything but boring as well. Her latest responsibility hit very close to home. The firm, with her name on the masthead now, was retained to defend a student at the college who was accused by another student of rape. Redding tried to handle the case internally, with the college's own legal team, but even their best efforts at proving all procedures had been followed correctly proved insufficient to satisfy the alleged victim. Her parents filed suit in state court, naming the boy and several college administrators as well, including Redding himself. The boy's parents then asked the firm of Smith, Jessup and Blake to take their case. The firm agreed, and in a smart strategic move, selected their one female partner to be lead attorney.

Since I was now retired, there was no conflict of interest this time. But I did learn a lot about the case from Kevin. It turned out that George Thomas had been taking courses in our department, so they knew him well. He was a mild-mannered and serious student, the last person they thought could do a thing like this. They were somewhat surprised he would have dated Nancy Parsons in the first place, since she was much more outgoing, and popular with the guys.

Being retired, I took the opportunity to attend the trial. I was anxious to see how Sarah would handle such a delicate situation.

When the trial began, the plaintiff's attorney put each of the college administrators on the stand, grilling them one by one, trying to get them to admit that the college's procedures for due process had not been followed correctly. He got little satisfaction from any of them, especially Redding, whose fine-tuned corporate sense allowed him to paint the college's performance as thorough to a fault. Then, with her subsequent cross-examinations Sarah was able to put an even finer point on it, exonerating the college completely of any wrong-doing. That left only the plaintiff herself and the defendant as witnesses to their own private encounter.

The plaintiff's attorney then put Nancy on the stand. Sarah knew she would have been coached on what to say and how to say it, just as she had done with George, and I could see her keeping careful notes as Nancy told her story.

"Please explain to the jury and this court, Nancy," her attorney began, "how you first met Mr. Thomas."

"OK. I was at a party with some friends when he approached me and we started talking. He seemed like a nice guy. At least other people said he was."

"Had you ever met him before?"

"Not that I recall. But I knew who he was from what I'd heard."

"Were you two alone, or were there others with you during this first meeting?"

"We were alone most of the time, but different people came and went."

"What did you talk about?"

"He said he was really into foreign languages and was planning to travel and see the world as soon as he graduated."

"And you, what did you say?"

"I don't really remember. I just listened mostly."

"How long did the conversation last?"

"I don't know, quite a while I think."

"And you kept quiet all this time?"

"Well, he was quite a talker, and had a lot to say."

"I see. So how did the conversation end?"

"He asked if I wanted to see some of the material he'd collected for his coming travels. And the itinerary he was planning."

"So you went to his place to see them?"

"Objection, Your Honor," Sarah interrupted. "Leading the witness."

"Sustained. Rephrase, counselor."

"Sorry, Your Honor. Did Mr. Thomas invite you to his place?"

"To see his stuff, yes."

"How did you get there?"

"In his car."

"And once you were there, what happened."

"He started showing me things. He had a whole library of stuff. Said he could teach a geography class with what he'd collected."

"And then?"

"After a while he made a pass at me."

"And how did you respond?"

"Well, again, I thought he was a nice guy, so I let him kiss me."

"And then what happened?"

"He started, you know, feeling me up."

"And then?"

"Well, one thing led to another, and before I could say anything, he was undressing me."

"Did you want him to stop?"

"Yes."

"What did you say to him?"

"I don't remember exactly."

"Try to remember. Did you say 'stop'?"

"Objection," Your Honor, Sarah shouted. "Counsel is deliberately leading the witness again."

"Sustained. Let her speak for herself, counselor?"

"Yes, Your Honor. So, Nancy, how did you tell him to stop?"

"I don't remember. I was really upset. Something like 'please' or 'no'. I don't know, but I meant for him to stop."

"And did he then have sex with you anyway?"

"Yes, he did."

"Did you try to get away?"

"I couldn't. He was on top of me."

"Did he penetrate you?"

"Yes."

After a long pause, her lawyer said, "Please tell us what happened afterwards."

"I just left his apartment and went home."

"Thank you, Nancy. That will be all."

It was good to have Sarah leading the defense team so there would be a woman cross-examining Nancy, not a man. It was also not lost on anyone that the judge chosen for the case was also a woman. Still, Sarah would have to ask some pretty tough questions in order to get at the truth. She began by showing sympathy for Nancy's situation, asking questions regarding her well-being since the incident.

"I understand this is difficult for you, Nancy. But I have to ask, did you see a doctor afterwards?"

"No, but I did buy a pregnancy test just to be sure."

"Did you tell anyone what happened afterwards, confide in anyone?"

"Yes, of course, that's why I'm here."

"I meant immediately afterwards, Nancy. You must have been distraught."

"I was too confused right after it happened. So no."

"Have you sought any counseling for mental distress since then?"

"No, I think I'm alright. I'm just angry."

"OK, then. Tell the court please, how old you are."

"I'm seventeen."

"Were you seventeen when this happened?"

"Yes."

"Then may I presume you knew you were at the age of consent in New York State at the time?"

"Yes, I knew that. Everybody knows that sort of thing."

"So if you were like everybody else, had you taken advantage of that before this incident?"

"I don't know what you mean."

"Would you say you have been sexually active, Nancy?"

I was surprised her lawyer hadn't objected to that last line of questioning before, but now he did.

"Objection," he yelled, jumping up. "My client's sexual behavior, past or present, has no relevance whatsoever here."

"I beg to differ, Your Honor," Sarah cut in before the judge had a chance to rule. "Since we have established that there was no statutory rape in this instance, the question goes to the very issue of character, which is central to the defense."

"Objection overruled," the judge said rather slowly and pensively. "You may answer, Nancy."

"I don't know what she means by active, judge. I don't sleep around, if that's what she's implying."

"Not at all," Sarah took over. "I don't mean to intrude, Nancy. I simply want to establish that you've had sex with boys before, that's all."

"Yes, I have, not that it's any of your business."

"Thank you. Let's move on. At the party that night, do you remember who approached whom? Did you approach George or did he approach you."

"I don't really remember. We just sort of met."

"You said you did not remember whether or not you had met him before that night. Is that so?"

"As far as I recall, yes."

"I see. You also said he did most of the talking when you met. Can you tell us what you said during that conversation?"

"Again, all I remember is that he was a big talker and I was happy to listen."

"There seems to be a lot you don't remember, Nancy. May I ask if you'd been drinking before the two of you met that night?"

That brought Nancy's lawyer to his feet again. "I object, Your Honor, to the insinuation counsel is making with this question."

"I'm going to allow it," the judge declared. "I would like to know as well."

"It was a party. Everyone was drinking."

"OK, so tell me, can you remember how many drinks you may already have consumed by the time the conversation started?"

"I really don't know. I wasn't counting. Like I said, we were having a party."

"Got it. So did George suggest you go to his place that night, or did he just say he'd love to show you his stuff some time?"

"What difference does it make? We just ended up at his place. Why do you keep asking me these questions?"

"Because I'm trying to get at the truth, Nancy. Trying to jog your memory."

"Whatever."

"So when you got to his place, did you have anything more to drink?"

"What does that matter? We had some wine, so what?"

"That would have been on top of what you'd been drinking before, from what you've told us, no?"

"Well, now that I think of it, I guess he did ask me if I wanted something. I thought he was just being a polite host, so I said sure."

"Did you still think he was acting as a polite host when he, as you said in your previous testimony, made a pass at you?"

"Well, it wouldn't be the first time someone's made a pass at me."

"So you were OK with that?"

"Up to that point, sure."

"And then when he started feeling you up, as you also stated, were you OK with that?"

"That was just necking. What's wrong with that? The point is he ended up raping me."

"That's what we're still trying to determine, Nancy. So let me ask you how you felt when he started undressing you. Was that still OK with you?"

"You don't understand anything," Nancy yelled. "All he did at first was take off my bra. Where I come from, that's still necking, in case you don't know."

"Oh, I know very well, Nancy. I've been there before myself."

The hushed snickers in the room almost brought the judge's gavel down, but she held back. Then Sarah continued.

"I'm trying to establish when exactly it was that you stopped cooperating that night, Nancy. From your previous testimony, it seems you don't even remember what you may have said to him, let alone what you did or didn't do to stop him. These are important facts, Nancy, so please try to be more specific."

When Nancy didn't answer after several minutes of silence, Sarah continued. "Could it be that you really don't remember, Nancy, what actually happened that night? Could it be you had so much to drink it was all a blur?"

Still no answer.

"Look, Nancy, I can put George on the stand and he will tell us how much he liked you and how disappointed he is that you saw things differently. Do you remember that the two of you talked about maybe going together on the trip he was planning after graduation?"

I noticed that Nancy's facial expression betrayed some recollection at that point, but still no verbal answer.

"Do you remember how you got back home that night, Nancy? George has told us that he ordered an Uber for you, and even called you later to make sure you got home safely. Could it possibly be that the two of you had consensual sex that night and you have felt guilty about it since then? I felt that way once myself too, Nancy, but I took full responsibility for my own actions at the time. And I have been glad I did ever since."

At this point, Nancy broke down in sobs, unable to say anything.

"That's alright, Nancy. I have no more questions."

Sarah then held Nancy's hand as she stepped down from the witness stand, hugged her close to comfort her and whispered something in her ear. She never told me what it was, but I could guess.

Once Nancy was seated again at the plaintiff's table, the judge asked her attorney if he had any other witnesses.

"No, Your Honor. The prosecution rests."

Then the judge turned to Sarah and asked, "Is the defense ready to call its first witness?"

"The defense also rests, Your Honor," was all she said.

The next day the *Syracuse Post-Standard* printed a short article below the fold on the front page.

Dateline June 10.

The trial in the George Thomas rape case ended rather unexpectedly yesterday without the accused taking the stand. In an abrupt move, the lawyer for plaintiff Nancy Parsons dropped all charges and the judge dismissed the case. After intense cross-examination by defense attorney Sarah Blake, the plaintiff broke down and admitted the encounter could have been consensual.

That might have been the end of the matter had the report of the trial not stirred up a torrent of commentary on the opinion pages of the paper. Not surprisingly, few if any of those venting their feelings had actually been in attendance at the trial. While some praised the justice system for getting at the truth, a lot of rancor was directed at Sarah. She was accused of "bullying the victim into submission." This in turn created a frenzy of even more uninformed commentary on social media masquerading as fact. And it continued for a long time, long enough to make Sarah's life miserable. There were even cartoons of her standing over the victim with snarling teeth and fangs. But hardly a word about how she comforted Nancy as she led her back to the plaintiff's table.

"Now we have two pariahs in the family," Sarah exclaimed one evening when we were by ourselves after dinner.

"And yet another system to fight," I added. "Now it's social media. I don't know how much fight we've got left in us."

"Well, we're not going to fight this one, Ike. They would love nothing more than for me to join the fray. The firm is not going to react, and I'm willing to bet Redding won't drag the college into this any further either."

"Wouldn't it be ironic, though, if we did, Sarah, after all we've been through together. Imagine, you having to justify the legal system and me the academic one. All in the name of challenging the social media system this time. Priceless!"

"I am worried, though," Sarah added, getting very serious, "about what a feeding frenzy like this might mean for my safety. The firm is taking precautions, of course, but I'm on my own when I'm not at the office. With all the stories lately about people taking things into their own hands to vent their stirred-up anger, we might want to get away for a while until things calm down."

"That's a good idea. But where would we go? Back to Oban to live it up with Tom and company?"

"That'd be nice, of course, but I have a better idea. I know how much Paris means to you, and I only got to know the city a little bit last time. I would love to go back, and Anna is old enough now she would get a lot out of such a trip."

"Probably even be speaking fluent French by the time we returned. She is of the age, you know, when kids pick up languages like they're candy."

"And I'd finally get to see Notre Dame the way it used to be, with its new roof and all."

"Maybe no cemeteries this time, though."

"Agreed."

"Oh Anna," I yelled to the other room, "how would you like to see Paris?"

"What's Paris?"

CHAPTER 52

It took Anna forever to finally fall asleep on the flight over, she was having such a good time with the flight attendants fussing over her. By the time the plane landed at Charles de Gaulle airport, she was already using a few French words. In her own way, of course. As we exited the plane, she answered the flight attendant's *au revoir* with her own cheery "oh reevwah," and the attendant's *bonne journée* with "bahn joonay."

"What do you bet she'll be pronouncing those French r's perfectly by the time we go home," I remarked as we schlepped our luggage up the gangway.

We got a taxi to the same hotel in the city as last time, next to the Place St. Germain des Prés. And we also had our first meal next door at the Café de Flore again. Once there, the waiter pampered Anna almost as much as the flight attendants had, proving that French waiters are not the surly sort Americans say they are. Of course it helped considerably that I spoke French; and Anna's attempts at mimicking what she heard didn't hurt either. Sarah couldn't resist commenting on all of it, which prompted me, forever the teacher, to give the culture lesson I loved to give in my classes.

"You know," I said, "this myth about Parisian waiters being obnoxious shows how little Americans understand French culture. The French waiter, who is almost always a man by the way, is not just a server trying to complement his meager wages with a tip. He is the person in charge of his domain at the front of the house, and it's his job to see that everything runs smoothly according to the expectations of the establishment. His is a position of responsibility and pride here."

"I see," Sarah remarked. "That explains why we were always treated so nicely last time we were in Paris. It was because you responded to them appropriately."

"You've probably also noticed from last time," I added, "that I only gave a small tip when the service was exceptional. Normally you don't give any tip because these people are properly paid, and what they call the *service* is normally *compris*, included in the price of the meal. If you really want to know, the word *service* actually stands for the table-setting the waiter has prepared for you, which will differ greatly depending on the type of meal the establishment offers."

Then, getting on a roll, I added, "There is another aspect to French culinary etiquette that we Americans don't understand, which really makes us look like the ugly Americans they think of us as. I don't know how many times I have cringed when I heard an American tourist ask for something different from what the chef had prepared, even something as seemingly harmless as extra salt or pepper, or God forbid, ketchup with the fries instead of the special dipping sauce the chef prepared. You can't imagine how insulting that is here. It says you think you know better than the chef how to prepare the meal."

Then I couldn't resist the temptation to mention that wonderful scene from the movie *A Good Year*. "Some American tourists ask for something different from what was on the menu at this Provençal café. The main character, himself a well-off but obnoxious Brit trying his best to woo the owner of the café, runs to her defense, grabs the menus out of the Americans' hands and says, 'There's a MacDonald's in the next village. Have a nice evening.' Absolutely priceless. What I loved about that movie was that it not only showed how hopeless Americans are but that the Brits, at least, are worth saving."

"I remember that film," Sarah remarked. "It had a British director, didn't it?"

"Yeah. Ridley Scott. Why?"

"That's what I thought."

Anna, of course, wasn't paying attention to any of this. She was too happy being treated like a princess again.

As for the rest of our itinerary, things were mostly different from last time Sarah and I were there alone. No more cemeteries or art museums. But we did spend another wonderful afternoon in the Jardin de Luxembourg, this time watching Anna play with the other children floating their toy boats on the pond. I was amazed at how she seemed to have no difficulty communicating with her new playmates. Made me wonder what sort of personal patois she must be using.

The highlight of the stay for Sarah this time was seeing Notre Dame in all her glory once again. For me, the restored inside of the cathedral was as much of a treat as the exterior. I was amazed at how much brighter and airier it seemed than when I was there as a student, even though everything had been put back exactly the way it was ages ago. The main reason, it turned out, was that the thick coat of soot and grime from centuries of incense burning had been meticulously removed from the limestone surfaces all the way up to the roof, restoring them to their original light patina. The same was true of the famous stained-glass windows, which had all been removed and cleaned during the restoration. As for Anna, she had never been in a building of such soaring height before, and seemed utterly enthralled. Her only complaint was the sore neck she got having to look up from her small-person's vantage point all the time.

Once back outside the church, I suggested we walk across the river and have lunch at a bistro I used to frequent, right next to the famous American bookstore, Shakespeare and Company. As we enjoyed eating under the trees at the river's edge, relishing the view of the cathedral right across from us, I recounted the history of the bookstore, how it was a favorite of the writers of Hemingway's generation and later became a hangout for those of the Beat Generation.

That prompted Sarah to remark, "I thought I knew why this city meant so much to you before, Ike, but I realize now that I only got half of it. It's what it has meant to so many people before, at one time or another: famous philosophers, writers, painters and so forth."

"And musicians," I added. "Think of all the black jazz greats who found Paris a haven from the life they had been subjected to in the States in those days. This city was an interracial mecca for them, back when they were inventing some of the world's greatest music."

Mostly, though, I wanted to appreciate the city from Anna's perspective. So I tried to keep these more serious discussions to a minimum. For the whole week we were there, I was fascinated by what she found fascinating, being in such a new and strange environment.

The Paris metro, for example, literally captivated her. She had never been on a train before, but she'd seen movies and had a general idea what they must be like. She was therefore surprised the first time we descended into the metro at the Place St. Germain des Prés. With me holding her back from the edge of the platform, she anxiously watched the train coming out of the tunnel into the station. She looked confused when she didn't hear anything that sounded like a train was supposed to. There was just a strange whooshing sound. I enjoyed telling her how Paris had pioneered the use of rubber tires for most of their subway trains, to make the ride quieter and more comfortable.

Then there was the time she saw a man standing by the side of the sidewalk, peeing into a bright red boxlike thing.

I hoped she hadn't noticed, but I should have known better. Kids don't miss a thing.

"Did you see that?" She asked with her eyes wide open. "He's peeing on the sidewalk."

"Well," I said hesitantly, knowing I was in for a long explanation, "not right on the sidewalk. That red thing he's actually peeing in is called a *uritrottoir*, a sidewalk urinal for men to use when they need to."

"That's disgusting," Sarah interrupted. "I don't remember seeing one of those when we were here before."

"Well, they are pretty new, the latest thing in fact. The new eco-friendly way, they say, to provide the service Parisians have enjoyed from time immemorial, a way to relieve themselves on the run, so to speak."

"That's not funny, Ike."

"No, I'm being serious. Would you like to hear the whole story?"

"I don't think so. We've got a young child here."

"But I want to know, too, mommy."

"OK, dad can tell you later. Just not here in public, sweetie."

That night we took Anna for a sunset dinner at the Eiffel Tower. It was to be Anna's last treat before returning home. She had noticed "that weird iron thing sticking up in the air like that", but had not yet gotten close enough to see for herself. Once inside on the second level where the restaurant was, she wanted to know why we were stopping there and not going all the way to the top.

"Maybe after dinner," Sarah told her, "if your dad will take you. There's no way I'm going up that high."

Once seated, I asked if they still wanted to hear the story about the urinals, now that we were in a more private space. I was hoping to distract Anna long enough to get her to eat her meal before scaling the heights.

"Maybe once we get back to the hotel," Sarah suggested. "I don't think it would make for good dinner conversation either."

Once dinner was finished and Anna's dream was about to be fulfilled, I excused myself for a moment to do, as I tried to joke, "what I would never think of doing in one of those *uritrottoirs*."

Sarah gave me a strange look as I left, and an even stranger one when I came back to the table.

"Are you OK, Ike? You seem a little off. Are you sure you're up to taking Anna to the top?"

"Not by the stairs, that's for sure," I said with a bit of a forced smile. "The elevator should be fine. I get these funny feelings every once in a while. Haven't had one on this trip until just now, so I should be OK."

Anna did get her ride to the top with her dad, but I also got a ride to the hospital as soon as the emergency medical team could get me back down to the ground. Not an easy feat when the elevators were crowded with tourists jostling for position in order to get the best view. The ambulance took us to the American Hospital, one of the best in Paris, known for its excellent cardiology unit.

The doctors didn't need to spend much time diagnosing my problem. I had brought records about my condition with me on the trip, just in case something like this might happen. I kept them with me all the time, in the man-purse I always liked to carry whenever I was in Europe. The main issue, they told me at the hospital, was not that I was in any imminent danger. It was how to get me home. I knew there was no way a commercial airline would allow a person in my condition to fly without a medical escort. I had learned that from my wonderful team in Siena. So before leaving the States, I had done what my students had been told to do, purchased an emergency evacuation policy along with the regular travel insurance ahead of time. So I was able to tell the wonderful people at the hospital that we had it all under control.

CHAPTER 53

The flight back to the States felt longer than it actually was, made all the more so by the connection we had to make from Kennedy airport to Syracuse. As soon as we got there, I was transported directly to the hospital for observation and more tests. They concluded there was nothing more they could do but have me keep up with my medications and get as much rest as possible.

By the time we returned, the social media frenzy over the rape case had tapered off, and the controversy caused by the Bell committee on campus had as well. For the next few years I could just revel in being part of Anna's life, watching her grow. I took her to school every day, made a real amateur chef out of her, spoke French with her when we were alone at home, and enrolled her in French classes in school at the earliest possible moment.

Although I was officially retired, I would get a call from Redding himself from time to time, seeking my advice and apprising me of the progress they were making. Slowly but surely, he informed me, the faculty were "coming around", acknowledging the new progressive spirit that was, as they put it, "infecting" the college. Although the word was sometimes meant to be pejorative, Redding took it as a compliment either way. He was especially pleased at how many of the younger faculty who were already on the tenure track when he arrived, were happy to accept one of the six-year renewable contracts instead. Most pleasing of all, he told me, was the successful campaign he had launched to woo established scholars to the campus without tenure.

Throughout this time, I didn't worry too much about my health. There wasn't much I could do about it anyway.

"That will take care of itself," I would tell Sarah, "one way or another." I did worry, though, about Anna becoming daddy's girl and leaving Sarah out. We never had an argument about it, but we did discuss it from time to time. Since Sarah was not inclined to learn French, given all the things she had to do at the firm, I made sure Anna and I spoke only English when Sarah was home. Except sometimes in the kitchen, when Anna would delight in showing her mom she knew how to *déglacer* the pan or *julienne* the vegetables. Sarah took particular delight in having Anna serve her a gourmet meal she had cooked herself, detailing all the ingredients and explaining the cooking process she had used.

One evening, when we were all relaxing in the living room after one of her special dinners, Anna reminded me that I never did finish the story I was going to tell her at the restaurant in the Eiffel Tower. Sarah was hoping she had forgotten about it, but we both knew better.

"Oh that one," I responded, giving Sarah a wink. "OK. Do you remember what those boxes were called, Anna?"

"Not really. *Uri*-something, I think."

"Yes, *uritrottoirs*. It means sidewalk urinals. They have a long tradition, a history that goes back centuries and explains a lot about why Paris is how it is today. You have to think about what the city was like in medieval times," I began, "when there was no indoor plumbing, no sewage systems and no paved streets. Like most cities at the time. People would throw their garbage in the muddy streets and relieve themselves wherever they could. Then someone would come along and haul the worst of it away. You can't imagine how the city smelled back then."

"That's even more disgusting than seeing these things on the sidewalk now," Sarah interrupted.

"That's exactly the point. They show how far things have evolved," I said, trying not to laugh. "Eventually, the streets began to be paved, but habits didn't change that quickly. So they built enclosed structures on the sidewalks for people to relieve themselves. Kind of like porta potties, only they weren't portable. You may not have realized, but those big round metal things with openings on the side that you walked by several times are some of the original urinals. I used to use them myself as a student, when the only other way to do what you had to do if you were out and about in the city was to go into a café and use one of their horrendous Turkish toilettes."

"What's a Turkish toilette?" Anna asked.

"Oh dear, do we have to go there too?" Sarah exclaimed with mock dismay.

Trying not to laugh too hard telling the story, I continued. "I always preferred to use one of those sidewalk urinals than have to go down into some café's *soussol*, or basement as we would call it, and discover there was nothing but a Turkish toilette down there. Just a dark room with a hole in the floor. You can't imagine how messy it gets in there. To make matters worse, the lights inside would always be on a timer, to save electricity of course, so if you didn't finish fast enough, you'd find yourself completely in the dark having to grope your way out. Then you'd have to find a way to clean your shoes."

Once we all stopped laughing hysterically, and Anna stopped holding her nose, I tried to sum things up. "So don't knock the urinals on the sidewalks. They are a great blessing, a true gift to mankind."

Then, trying to get serious, I added, "Actually, maintaining the sidewalk tradition in Paris with these new contraptions has now become rather controversial. For one thing, it promotes the notion that men are slobs who can't hold it until they find a proper place. And most of those Turkish toilettes have long been replaced with modern ones, so there's really no excuse anymore. But the worst criticism is the way the Paris city council decided to go all eco-friendly.

We whisked you away from what you saw that day, Anna, but if you had looked carefully, you would have noticed that those boxes are actually flower boxes, with pretty plants and flowers on top."

"So what do the men do, pee on the flowers?" Anna asked in her way-too-smart-for-her-age tone of voice.

"No, they pee into a drawer in the front, so they can water the flowers from the roots up," I said, causing another eruption of laughter. "But that's not what bothers people the most. Each of these contraptions is not only painted bright red, it has a red flag on top, too, so you can't miss it. Like waiving a red flag in front of a bull!"

I was in such great form that evening, having such a good time with my family, you'd never know my health was so precarious.

EPILOGUE

If Ike and Sarah's was a match made in heaven, heaven did come calling one day not long after, when they least expected it. Redding had phoned earlier in the day to let Ike know he was planning a ceremony to celebrate what had already been accomplished in the initial years of the college's new venture. The person of honor, he insisted even as Ike protested, was to be the chair of the committee that set it all in motion, now officially known as the Isaac Bell committee.

With the thought of this honor still ringing in his ears, Ike succumbed to his illness at ten o'clock that evening, quietly asleep with Sarah at his side.

With Sarah's permission, the college decided to make Ike's funeral the event Redding had arranged to celebrate what the college had become, and to highlight his role in it. Like their marriage, it was to be held in the college chapel with the president presiding and the pastor of a local church leading the service.

People said it was one of the most moving ceremonies the campus had ever seen. Redding's eulogy was magnanimous, giving Ike more credit than he would ever have thought to give himself. Tom and Bill were there, Tom telling stories of Ike's past, painting an unforgettable portrait of a modern-day Don Quixote, jousting with the evils of one system after another.

"Only this Don Quixote," he ended by saying, "did not die in vain like Cervantes' tragic hero. Our hero left the legacy of accomplishment we all celebrate here today."

As moving as the previous tributes were, no one could forget Sarah's closing remarks. She talked about Ike having finally received the ultimate tenure, God's tenure in heaven.

Then she went on to declare that naming their daughter after Poe's cherished love was the most prescient thing they ever did. Many still recall her exact words.

"Ike may have left me now, but he left me with a wonderful child. Our lovely Anna Bell will forever embody the love between Ike and me that not even death can take away."

Ike was buried in the beautiful cemetery at the edge of the college campus, in the bucolic setting he loved so much. Then Sarah invited everyone to join her at the apartment to relax and reminisce. There was plenty to eat and drink, and the mood lightened considerably, like the wake it was supposed to be. Everyone was trying to one-up somebody else with a different Ike story.

Through all of this Tom remained rather quiet, and those who knew him wondered why. He had always been the life of the party. Finally it came his turn, and he surprised them all. He had helped Sarah sort through some of Ike's papers after he died and had found a diary of sorts. Mostly it was notes on things Ike was working on or thinking about at the time. Needless to say, Ike had thought a lot about the tenure issue, and apparently, to keep his spirits up, he had taken to writing private jokes about it. Some of the jokes he had turned into limericks, and those are what caught Tom's eye.

So instead of telling a story, Tom asked if they would like to hear a couple of Ike's limericks about the tenure issue. Redding was there, and seeing him nodding enthusiastically, Tom began by waving the paper he retrieved from his jacket pocket and said, "I have Sarah's permission to let you frame these for your office, sir, if you'd like."

When the laughter died down, he began reading.

"There once was a professor with tenure
Who craved a bit more adventure

He gave it away
On a bright summer day
And lived happily ever after"

That brought appreciative applause, with Redding leading the way.

"Now this second one," Tom went on, "is a bit risqué, so Mr. President, you may want to put this one away in a drawer somewhere."

As the laughter died down, Tom checked to see if Sarah, on cue, had led Anna out of the room. Seeing she had, he began.

"There once was a professor with tenure
Who basked in the light of his sinecure
He never did anything
But play with his ding-a-ling
And finally got put out to pasture"

Back in the kitchen, Sarah was trying to explain to Anna what the word 'risqué' meant.

Several years later they erected a memorial on the Grosvenor Grove campus in honor of Isaac Bell. And some years after that, young Anna Bell enrolled in a Junior Year in France program, headed to Paris. She told her mother she would be getting involved with the movement to have all sidewalk urinals removed. Parisians are always protesting and marching against something, she had learned, so why not this one.

"Who knows," she said, "it might change the world."

* * * * * *

The End

Yonder Blair is the nom de plume of Rodney Blair Sangster. A retired professor himself, he knows of what he writes. He is grateful his experience in academia has not yet been matched by any personal involvement in the legal system. But as a news junkie and an avid reader of crime novels and Law and Order television, he has developed an acute sense of the limits of justice in both academia and the so-called justice system itself. He enjoys his retirement years writing and cultivating his garden in Santa Barbara, California alongside his long-time partner, Rebecca. He welcomes feedback at rsangster1@cox.net.

ACKNOWLEDGMENTS

Most of the places in the story are real, some are made up. There is a well-known town in Scotland named Oban, famous for its Scotch, but there is no Oban in Upstate New York. Macallan Scotch is definitely real, but there is no Macallan University in New York either. Nor is there a college called Grosvenor Grove in Syracuse. The reputation of the Otisville Prison Camp is well-known by those who've had the pleasure of staying there. The reputations of Paris, Siena, and Prescott, Arizona speak for themselves.

The author wishes to thank those who have contributed ideas and, equally important, encouragement at critical times during the process of creating a first novel. To Joan Tapper, whose critique of the initial draft led to substantial rewriting and refocusing of the story. To Kathryn Dinkin, who taught this academic how to stop writing like one who has published too many scientific manuscripts. To my former colleague and best friend Andy Kerek and his daughter Viki who engaged in the project as if it was their own, spearheading the quest for the perfect title. To Antonio Artese, gifted musician and resourceful study abroad director, whose work with American students inspired the description of the Siena program in the story. To others who made helpful comments along the way, including Elissa Rubin, Pat Cavit, Ines de Romana, Kathy Sideli, Nancy Clayton, and my niece, Jeannie Coy.

Thanks must also go to Wikipedia for being the author's faithful research assistant.

Special thanks to Bill Dalziel, colorful companion at Lucky's bar on Saturday mornings, whose artistic mind and imaginative eye captured the essence of the story perfectly in producing the cover art for the book.

And finally, to Louis Torres, indefatigable book man at Bookchurch and Polyverse Publications, who took on this project without hesitation, and gave it a home.

This book is dedicated to my partner, my best friend and soulmate, Rebecca Morrison.

9 781959 111153